Classic Tales of Horror

BLOODY BOOKS

First published 2006
Published by Bloody Books™

9 8 7 6 5 4 3 2 1

A catalogue of this book is available from the British Library.

ISBN 0954947681
ISBN 9780954947682

Bloody Books™ is an imprint of Beautiful Books Limited,
117 Sugden Road, London SW11 5ED.

www.beautiful-books.co.uk

Printed in Italy by Legoprint.

Contents

The Man and the Snake

Ambrose Bierce

It is of veritabyll report, and attested of so many that there be nowe of wyse and learned none to gaynsaye it, that ye serpente hys eye hath a magnetick propertie that whosoe falleth into its svasion is drawn forwards in despyte of his wille, and perisheth miserabyll by ye creature hys byte.

Stretched at ease upon a sofa, in gown and slippers, Harker Brayton smiled as he read the foregoing sentence in old Morryster's 'Marvels of Science'. 'The only marvel in the matter,' he said to himself, 'is that the wise and learned in Morryster's day should have believed such nonsense as is rejected by most of even the ignorant in ours.'

A train of reflection followed – for Brayton was a man of thought – and he unconsciously lowered his book without altering the direction of his eyes. As soon as the volume had gone below the line of sight, something in an obscure corner of the room recalled his attention to his surrounding. What he saw, in the shadow under his bed, were two small points of light, apparently about an inch apart. They might have been reflections of the gas jet above him, in metal nail heads; he gave them but little thought and resumed his reading. A moment later something – some impulse which it did not occur to him to analyse – impelled him to lower the book again and seek for what he saw before. The points of light were still there. They seemed to have become brighter than before, shining with a greenish luster which he had not at first observed. He thought, too, that they might have moved a trifle

– were somewhat nearer. They were still too much in the shadow, however, to reveal their nature and origin to an indolent attention, and he resumed his reading. Suddenly something in the text suggested a thought which made him start and drop the book for the third time to the side of the sofa, whence, escaping from his hand, it fell sprawling to the floor, back upward. Brayton, half-risen, was staring intently into the obscurity beneath the bed, where the points of light shone with, it seemed to him, an added fire. His attention was now fully aroused, his gaze eager and imperative. It disclosed, almost directly beneath the foot rail of the bed, the coils of a large serpent – the points of light were its eyes! Its horrible head, thrust flatly forth from the innermost coil and resting upon the outermost, was directed straight toward him, the definition of the wide, brutal jaw and the idiotlike forehead serving to show the direction of its malevolent gaze. The eyes were no longer merely luminous points; they looked into his own with a meaning, a malign significance.

A snake in a bedroom of modern city dwelling of the better sort is, happily, not so common a phenomenon as to make explanation altogether needless. Harker Brayton a bachelor of thirty-five, a scholar, idler, and something of an athlete, rich, popular, and of sound health, had returned to San Francisco from all manner of remote and unfamiliar countries. His tastes, always a trifle luxurious, had taken on an added exuberance from long privation; and the resources of even the Castle Hotel being inadequate for their perfect gratification, he had gladly accepted the hospitality of his friend, Dr Druring, the distinguished scientist. Dr Druring's house, a large, old-fashioned one in what was now an obscure quarter of the city, had an outer and visible aspect of reserve. It plainly would not associate with the contiguous elements of its altered environment, and appeared to have developed some of the eccentricities which come of isolation. One of these was a 'wind', conspicuously irrelevant in point of architecture, and no less rebellious in the matter of purpose; for it was a combination of laboratory, menagerie, and museum. It was here that the doctor indulged the scientific side of his nature in the study of such forms of animal life as engaged his interest and comforted his taste – which, it must be confessed, ran rather to the lower forms. For one of the higher types nimbly and sweetly to recommend itself unto his gentle senses, it had at least to retain certain rudimentary characteristics allying it to such 'dragons of the prime' as toads and snakes. His scientific sympathies were distinctly reptilian; he loved nature's vulgarians and described himself as the Zola of Zoology. His wife and daughters, not having the advantage to share his enlightened curiosity regarding the works and ways of our ill-starred fellow-creatures, were, with needless austerity, excluded from what he called the Snakery, and doomed to companionship with their own kind; though, to soften the rigors of their lot, he had permitted them, out of his great wealth, to outdo the reptiles in the gorgeousness of their surroundings and to shine with a superior splendour.

Architecturally, and to point of 'furnishing', the Snakery had a severe simplicity befitting the humble circumstances of its occupants, many of whom, indeed, could not safely have been intrusted with the liberty which is necessary to the full enjoyment of luxury, for they had the troublesome peculiarity of being alive. In their own apartments, however, they were under as little personal restraint as was compatible with their protection from the baneful habit of swallowing one another; and, as Brayton had thoughtfully been apprised it was more than a tradition that some of them had at diverse times been found in parts of the premises where it would have embarrassed them to explain their presence. Despite the Snakery and its uncanny associations – to which, indeed, he gave little attention – Brayton found life at the Druring mansion very much to his mind.

Beyond a smart shock of surprise and a shudder of mere loathing, Mr. Brayton was not greatly affected. His first thought was to ring the call bell and bring a servant; but, although the bell cord dangled within easy reach, he made no movement toward it; it had occurred to his mind that the act might subject him to the suspicion of fear, which he certainly did not feel. He was more keenly conscious of the incongruous nature of the situation than affected by its perils; it was revolting, but absurd.

The reptile was of a species with which Brayton was unfamiliar. Its length he could only conjecture; the body at the largest visible part seemed about as thick as his forearm. In what way was it dangerous, if in any way? Was it venomous? Was it a constrictor? His knowledge of nature's danger signals did not enable him to say; he had never deciphered the code.

If not dangerous, the creature was at least offensive. It was *de trop* – 'matter out of place' – an impertinence. The gem was unworthy of the setting. Even the barbarous taste of our time and country, which had loaded the walls of the room with pictures, the floor with furniture, and the furniture with *bric-a-brac*, had not quite fitted the place for this bit of the savage life of the jungle. Beside – insupportable thought! - the exhalations of its breath mingled with the atmosphere which he himself was breathing!

These thoughts shaped themselves with the greater or less definition in Brayton's mind, and begot action. The process is what we call consideration and decision. It is thus that we are wise and unwise. It is thus that the withered leaf in an autumn breeze shows greater or less intelligence than its fellows, falling upon the land or upon the lake. The secret of human action is an open one – something contracts our muscles. Does it matter if we give to the preparatory molecular changes the name of will?

Brayton rose to his feet and prepared to back softly away from the snake, without disturbing it, if possible, and through the door. People retire so from the presence of the great, for greatness is power, and power is a menace. He knew that he could walk backward without obstruction, and find the door without error. Should the monster follow, the taste which had plastered the walls with paintings had consistently supplied a rack of murderous Oriental weapons from which he could snatch one to suit the occasion. In the meantime the snake's eyes burned with a more pitiless malevolence than ever.

Brayton lifted his right foot free of the floor to step backward. That moment he felt a strong aversion to doing so.

'I am accounted brave,' he murmured; 'is bravery, then, no more than pride? Because there are none to witness the shame shall I retreat?'

He was steadying himself with his right hand upon the back of a chair, his foot suspended.

'Nonsense!' he said aloud; 'I am not so great a coward as to fear to seem to myself afraid.'

He lifted the foot a little higher by slightly bending the knee, and thrust it sharply to the floor – an inch in front of the other! He could not think how that occurred. A trial with the left foot had the same result; it was again in advance of the right. The hand upon the chair back was grasping it; the arm was straight, reaching somewhat backward. One might have seen that he was reluctant to lose his hold. The snake's malignant head was still thrust forth from the inner coil as before, the neck level. It had not moved, but its eyes were now electric sparks, radiating an infinity of luminous needles.

The man had an ashy pallor. Again he took a step forward, and another, partly dragging the chair, which, when finally released, fell upon the floor with a crash. The man groaned; the snake made neither sound nor motion, but its eyes were two dazzling suns. The reptile itself was wholly concealed by them. They gave off enlarging rings of rich and vivid colours, which at their greatest expansion successively vanished like soap bubbles; they seemed to approach his very face, and anon were an immeasurable distance away. He heard, somewhere, the continual throbbing of a great drum, with desultory bursts of far music, inconceivably sweet, like the tones of an Aeolian harp. He knew it for the sunrise melody of Memnon's statue, and thought he stood in the Nileside reeds, hearing, with exalted sense, that immortal anthem through the silence of the centuries.

The music ceased; rather it became by insensible degrees the distant roll of a retreating thunderstorm. A landscape, glittering with sun and rain, stretched before him, arched with a vivid rainbow, framing in its giant curve a hundred visible cities. In the middle distance a vast serpent, wearing a crow reared its head out of its voluminous convolutions and looked at him with his dead mother's eyes. Suddenly this enchanting landscape seemed to rise swiftly upward, like the drop scene at a theatre, and vanished in a blank. Something struck him a hard blow upon the face and breast. He had fallen to the floor; the blood ran from his broken nose and his bruised lips. For a moment he was dazed and stunned, and lay with closed eyes, his face against the door. In a few moments he had recovered, and then realised that his fall, by withdrawing his eyes, had broken the spell which held him. He felt that now, by keeping his gaze averted, he would be able to retreat. But the thought of the serpent within a few feet of his head, yet unseen – perhaps in the very act of springing upon him and throwing its coils about his throat – was too horrible. He lifted his head, stared again into those baleful eyes, and was again in bondage.

The snake had not moved, and appeared somewhat to have lost its power upon the imagination; the gorgeous illusions of a few moments before were not repeated. Beneath that flat and brainless brow its black, beady eyes simply glittered, as at first, with an expression unspeakably malignant. It was as if the creature, knowing its triumph assured, had determined to practice no more alluring wiles.

Now ensued a fearful scene. The man, prone upon the floor, within a yard of his enemy, raised the upper part of his body upon his elbows, his head thrown back, his legs extended to their full length. His face was white between its gouts of blood; his eyes were strained open to their uttermost expansion. There was froth upon his lips; it dropped off in flakes. Strong convulsions ran through his body, making almost serpentine undulations. He bent himself at the waist, shifting his legs from side to side. And every movement left him a little nearer to the snake. He thrust his hands forward to brace himself back, yet constantly advanced upon his elbows.

Dr. Druring and his wife sat in the library. The scientist was in rare good humour.

'I have just obtained, by exchange with another collector,' he said, 'a splendid specimen of the *Ophiophagus*.'

'And what may that be?' the lady enquired with a somewhat languid interest.

'Why, bless my soul, what profound ignorance! My dear, a man who ascertains after marriage that his wife does not know Greek, is entitled to a divorce. The *Ophiophagus* is a snake which eats other snakes.'

'I hope it will eat all yours,' she said, absently shifting the lamp. 'But how does it get the other snakes? By charming them, I suppose.'

'That is just like you, dear,' said the doctor, with an affection of petulance. 'You know how irritating to me is any allusion to that vulgar superstition about the snake's power of fascination.'

The conversation was interrupted by a mighty cry which rang through the silent house like the voice of a demon shouting in a tomb. Again and yet again it sounded, with terrible distinctness. They sprang to their feet, the man confused, the lady pale and speechless with fright. Almost before the echoes of the last cry had died away the doctor was out of the room, springing up the staircase two steps at a time. In the corridor, in front of Brayton's chamber, he met some servants who had come from the upper floor. Together they rushed at the door without knocking. It was unfastened, and gave way. Brayton lay partly upon his stomach on the floor, dead. His head and arms were partly concealed under the foot rail of the bed. They pulled the body away, turning it upon the back. The face was daubed with blood and froth, the eyes were wide open, staring – a dreadful sight!

'Died in a fit,' said the scientist, bending his knee and

placing his hand upon the heart. While in that position he happened to glance under the bed. 'Good God!' he added; 'how did this thing get in here?'

He reached under the bed, pulled out the snake, and flung it, still coiled, to the centre of the room, whence, with a harsh, shuffling sound, it slid across the polished floor till stopped by the wall, where it lay without motion. It was a stuffed snake; its eyes were two shoe buttons.

The Ghostly Rental

Henry James

I was in my twenty-second year, and I had just left college. I was at liberty to choose my career, and I chose it with much promptness. I afterwards renounced it, in truth, with equal ardour, but I have never regretted those two youthful years of perplexed and excited, but also of agreeable and fruitful experiment. I had a taste for theology, and during my college term I had been an admiring reader of Dr. Channing. This was theology of a grateful and succulent savour; it seemed to offer one the rose of faith delightfully stripped of its thorns. And then (for I rather think this had something to do with it), I had taken a fancy to the Old Divinity School. I have always had an eye to the back scene in the human drama, and it seemed to me that I might play my part with a fair chance of applause (from myself at least), in that detached and tranquil home of mild casuistry, with its respectable avenue on one side, and its prospect of green fields and contact with acres of woodland on the other. Cambridge, for the lovers of woods and fields, has changed for the worse since those days, and the precinct in question has forfeited much of its mingled pastoral and scholastic quietude. It was then a College-hall in the woods – a charming mixture. What it is now has nothing to do with my story; and I have no doubt that there are still doctrine-haunted young seniors who, as they stroll near it in the summer dusk, promise themselves, later, to taste of its fine leisurely quality. For myself, I was not disappointed. I established myself in a great square, low-browed room, with deep window-benches; I hung prints from Overbeck and Argy

Scheffer on the walls; I arranged my books, with great refinement of classification, in the alcoves beside the high chimney-shelf, and I began to read Plotinus and St. Augustine. Among my companions were two or three men of ability and of good fellowship, with whom I occasionally brewed a fireside bowl; and with adventurous reading, deep discourse, potations conscientiously shallow, and long country walks, my initiation into the clerical mystery progressed agreeably enough.

With one of my comrades I formed an especial friendship, and we passed a great deal of time together. Unfortunately he had a chronic weakness of one of his knees, which compelled him to lead a very sedentary life, and as I was a methodical pedestrian, this made some difference in our habits. I used often to stretch away for my daily ramble, with no companion but the stick in my hand or the book in my pocket. But in the use of my legs and the sense of unstinted open air, I have always found company enough. I should, perhaps, add that in the enjoyment of a very sharp pair of eyes, I found something of a social pleasure. My eyes and I were on excellent terms; they were indefatigable observers of all wayside incidents, and so long as they were amused I was contented. It is, indeed, owing to their inquisitive habits that I came into possession of this remarkable story. Much of the country about the old College town is pretty now, but it was prettier thirty years ago. That multitudinous eruption of domiciliary pasteboard which now graces the landscape, in the direction of the low, blue Waltham Hills, had not yet taken place; there were no genteel cottages to put the shabby meadows and scrubby orchards to shame – a juxtaposition by which, in later years, neither element of the contrast has gained. Certain crooked cross-roads, then, as I remember them, were more deeply and naturally rural, under the tall, customary elm that curved its foliage in mid-air like the outward dropping ears of a girdled wheat-sheaf, sat with their shingled hoods well pulled down on their ears, and no prescience whatever of the fashion of French roofs – weather-wrinkled old peasant women, as you might call them, quietly wearing the native coif, and never dreaming of mounting bonnets, and indecently exposing their venerable brows. That winter was what is called an 'open' one; there was much cold, but little snow; the roads were firm and free, and I was rarely compelled by the weather to forego my exercise. One grey December afternoon I had sought it in the direction of the adjacent town of Medford, and I was retracing my steps at an even pace, and watching the pale, cold tints – the transparent amber and faded rose-colour – which curtained, in wintery fashion, the western sky, and reminded me of a sceptical smile on the lips of a beautiful woman. I came, as dusk was falling, to a narrow road which I had never traversed and which I imagined offered me a short cut homeward. I was about three miles away; I was late, and would have been thankful to make them two. I diverged, walked some ten minutes, and then perceived that the road had a very unfrequented air. The wheel-ruts looked old; the stillness seemed peculiarly sensible. And yet down the road stood a house, so that it must in some degree have been a thoroughfare. On one side was a high, natural embankment, on the top of which was perched an apple-orchard, whose tangled boughs made a stretch of coarse black lace-work, hung across the coldly rosy west. In a short time I came to the house, and I immediately found myself interested in it. I stopped in front of it gazing hard, I hardly knew why, but with a vague mixture of curiosity and timidity. It was a house like most of the houses thereabouts, except that it was decidedly a handsome specimen of its class. It stood on a grassy slope, it had its tall, impartially drooping elm beside it, and its old black well-cover at its shoulder. But it was of very large proportions, and it had a striking look of solidity and stoutness of timber. It had lived to a good old age, too, for the wood-work on its door-way and under its eaves, carefully and abundantly carved, referred it to the middle, at the latest, of the last century. All this had once been painted white, but the broad back of time, leaning against the door-posts for a hundred years, had laid bare the grain of the wood. Behind the house stretched an orchard of apple-trees, more gnarled and fantastic than usual, and wearing in the deepening dusk, a blighted and exhausted aspect. All the windows of the house had rusty shutters, without slats, and these were closely drawn. There was no sign of life about it; it looked blank, bare and vacant, and yet, as I lingered near it, it seemed to have a familiar meaning – an audible eloquence. I have always thought of the impression made upon me at first sight, by that grey colonial dwelling, as a proof that induction may sometimes be near akin to divination; for after all, there was nothing on the face of the matter to warrant the very serious induction that I made. I fell back and crossed the road. The last red light of the sunset disengaged itself, as it was about to vanish, and rested faintly for a moment on the time-silvered front of the old house. It touched, with perfect regularity, the series of small panes in the fan-shaped window above the door, and twinkled there fantastically. Then it died away, and left the place more intensely sombre. At this moment I said to myself with the accent of profound conviction – 'The house is simply haunted!'

Somehow, immediately, I believed it, and so long as I was not shut up inside, the idea gave me pleasure. It was implied in the aspect of the house, and it explained it. Half an hour before, if I had been asked, I would have said, as befitted a young man who was explicitly cultivating cheerful views of the supernatural, that there were no such things as haunted houses. But the dwelling before me gave a vivid meaning to the empty words; it had been spiritually blighted.

The longer I looked at it, the intenser seemed the secret that it held. I walked all round it, I tried to peep here and there, through a crevice in the shutters, and I took a puerile satisfaction in laying my hand on the door-knob and gently turning it. If the door had yielded, would I have gone in? – would I have penetrated the dusky stillness? My audacity, fortunately, was not put to the test. The portal was admirably solid, and I was unable even to shake it. At last I turned away, casting many looks behind me. I pursued my way, and, after a longer walk than I had bargained for, reached the high-road. At a certain distance below the point at which the long lane I have mentioned entered it, stood a comfortable, tidy dwelling, which might have offered itself as the model of the house which is in no sense haunted – which has no sinister secrets, and knows nothing but blooming prosperity. Its clean white paint stared placidly through the dusk, and its vine-covered porch had been dressed in straw for the winter. An old, one-horse chaise, freighted with two departing visitors was leaving the door, and through the undraped windows, I saw the lamp-lit sitting-room, and the table spread with the early 'tea', which had been improvised for the comfort of the guests. The mistress of the house had come to the gate with her friends; she lingered there after the chaise had wheeled creakingly away, half to watch them down the road, and half to give me as I passed I the twilight, a questioning look. She was a comely, quick young woman, with a sharp, dark eye, and I ventured to speak to her.

'That house down that side-road,' I said, 'about a mile from here – the only one – can you tell whom it belongs to?'

She stared at me a moment, and, I thought, coloured a little. 'Our folks never go down that road,' she said, briefly.

'But it's a short way to Medford,' I answered.

She gave a little toss of her head. 'Perhaps it would turn out a long way. At any rate, we don't use it.'

This was interesting. A thrifty Yankee household must have good reasons for this scorn of time-saving processes. 'But you know the house, at least?' I said.

'Well, I have seen it.'

'And to whom does it belong?'

She gave a little laugh and looked away as if she were aware that, to a stranger, her words might seem to savour of agricultural superstition. 'I guess it belongs to them that are in it.'

But I laid my hand on her arm, respectfully. 'You mean,' I said, 'that the house is haunted?'

She drew herself away, coloured, raised her finger to her

lips, and hurried into the house, where in a moment, the curtains were dropped over the windows.

For several days, I thought repeatedly of this little adventure, but I took some satisfaction in keeping it to myself. If the house was not haunted, it was useless to expose my imaginative whims, and if it was, it was agreeable to drain the cup of horror without assistance. I determined, of course, to pass that way again; and a week later – it was the last day of the year – I retraced my steps. I approached the house from the opposite direction, and found myself before it at about the same hour as before. The light was failing, the sky low and grey; the wind wailed along the hard, bare ground, and made slow eddies of the frost-blackened leaves. The melancholy mansion stood there, seemingly to gather the winter twilight around it, and mask itself in it, inscrutably. I hardly knew on what errand I had come, but I had a vague feeling that if this time the door-knob were to turn and the door to open, I should take my heart in my hands, and let them close behind me. Who were the mysterious tenants to whom the good woman at the corner had alluded? What had been seen or heard – what was related? The door was as stubborn as before, and my impertinent fumblings with the latch caused no upper window to be thrown open, nor any strange, pale face to be thrust out. I ventured even to raise the rusty knocker and give it half-a-dozen raps, but they made a flat, dead sound, and aroused no echo. Familiarity breeds contempt; I don't know what I should have done next, if, in the distance, up the road (the same one I had followed), I had not seen a solitary figure advancing. I was unwilling to be observed hanging about this ill-famed dwelling, and I sought refuge among the dense shadows of a grove of pines near by, where I might peep forth, and yet remain invisible. Presently, the new-comer drew near, and I perceived that he was making straight for the house. He was a little, old man, the most striking feature of whose appearance was a voluminous cloak, of a sort of military cut. He carried a walking-stick, and advanced in a slow, painful, somewhat hobbling fashion, but with an air of extreme resolution. He turned off from the road, and followed the vague wheel-track, and within a few yards of the house he paused. He looked up at it, fixedly and searchingly, as if he were counting the windows, or noting certain familiar marks. Then he took off his hat, and bent over slowly and solemnly, as if he were performing an obeisance. As he stood uncovered, I had a good look at him. He was, as I have said, a diminutive old man, but it would have been hard to decide whether he belonged to this world or to the other. His head reminded me, vaguely, of the portraits of Andrew Jackson. He had a crop of grizzled hair, as stiff as a brush, a lean, pale, smooth-shaved face, and an eye of intense brilliancy, surmounted with thick brows, which had remained perfectly black. His face, as well as his cloak, seemed to belong to an old soldier; he looked like a retired military man of a modest rank; but he struck me as exceeding the classic privilege of even such a personage to be eccentric and grotesque. When he had finished his salute, he advanced to the door, fumbled in the folds of his cloak, which hung down much further in front than behind, and produced a key. This he slowly and carefully inserted into the lock, and then, apparently, he turned it. But the door did not immediately open; first he bent his head, turned his ear, and stood listening, and then he looked up and down the road. Satisfied or reassured, he applied his aged shoulder to one of the deep-set panels, and pressed a moment. The door yielded – opening into perfect darkness. He stopped again on the threshold, and again removed his hat and made his bow. Then he went in, and carefully closed the door behind him.

Who in the world was he, and what was his errand? He might have been a figure out of one of Hoffman's tales. Was he vision or a reality – an inmate of the house, or a familiar, friendly visitor? What had been the meaning, in either case, of his mystic genuflexions, and how did he propose to proceed, in that inner darkness? I emerged from my retirement and observed narrowly, several of the windows. In each of them, at an interval, a ray of light became visible in the chink between the two leaves of the shutters. Evidently, he was lighting up; was he going to throw a party – a ghostly revel? My curiosity grew intense, but I was quite at a loss how to satisfy it. For a moment I thought of rapping peremptorily at the door; but I dismissed this idea as unmannerly, and calculated to break the spell, if spell there was. I walked round the house and tried, without violence, to open one of the lower windows. It resisted, but I had better fortune, in a moment, with another. There was a risk, certainly, in the trick I was playing – a risk of being seen from within, or (worse) seeing, myself, something that I should repent of seeing. But curiosity, as I say, had become an inspiration, and the risk was highly agreeable. Through the parting of the shutters I looked into a lighted room – a room lighted by two candles in old brass flambeaux, placed upon the mantel-shelf. It was apparently a sort of back parlour, and it had retained all its furniture. This was of a homely, old-fashioned pattern, and consisted of hair-cloth chairs and sofas, spare mahogany tables, and framed samplers hung upon the walls. But although the room was furnished, it had a strangely uninhabited look; the tables and chairs were in rigid positions, and no small, familiar objects were visible. I could not see everything, and I could only guess at the existence, on my right, of a large folding-door. It was apparently open, and the light of the neighbouring room passed through it. I waited for some time, but the room remained empty. At last I became conscious that a large shadow was projected upon the wall opposite the folding-door – the shadow, evidently, of a figure in the adjoining room. It was tall and grotesque, and seemed to represent a person sitting perfectly motionless, in profile. I thought I recognized the perpendicular bristles and far-arching nose of my little old man. There was a strange fixedness in his posture; he appeared to be seated, and looking intently at something. I watched the shadow a long time, but it never stirred. At last, however, just as my patience began to ebb, it moved slowly, rose to the ceiling, and became indistinct.

I don't know what I should have seen next, but by an irresistible impulse, I closed the shutter. Was it delicacy? – was it pusillanimity? I can hardly say. I lingered, nevertheless, near the house, hoping that my friend would re-appear. I was not disappointed; for he at last emerged, looking just as when he had gone in, and taking his leave in the same ceremonious fashion. (The lights, I had already observed, had disappeared from the crevice of each of the windows.) He faced about before the door, took off his hat, and made an obsequious bow. As he turned away I had a hundred minds to speak to him, but I let him depart in peace. This, I may say, was pure delicacy; – you will answer, perhaps, that it came too late. It seemed to me that he had a right to resent my observation; though my own right to exercise it (if ghosts were in the question) struck me as equally positive. I continued to watch him as he hobbled softly down the bank, and along the lonely road. Then I musingly retreated in the opposite direction. I was tempted to follow him, at a distance, to see what became of him; but this, too, seemed indelicate; and I confess, moreover, that I felt the inclination to coquet a little, as it were, with my discovery – to pull apart the petals of the flower one by one.

I continued to smell the flower, from time to time, for its oddity of perfume had fascinated me. I passed by the house on the cross-road again, but never encountered the old man in the cloak, or any other wayfarer. It seemed to keep observers at a distance, and I was careful not to gossip about it: one inquirer, I said to myself, may edge his way into the secret, but there is no room for two. At the same time, of course, I would have been thankful for any chance side-light that might fall across the matter – though I could not well see whence it was to come. I hoped to meet the old man in the cloak elsewhere, but as the days passed by without his reappearing, I ceased to expect it. And yet I reflected that he probably lived in that neighbourhood, inasmuch as he had made his pilgrimage to the vacant house on foot. If he had come from a distance, he would have been sure to arrive in some old deep-hooded gig with yellow wheels – a vehicle as venerably grotesque as himself. One day I took a stroll in Mount Auburn cemetery – an institution at that period in its infancy, and full of a sylvan charm which it has now completely forfeited. It contained more maple and birch than willow and cypress, and the sleepers had ample elbow room. It was not a city of the dead, but at the most a village, and a meditative pedestrian might stroll there without too importunate reminder of the grotesque side of our claims to posthumous consideration. I had come out to enjoy the first foretaste of Spring – one of those mild days of late winter, when the torpid earth seems to draw the first long breath that marks the rupture of the spell of sleep. The sun was veiled in haze, and yet warm, and the frost was oozing from its deepest lurking-places. I had been treading for half an hour the winding ways of the cemetery, when suddenly I perceived a familiar figure seated on a bench against a southward-facing evergreen hedge. I call the figure familiar, because I had seen it often in memory and in fancy; in fact, I had beheld it but once. Its back was turned to me, but it wore a voluminous cloak, which there was no mistaking. Here, at last, was my fellow-visitor at the haunted house, and here was my chance, if I wished to approach him! I made a circuit, and came towards him from in front. He saw me, at the end of the alley, and sat motionless, with his hands on the head of his stick, watching me from under his black eyebrows as I drew near. At a distance these black eyebrows looked formidable; they were the only thing I saw in his face. But on closer view I was reassured, simply because I immediately felt that no man could really be as fantastically fierce as this poor old gentleman looked. His face was a kind of caricature of martial truculence. I stopped in front of him, and respectfully asked leave to sit and rest upon his bench. He granted it with a silent gesture, of much dignity, and I placed myself beside him. In this position I was able, covertly, to observe him. He was quite as much an oddity in the morning sunshine, as he had been in the dubious twilight. The lines in his face were as rigid as if they had been hacked out of a block by a clumsy wood-carver. His eyes were flamboyant, his nose terrific, his mouth implacable. And yet, after awhile, when he slowly turned and looked at me, fixedly, I perceived that in spite of this portentous mask, he was a very mild old man. I was sure he even would have been glad to smile, but, evidently, his facial muscles were too stiff – they had taken a different fold, once for all. I wondered whether he was demented, but I dismissed the idea; the fixed glitter in his eye was not that of insanity. What his face really expressed was deep and simple sadness; his heart perhaps was broken, but his brain was intact. His dress was shabby but neat, and his old blue cloak had known half a century's brushing.

I hastened to make some observation upon the exceptional softness of the day, and he answered me in a gentle, mellow voice, which it was almost startling to hear proceed from such bellicose lips.

'This is a very comfortable place,' he presently added.

'I am fond of walking in graveyards,' I rejoined deliberately; flattering myself that I had struck a vein that might lead to something.

I was encouraged; he turned and fixed me with his duskily glowing eyes. Then very gravely, - 'Walking, yes. Take all your exercise now. Some day you will have to settle down in a graveyard in a fixed position.'

'Very true,' said I. 'But you know there are some people who are said to take exercise even after that day.'

He had been looking at me still; at this he looked away.

'You don't understand?' I said, gently.

He continued to gaze straight before him.

'Some people, you know, walk about after death,' I went on.

At last he turned, and looked at me more portentously than ever. 'You don't believe that,' he said simply.

'How do you know I don't.'

'Because you are young and foolish.' This was said without acerbity – even kindly; but in the tone of an old man whose consciousness of his own heavy experience made everything else seem light.

'I am certainly young,' I answered; 'but I don't think that, on the whole, I am foolish. But say I don't believe in ghosts – most people would be on my side.'

'Most people are fools!' said the old man.

I let the question rest, and talked of other things. My companion seemed on his guard, he eyed me defiantly, and made brief answers to my remarks; but I nevertheless gathered an impression that our meeting was an agreeable thing to him, and even a social incident of some importance. He was evidently a lonely creature, and his opportunities for gossip were rare. He had had troubles, and they had detached him from the world, and driven him back upon himself; but the social chord in his antiquated soul was not entirely broken, and I was sure he was gratified to find that it could still feebly resound. At last, he began to ask questions himself; he inquired whether I was a student.

'I am a student of divinity,' I answered.

'Of divinity?'

'Of theology. I am studying for the ministry.'

At this he eyed me with peculiar intensity – after which his gaze wandered away again. 'There are certain things you ought to know, then,' he said at last.

'I have a great desire for knowledge,' I answered. 'What things do you mean?'

He looked at me again awhile, but without heeding my question.

'I like your appearance,' he said. 'You seem to me a sober lad.'

'Oh, I am perfectly sober!' I exclaimed – yet departing for a moment from my soberness.

'I think you are fair-minded,' he went on.

'I don't any longer strike you as foolish then? I asked.

'I stick to what I said about people who deny the power of departed spirits to return. They *are* fools!' And he rapped fiercely with his staff on the earth.

I hesitated a moment, and then, abruptly, 'You have seen a ghost!' I said.

He appeared not at all startled.

'You are right, sir!' he answered with great dignity. 'With me it's not a matter of cold theory – I have not had to pry into old books to learn what to believe. I *know*! With these eyes I have beheld the departed spirit standing before me as near as you are!' And his eyes, as he spoke, certainly looked as if they had rested upon strange things.

I was irresistibly impressed – I was touched with credulity.

'And was it very terrible?' I asked.

'I am an old soldier – I am not afraid!'

'When was it? – where was it?' I asked.

He looked at me mistrustfully, and I saw that I was going too fast.

'Excuse me from going into particulars,' he said. 'I am not at liberty to speak more fully. I have told you so much, because I cannot bear to hear this subject spoken of lightly. Remember in future, that you have seen a very honest old man who told you – on his honour – that he had seen a ghost!' And he got up, as if he thought he had said enough. Reserve, shyness, pride, the fear of being laughed at, the memory, possibly, of former strokes of sarcasm – all this, on one side, had its weight with him; but I suspected that on the other, his tongue was loosened by the garrulity of old age, the sense of solitude, and the need of sympathy – and perhaps, also, by the friendliness which he had been so good as to express towards myself. Evidently it would be unwise to press him, but I hoped to see him again.

'To give greater weight to my words,' he added, 'let me mention my name – Captain Diamond, sir. I have seen service.'

'I hope I may have the pleasure of meeting you again,' I said.

'The same to you, Sir!' And brandishing his stick portentously – though with the friendliest intentions – he marched stiffly away.

I asked two or three persons – selected with discretion – whether they knew anything about Captain Diamond, but they were quite unable to enlighten me. At last, suddenly, I smote my forehead, and dubbing myself a dolt, remembered that I was neglecting a source of information to which I had never applied in vain. The excellent person at whose table I habitually dined, and who dispensed hospitality to students at so much a week, had a sister as good as herself, and of conversational powers more varied. This sister, who was known as Miss Deborah, was an old maid in all the force of the term. She was deformed, and she never went out of the house; she sat all day at the window, between a bird-cage and a flower-pot, stitching small linen articles – mysterious bands and frills. She wielded, I was assured, an exquisite needle, and her work was highly prized. In spite of her deformity and her confinement, she had a little, fresh, round face, and an imperturbable serenity of spirit. She had also a very quick little wit of her own, she was extremely observant, and she had a high relish for a friendly chat. Nothing pleased her so much as to have you – especially, I think, if you were a young divinity student – move your chair near her sunny window, and settle yourself for twenty minutes' 'talk'. 'Well, sir,' she used always to say, 'what is the latest monstrosity in Biblical criticism?' – for she used to pretend to be horrified at the rationalistic tendency of the age. But she was an inexorable little philosopher, and I am convinced that she was a keener rationalist than any of us, and that, if she had chosen, she could have propounded questions that would have made the boldest of us wince. Her window commanded that whole town – or rather, the whole county. Knowledge came to her as she sat singing, with her little, cracked voice, in her low rocking chair. She was the first to learn everything, and the last to forget it. She had the town gossip at her fingers' ends, and she knew everything about people she had never seen. When I asked her how she had acquired her learning, she said simply – 'Oh, I observe!' 'Observe closely enough,' she once said, 'and it doesn't matter where you are. You may be in a pitch-dark closet. All you want is something to start with; one thing leads to another, and all things are mixed up. Shut me up in a dark closet and I will observe after a while, that some places in it are darker than others. After that (give me time), and I will tell you what the President of the United States is going to have for dinner.' Once I paid her a compliment. 'Your observation,' I said, 'is as fine as your needle, and your statements are as true as your stitches.'

Of course Miss Deborah had heard of Captain Diamond. He had been much talked about many years before, but he had survived the scandal that attached to his name.

'What was the scandal?' I asked.

'He killed his daughter.'

'Killed her?' I cried; 'how so?'

'Oh, not with a pistol, or a dagger, or a dose of arsenic! With his tongue. Talk of women's tongues! He cursed her – with some horrible oath – and she died!'

'What had she done?'

'She had received a visit from a young man who loved her, and whom he had forbidden in the house.'

'The house,' I said – 'ah yes! The house is out in the country, two or three miles from here, on a lonely cross-road.'

Miss Deborah looked sharply at me, as she bit her thread.

'Ah, you know about the house?' she said.

'A little,' I answered; 'I have seen it. But I want you to tell me more.'

But here Miss Deborah betrayed an incommunicativeness which was most unusual.

'You wouldn't call me superstitious, would you?' she asked.

'You? – you are the quintessence of pure reason.'

'Well, every thread has its rotten place and every needle its grain of rust. I would rather not talk about that house.'

'You have no idea how you excite my curiosity!' I said.

'I can feel for you. But it would make me very nervous.'

'What harm can come to you?' I asked.

'Some harm came to a friend of mine.' And Miss Deborah gave a very positive nod.

'What had your friend done?'

'She had told me Captain Diamond's secret, which he had told her with a mighty mystery. She had been an old flame of his, and he took her into his confidence. He bade her tell no one, and assured her that if she did, something dreadful would happen to her.'

'And what happened to her?'

'She died.'

'Oh, we are all mortal!' I said. 'Had she given him a promise?'

'She had not taken it seriously, she had not believed him. She repeated the story to me, and three days afterwards, here where I sit now, I was stitching her grave-clothes. Since then, I have never mentioned what she told me.'

'Was it very strange?'

'It was strange, but it was ridiculous too. It is a thing to make you shudder and to make you laugh, both. But you can't worry it out of me. I am sure that if I were to tell you, I should immediately break a needle in my finger, and die the next week of lock-jaw.'

I retired, and urged Miss Deborah no further; but every two or three days, after dinner, I came and sat down by her rocking-chair. I made no further allusion to Captain Diamond; I sat silent, clipping tape with her scissors. At last, one day, she told me I was looking poorly. I was pale.

'I am dying of curiosity,' I said. 'I have lost my appetite. I have eaten no dinner.'

'Remember Bluebeard's wife!' said Miss Deborah.

'One may as well perish by the sword as by famine!' I answered.

Still she said nothing, and at last I rose with a melodramatic sigh and departed. As I reached the door she called me and pointed to the chair I had vacated. 'I never was hard-hearted,' she said. 'Sit down, and if we are to perish, may we at least perish together.' And then, in very few words, she communicated what she knew of Captain Diamond's secret. 'He was a very high-tempered old man, and though he was very fond of his daughter, his will was law. He had picked out a husband for her, and given her due notice. Her mother was dead, and they lived alone together. The house had been Mrs. Diamond's own marriage portion; the Captain, I believe, hadn't a penny. After his marriage they had come to live there, and he had begun to work the farm. The poor girl's lover was a young man with whiskers from Boston. The Captain came in one evening and found them together; he collared the young man, and hurled a terrible curse at the poor girl. The young man cried that she was his wife, and he asked her if it was true. She said, No! Thereupon Captain Diamond, his fury growing fiercer, repeated his imprecation, ordered her out of the house, and disowned her forever. She swooned away, but her father went raging off and left her. Several hours later, he came back and found the house empty. On the table was a note from the young man telling him that he had killed his daughter, repeating assurance that she was his own wife, and declaring that he himself claimed the sole right to commit her remains to earth. He had carried the body away in a gig! Captain Diamond wrote him a dreadful note in answer, saying that he didn't believe his daughter was dead, but that whether or no, she was dead to him. A week later, in the middle of the night, he saw her ghost. Then, I suppose, he was convinced. The ghost reappeared several times, and finally began regularly to haunt the house. It made the old man very uncomfortable, for little by little his passion had passed away, and he was given up to grief. He determined at last to leave the place, and tried to sell or rent it; but meanwhile the story had gone abroad, the ghost had been seen by other persons, the house had a bad name, and it was impossible to dispose of it. With the farm, it was the old man's only property, and his only means of subsistence; if he could neither live in it nor rent it, he was beggared. But the ghost had no mercy, as he had had none. He struggled for six months, and at last he broke down. He put on his old blue cloak and took up his staff, and prepared to wander away and beg his bread. Then the ghost relented, and proposed a compromise. "Leave the house to me!" it said; "I have marked it for my own. Go off and live elsewhere. But to enable you to live, I will be your tenant, since you can find no other. I will hire the house off you and pay you a certain rent." And the ghost named a sum. The old man consented, and he goes every quarter to collect his rent!'

I laughed at this recital, but I confess I shuddered too, for my own observation had exactly confirmed it. Had I not been witness of one of the Captain's quarterly visits, had I not all but seen him sit watching his spectral tenant count out the rent-money, and when he trudged away in the dark, had he not a little bag of strangely gotten coin hidden in the folds of his old blue cloak? I imparted none of these reflections to Miss Deborah, for I was determined that my observations should have a sequel, and I promised myself that pleasure of treating her to my story in its full maturity. 'Captain Diamond,' I asked, 'has no other known means of subsistence?'

'None whatever. He toils not, neither does he spin – his ghost supports him. A haunted house is valuable property!'

'And in what coin does the ghost pay?'

'In good American gold and silver. It has only this peculiarity – that the pieces are all dated before the young girl's death. It's a strange mixture of matter and spirit!'

'And does that ghost do things handsomely; is the rent large?'

'The old man, I believe, lives decently, and has his pipe and his glass. He took a little house down by the river; the door is sidewise to the street, and there is a little garden before it. There he spends his days, and has an old coloured woman to do for him. Some years ago, he used to wander about a good deal, he was a familiar figure in the town, and most people knew his legend. But of late he has drawn back into his shell; he sits over his fire, and curiosity has forgotten him. I suppose he is falling into his dotage. But I am sure, I trust,' said Miss Deborah in conclusion, 'that he won't outlive his faculties or his powers of locomotion, for, if I remember rightly, it was part of the bargain that he should come in person to collect his rent.'

We neither of us seemed likely to suffer any especial penalty for Miss Deborah's indiscretion; I found her, day after day, singing over her work, neither more nor less active than usual. For myself, I boldly pursued my observations. I went again, more than once, to the great graveyard, but I was disappointed in my hope of finding Captain Diamond there. I had a prospect, however, which afforded me compensation. I shrewdly inferred that the old man's quarterly pilgrimages were made upon the last day of the old quarter. My first sight of him had been on the 31st December, and it was probable that he would return to his haunted home on the last day of March. This was near at hand; at last it arrived. I betook myself late in the afternoon to the old house on the cross-road, supposing that the hour of twilight was the appointed season. I was not wrong. I had been hovering about for a short time, feeling very much like a restless ghost myself, when he appeared in the same manner as before, and wearing the same costume. I again concealed myself, and saw him enter the house with the ceremonial which he had used on the former occasion. A light appeared successively in the crevice of each pair of shutters, and I opened the window which had yielded to my importunity before. Again I saw the great shadow on the wall, motionless and solemn. But I saw nothing else. The old man reappeared at last, made his fantastic salaam before the house, and crept away into the dusk.

One day, more than a month after this, I met him again at Mount Auburn. The air was full of the voice of Spring; the birds had come back and were twittering over their Winter's travels, and a mild west wind was making a thin murmur in the raw verdure. He was seated on a bench in the sun, still muffled in his enormous mantle, and he recognized me as soon as I approached him. He nodded at me as if he were an old Bashaw giving the signal for my decapitation, but it was apparent that he was pleased to see me.

'I have looked for you here more than once,' I said. 'You

don't come very often.'

'What did you want of me?' he asked.

'I wanted to enjoy your conversation. I did so greatly when I met you here before.'

'You found me amusing?'

'Interesting!' I said.

'You didn't think me cracked?'

'Cracked? – My dear sir - !' I protested.

'I'm the sanest man in the country. I know that is what insane people always say; but generally they can't prove it. I can!'

'I believe it,' I said. 'But I am curious to know how such a thing can be proved.'

He was silent awhile.

'I will tell you. I once committed, unintentionally, a great crime. Now I pay the penalty. I give up my life to it. I don't shirk it; I face it squarely, knowing perfectly what it is. I haven't tried to bluff it off; I haven't begged off from it; I haven't run away from it. The penalty is terrible, but I have accepted it. I have been a philosopher!'

'If I were a Catholic, I might have turned monk, and spent the rest of my life in fasting and praying. That is no penalty; that is an evasion. I might have blown my brains out – I might have gone mad. I wouldn't do either. I would simply face the music, take the consequences. As I say, they are awful! I take them on certain days, four times a year. So it has been these twenty years; so it will be as long as I last. It's my business; it's my avocation. That's the way I feel about it. I call that reasonable!'

'Admirably so!' I said. 'But you fill me curiosity and with compassion.'

'Especially with curiosity,' he said cunningly.

'Why,' I answered, 'if I know exactly what you suffer I can pity you more.'

'I'm much obliged. I don't want your pity; it won't help me. I'll tell you something, but it's not for myself; it's for your own sake.' He paused a long time and looked all round him, as if for chance eavesdroppers. I anxiously awaited his revelation, but he disappointed me. 'Are you still studying theology?' he asked.

'Oh, yes,' I answered, perhaps with a shade of irritation. 'It's a thing one can't learn in six months.'

'I should think not, so long as you have nothing but your books. Do you know the proverb, "A grain of experience is worth a pound of precept?" I'm a great theologian.'

'Ah, you have had experience,' I murmured sympathetically.

'You have read about the immortality of the soul; you have seen Jonathan Edwards and Dr. Hopkins chopping logic over it, and deciding, by chapter and verse, that it is true. But I have seen it with these eyes; I have touched it with these hands!' And the old man held up his rugged fists and shook them portentously. 'That's better!' he went on; 'but I have bought it dearly. You had better take it from the books – evidently you always will. You are a very good young man; you will never have a crime on your conscience.'

I answered with some juvenile fatuity, that I certainly hoped I had my share of human passions, good young man and prospective Doctor of Divinity as I was.

'Ah, but you have a nice, quiet little temper,' he said. 'So have I – now! But once I was very brutal – very brutal. You ought to know that such things are. I killed my own child.'

'Your own child?'

'I struck her down to the earth and left her to die. They could not hang me, for it was not with my hand I struck her. It was with foul and damnable words. That makes a difference; it's a grand law we live under! Well, sir, I can answer for it that *her* soul is immortal. We have an appointment to meet four times a year, and then I catch it!'

'She has forgiven you?'

'She has forgiven me as the angels forgive! That's what I can't stand – the soft, quiet way she looks at me. I'd rather she twisted a knife about in my heart – O Lord, Lord, Lord!' And Captain Diamond bowed his head over his stick, and leaned his forehead on his crossed hands.

I was impressed and moved, and his attitude seemed for the moment a check to further questions. Before I ventured to ask him anything more, he slowly rose and pulled his old cloak around him. He was unused to talking about his troubles, and his memories overwhelmed him. 'I must go my way,' he said. 'I must be creeping along.'

'I shall perhaps meet you here again,' I said.

'Oh, I'm a stiff-jointed old fellow,' he answered, 'and this is rather far for me to come. I have to reserve myself. I have sat sometimes a month at a time smoking my pipe in my chair. But I should like to see you again.' And he stopped and looked at me, terribly and kindly. 'Some day, perhaps, I shall be glad to be able to lay my hand on a young, unperverted soul. If a man can make a friend, it is always something gained. What is your name?'

I had in my pocket a small volume of Pascal's *Thoughts* on the fly leaf of which were written my name and address. I took it out and offered it to my old friend. 'Pray keep this little book,' I said. 'It is one I am very fond of, and it will tell you something about me.'

He took it and turned it over slowly, then looking up at me with a scowl of gratitude, 'I'm not much of a reader,' he said; 'but I won't refuse the first present I shall have received since – my troubles; and the last. Thank you, sir!' And with the little book in his hand he took his departure. I was left to imagine him for some weeks after that sitting solitary in his arm-chair with his pipe. I had not another glimpse of him. But I was awaiting my chance, and on the last day of June, another quarter having elapsed, I deemed that it had come. The evening dusk in June falls late, and I was impatient for its coming. At last, towards the end of a lovely summer's day, I revisited Captain Diamond's property. Everything now was green around it save the blighted orchard in its rear, but its own immitigable greyness and sadness were as striking as when I had first beheld it beneath a December sky. As I drew near, it, I saw that I was late for my purpose, for my purpose had simply been to step forward on Captain Diamond's arrival, and bravely ask him to let me go in with him. He had preceded me, and there were lights already in the windows. I was unwilling, of course, to disturb him during his ghostly interview, and I waited till he came forth. The lights disappeared in the course of time; then the door opened and Captain Diamond stole out. That evening he made no bow to the haunted house, for the first object he beheld was his fair-minded young friend planted, modestly but firmly, near the doorstep. He stopped short, looking at me, and this time his terrible scowl was in keeping with the situation.

'I knew you were here,' I said. 'I came on purpose.'

He seemed dismayed, and looked round at the house uneasily.

'I beg your pardon if I have ventured too far,' I added, 'but you know you have encouraged me.'

'How did you know I was here?'

'I reasoned it out. You told me half your story, and I guessed the other half. I am a great observer, and I had noticed this house in passing. It seemed to me to have a mystery. When you kindly confided to me that you saw spirits, I was sure that it could only be here that you saw them.'

'You are mighty clever,' cried the old man. 'And what brought you here this evening?'

I was obliged to evade this question.

'Oh, I often come; I like to look at the house – it fascinates me.'

He turned and looked up at it himself. 'It's nothing to look at outside.' He was evidently quite unaware of its peculiar outward appearance, and this odd fact, communicated to me thus in the twilight, and under the very brow of the sinister dwelling, seemed to make his vision of the strange things within more real.

'I have been hoping,' I said, 'for a chance to see the inside. I thought I might find you here, and that you would let me go in with you. I should like to see what you see.'

He seemed confounded by my boldness, but not altogether displeased. He laid his hand on my arm. 'Do you know what I see?' he asked.

'How can I know, except as you said the other day, by experience? I want to have the experience. Pray, open the door and take me in.'

Captain Diamond's brilliant eyes expanded beneath their dusky brows, and after holding his breath a moment, he indulged in the first and last apology for a laugh by which I was to see his solemn visage contorted. It was profoundly grotesque, but it was perfectly noiseless. 'Take you in?' he softly growled. 'I wouldn't go in again before my time's up for a thousand times that sum.' And he thrust out his hand from the folds of his cloak and exhibited a small agglomeration of a coin, knotted into the corner of an old silk pocket-handkerchief. 'I stick to my bargain no less, but no more!'

'But you told me that first time I had pleasure of talking with you that it was not so terrible.'

'I don't say it's terrible – now. But it's damned disagreeable!'

This adjective was uttered with a force that made me hesitate and reflect. While I did so, I thought I heard a slight movement of one of the window-shutters above us. I looked up, but everything seemed motionless. Captain Diamond, too, had been thinking; suddenly he turned towards the house. 'If you will go in alone,' he said, 'you are welcome.'

'Will you wait for me here?'

'Yes, you will not stop long.'

'But the house is pitch dark. When you go you have lights.'

He thrust his hand into the depths of his cloak and produced some matches. 'Take these,' he said. 'You will find two candlesticks with candles on the table in the hall. Light them, take one in each hand and go ahead.'

'Where shall I go?'

'Anywhere – everywhere. You can trust the ghost to find you.'

I will not pretend to deny that by this time my heart was beating. And yet I imagine I motioned the old man with a sufficiently dignified gesture to open the door. I had made up my mind that there was in fact a ghost. I had conceded the premise. Only I had assured myself that once the mind was prepared, and the thing was not a surprise, it was possible to keep cool. Captain Diamond turned the lock, flung open the door, and bowed low to me as I passed in. I stood in the darkness, and heard the door close behind me. For some moments, I stirred neither finger nor toe; I stared bravely into the impenetrable dusk. But I saw nothing and heard nothing, and at last I struck a match. On the table were two brass candlesticks rusty from disuse. I lighted the candles and began my tour of exploration.

A wide staircase rose in front of me, guarded by an antique balustrade of that rigidly delicate carving which is found so often in old New England houses. I postponed ascending it, and turned into the room on my right. This was an old-fashioned parlour meagrely furnished, and musty with the absence of human life. I raised my two lights aloft and saw nothing but its empty chairs and its blank walls. Behind it was the room into which I had peeped from without, and which, in fact, communicated with it, as I had supposed, by folding doors. Here, too, I found myself confronted by no menacing spectre. I crossed the hall again, and visited the rooms on the other side; a dining-room in front, where I might have written my name with my finger in the dust of the great square table; a kitchen behind with its pots and pans eternally cold. All this was hard and grim, but it was not formidable. I came back into the hall, and walked to the foot of the staircase, holding up my candles; to ascend required a fresh effort, and I was scanning the gloom above. Suddenly, with an inexpressible sensation, I became aware that this gloom was animated; it seemed to move and gather itself together. Slowly – I say slowly, for to my tense expectancy the instants appeared ages – it took the shape of a large, definite figure, and this figure advanced and stood at the top of the stairs. I frankly confess that by this time I was conscious of a feeling to which I am in duty bound to apply the vulgar name of fear. I may poetize it and call it Dread, with a capital letter; it was at any rate the feeling that makes a man yield ground. I measured it as it grew, and it seemed perfectly irresistible; for it did not appear to come from within but from without, and to be embodied in the dark image at the head of the staircase. After a fashion I reasoned – I remember reasoning. I said to myself, 'I had always thought ghosts were white and transparent; this is a thing of thick shadows, densely opaque.' I reminded myself that the occasion was momentous, and that if fear were to overcome me I should gather all possible impressions while my wits remained. I stepped back, foot behind foot, with my eyes still on the figure and placed my candles on the table. I was perfectly conscious that the proper thing was to ascend the stairs resolutely, face to face with the image, but the soles of my shoes seemed suddenly to have been transformed into leaden weights. I had got what I wanted; I was seeing the ghost. I tried to look at the figure distinctly so that I could remember it, and fairly claim, afterwards, not to have lost my self-possession. I even asked myself how long it was expected I should stand looking, and how soon I could honourably retire. All this, of course, passed through my mind with extreme rapidity, and it was checked by a further movement on the part of the figure. Two white hands appeared in the dark perpendicular mass, and were slowly raised to what seemed to be the level of the head. Here they were pressed together, over the region of the face, and then they were removed, and the face was disclosed. It was dim, white, strange. In every way ghostly. It looked down at me for an instant, after which one of the hands was raised again, slowly, and waved to and fro before it. There was something very singular in this gesture; it seemed to denote resentment and dismissal, and yet had a sort of trivial, familiar motion. Familiarity on the part of the haunting Presence had not entered into my calculations, and did not strike me pleasantly. I agreed with

Captain Diamond that it was 'damned disagreeable.' I was pervaded by an intense desire to make an orderly, and if possible, a graceful retreat. I wished to do it gallantly, and it seemed to me that it would be gallant to blow out my candles. I turned and did so, punctiliously, and then I made my way to the door, groped a moment and opened it. The outer light, almost extinct as it was, entered for a moment, played over the dusty depths of the house and showed me the solid shadow.

Standing on the grass bent over his stick, under the early glimmering stars, I found Captain Diamond. He looked up at me fixedly for a moment, but asked no questions, and then he went and locked the door. This duty performed, he discharged the other – made his obeisance like the priest before the alter – and then without heeding me further, took his departure.

A few days later, I suspended my studies and went off for the summer's vacation. I was absent for several weeks, during which I had plenty of leisure to analyse my impressions of the supernatural. I took some satisfaction in the reflection that I had not been ignobly terrified; I had not bolted nor swooned – I had proceeded with dignity. Nevertheless, I was certainly more comfortable when I had put thirty miles between me and the scene of my exploit, and I continued for many days to prefer the daylight to the dark. My nerves had been powerfully excited; of this I was particularly conscious when, under the influence of the drowsy air of the sea-side, my excitement began slowly to ebb. As it disappeared, I attempted to take a sternly rational view of my experience. Certainly I had seen *something* – that was not fancy; but what had I seen? I regretted extremely now that I had not been bolder, that I had not gone nearer and inspected the apparition more minutely. But it was very well to talk; I had done as much as any man in the circumstances would have dared; it was indeed a physical impossibility that I should have advanced. Was not this paralysis of my powers in itself a supernatural influence? Not necessarily perhaps, for a sham ghost that one accepted might do as much execution as a real ghost. But why had I so easily accepted the sable phantom that waved its hand? Why had it so impressed itself? Unquestionably, true or false, it was a very clever phantom. I greatly preferred that it should have been true – in the first place because I did not care to have shivered and shaken for nothing, and in the second place because to have seen a well-authenticated goblin is, as things go, a feather in a quiet man's cap. I tried, therefore, to let my vision rest and to stop turning it over. But an impulse stronger than my will recurred at intervals and set a mocking question on my lips. Granted that the apparition was Captain Diamond's daughter; if it was she it certainly was her spirit. But was it not her spirit and something more?

The middle of September saw me again establishing among the theologic shades, but I made no haste to revisit the haunted house.

The last of the month approached – the term of another quarter with poor Captain Diamond – and found me indisposed to disturb his pilgrimage on this occasion; though I confess that I thought with a good deal of compassion, of the feeble old man trudging away, lonely, in the Autumn dusk, on his extraordinary errand. On the thirtieth of September, at noonday, I was drowsing over a heavy octavo, when I heard a feeble rap at my door. I replied with an invitation to enter it. Before me stood an elderly negress with her head bound in a scarlet turban, and a white handkerchief folded across her bosom. She looked at me intently and in silence; she had that air of supreme gravity and decency which aged persons of her race so often wear. I stood interrogative, and at last, drawing her hand from her ample pocket, she held up a little book. It was the copy of Pascal's *Thoughts* that I had given to Captain Diamond.

'Please sire,' she said, very mildly, 'do you know this book?'

'Perfectly,' said I, 'my name is on the fly-leaf.'

'It is your name – no other?'

'I will write my name if you like, and you can compare them,' I answered.

She was silent a moment and then, with dignity – 'It would be useless sir,' she said, 'I can't read. If you will give me your word that is enough. I come,' she went on, 'from the gentleman to whom you gave the book. He told me to carry it as a token – a token – that is what he called it. He is right down sick, and he wants to see you.'

'Captain Diamond – sick?' I cried. 'Is his illness serious?'

'He is very bad – he is all gone.'

I expressed my regret and sympathy, and offered to go to him immediately, if his sable messenger would show me the way. She assented deferentially, and in a few minutes I was following her along the sunny streets, feeling very much like a personage in the Arabian Nights led to a postern gate by an Ethiopian slave. My own conductress directed her steps towards the river and stopped at a decent little yellow house in one of the streets that descend to it. She quickly opened the door and led me in, and I very soon found myself in the presence of my old friend. He was in bed, in a darkened room, and evidently in a very feeble state. He lay back on his pillow staring before him, with his bristling hair more erect than ever, and his intensely dark and bright old eyes touched with the glitter of fever. His apartment was humble and scrupulously neat and I could see that my dusky guide was a faithful servant. Captain Diamond lying there rigid and pale on his white sheets, resembled some ruggedly carven figure on the lid of a Gothic tomb. He looked at me silently, and my companion withdrew and left us alone.

'Yes, it's you,' he said, at last, 'it's you, that good young man. There is no mistake, is there?'

'I hope not; I believe I'm a good young man. But I am very sorry you are ill. What can I do for you?'

'I am very bad, very bad; my poor old bones ache so!' and, groaning portentously, he tried to turn towards me.

I questioned him about the nature of his malady and the length of time he had been in bed, but he barely heeded me; he seemed impatient to speak of something else. He grasped my sleeve, pulled me towards him and whispered quickly:

'You know my time's up!'

'Oh, I trust not,' I said, mistaking his meaning. 'I shall certainly see you on your legs again.'

'God knows!' he cried. 'But I don't mean I'm dying; not yet a bit. What I mean is, I'm due at the house. This is rent-day.'

'Oh, exactly! But you can't go.'

'I can't go. It's awful. I shall lose my money. If I am dying, I want it all the same. I want to pay the doctor. I want to be buried like a respectable man.'

'Is it this evening?' I asked.

'This evening at sunset, sharp.'

He lay staring at me, and as I looked at him in return, I suddenly understood his motive for sending for me. Morally, as it came into my thought, I winced. But, I suppose I looked unperturbed, for he continued in the same tone. 'I can't lose my money. Some one else must go. I asked Belinda; but she won't hear of it.'

'You believe the money will be paid to another person?'

'We can try, at least. I have never failed before and I don't know. But, if you say I'm as sick as a dog, that my old bones ache, that I'm dying, perhaps she'll trust you. She doesn't want me to starve!'

'You would like me to go in your place, then?'

'You have been there once; you know what it is. Are you afraid?'

I hesitated.

'Give me three minutes to reflect,' I said, 'and I will tell you.' My glance wandered over the room and rested on the various objects that spoke of the threadbare, decent poverty of its occupant. There seemed to be a mute appeal to my pity and my resolution in their cracked and faded sparseness. Meanwhile Captain Diamond continued, feebly:

'I think she'd trust you, as I have trusted you; she'll like your face; she'll see there is no harm in you. It's a hundred and thirty-three dollars, exactly. Be sure you put them into a safe place.'

'Yes,' I said at last, 'I will go, and, so far as it depends upon me, you shall have the money by nine o'clock tonight.'

He seemed greatly relieved; he took my hand and faintly pressed it, and soon afterwards I withdrew. I tried for the rest of the day not to think of my evening's work, but, of course, I thought of nothing else. I will not deny that I was nervous; I was, in fact, greatly excited, and I spent my time in alternately hoping that the mystery should prove less deep than it appeared, and yet fearing that it might prove too shallow. The hours passed very slowly, but, as the afternoon began to wane, I started on my mission. On the way, I stopped at Captain Diamond's modest dwelling, to ask how he was doing, and to receive such last instructions as he might desire to lay upon me. The old negress, gravely and inscrutably placid, admitted me, and, in answer to my inquiries, said that the Captain was very low; he had sunk since the morning.

'You must be right smart,' she said, 'if you want to get back before he drops off.'

A glance assured me that she knew of my projected expedition, though, in her own opaque black pupil, there was not a gleam of self-betrayal.

'But why should Captain Diamond drop off?' I asked. 'He certainly seems very weak; but I cannot make out that he has any definite disease.'

'His disease is old age,' she said, sententiously.

'But he is not so old as that; sixty-seven or sixty-eight, at most.'

She was silent a moment.

'He's worn out; he's used up; he can't stand it any longer.'

'Can I see him a moment?' I asked; upon which she led me again to his room.

He was lying in the same way as when I had left him, except that his eyes were closed. But he seemed very 'low', as she had said, and he had very little pulse. Nevertheless, I further learned the doctor had been there in the afternoon and professed himself satisfied. 'He don't know what's been going on,' said Belinda curtly.

The old man stirred a little, opened his eyes, and after some time recognized me.

'I'm going, you know,' I said. 'I'm going for your money. Have you anything more to say?' He raised himself slowly, and with a painful effort, against his pillows; but he seemed hardly to understand me. 'The house, you know,' I said. 'Your daughter.'

He rubbed his forehead, slowly, awhile, and at last, his comprehension awoke. 'Ah, yes,' he murmured, 'I trust you. A hundred and thirty-three dollars. In old pieces – all in old pieces.' Then he added more vigorously, and with a brightening eye: 'Be very respectful – be very polite. If not – if not –' and his voice failed again.

'Oh, I certainly shall be,' I said, with a rather forced smile. 'But, if not?'

'If not, I shall know it!' he said, very gravely. And with this, his eyes closed and he sunk down again.

I took my departure and pursued my journey with a sufficiently resolute step. When I reached the house, I made a propitiatory bow in front of it, in emulation of Captain Diamond. I had timed my walk so as to be able to enter without delay; night had already fallen. I turned the key, opened the door and shut it behind me. Then I struck a light, and found the two candlesticks I had used before, standing on the tables in the entry. I applied a match to both of them, took them up and went into the parlour. It was empty, and though I waited awhile, it remained empty. I passed then into the other rooms on the same floor, and no dark image rose before me to check my steps. At last, I came out into the hall again, and stood weighting the question of going upstairs. The staircase had been the scene of my discomfiture before, and I approached it with profound mistrust. At the foot, I paused, looking up, with my hand on the balustrade. I was acutely expectant, and my expectation was justified. Slowly, in the darkness above, the black figure that I had seen before took shape. It was not an illusion; it was a figure, and the same. I gave it time to define itself, and watched it stand and look down at me with its hidden face. Then, deliberately, I lifted up my voice and spoke.

'I have come in place of Captain Diamond, at his request,' I said. 'He is very ill; he is unable to leave his bed. He earnestly begs that you will pay the money to me; I will immediately carry it to him.' The figure stood motionless, giving no sign. 'Captain Diamond would have come if he were able to move,' I added, in a moment, appealingly; 'but he is utterly unable.'

At this the figure slowly unveiled its face and showed me a dim, white mask; then it began slowly to descend the stairs. Instinctively I fell back before it, retreating to the door of the front sitting-room. With my eyes still fixed on it, I moved backward across the threshold; then I stopped in the middle of the room and set down my lights. The figure advanced; it seemed to be that of a tall woman, dressed in vaporous black crepe. As it drew near, I saw that it had a perfectly human face, though it looked extremely pale and sad. We stood gazing at each other; my agitation had completely vanished; I was only deeply interested.

'Is my father dangerously ill?' said the apparition.

At the sound of its voice – gentle, tremulous, and perfectly human – I started forward; I felt a rebound of excitement. I drew a long breath, I gave a sort of cry, for what I saw before me was not a disembodied spirit, but a beautiful woman, an audacious actress. Instinctively, irresistibly, by the force of reaction against my credulity, I stretched out my hand and seized the long veil that muffled her head. I gave it a violent jerk, dragged it nearly off, and stood staring at a large fair person, of about five-and-thirty. I comprehended her at a glance; her long black dress, her pale, sorrow-worn eyes, – the colour of her father's, – and her sense of outrage at my movement.

'My father, I suppose,' she cried, 'did not send you here to insult me!' and she turned away rapidly, took up one of the candles and moved towards the door. Here she paused, looked at me again, hesitated, and then drew a purse from her pocket and flung it down on the floor. 'There is your money!' she said majestically.

I stood there, wavering between amazement and shame, and saw her pass out into the hall. Then I picked up the purse. The next moment, I heard a loud shriek and a crash of something dropping, and she came staggering back into the room without her light.

'My father – my father!' she cried, and with parted lips and dilated eyes, she rushed towards me.

'Your father – where?' I demanded.

'In the hall, at the foot of the stairs.'

I stepped forward to go out, but she seized my arm.

'He is in white,' she cried, 'in his shirt. It's not he!'

'Why, your father is in his house, in his bed extremely ill,' I answered.

She looked fixedly, with searching eyes.

'Dying?'

'I hope not,' I stuttered.

She gave a long moan and covered her face with her hands.

'Oh, heavens, I have seen his ghost!' she cried.

She still held my arm; she seemed terrified to release it.

'His ghost!' I echoed, wondering.

'It's the punishment of my long folly!' she went on.

'Ah,' said I, 'it's the punishment of my indiscretion – of my violence!'

'Take me away, take me away!' she cried, still clinging to my arm. 'Not there' – as I was turning towards the hall and the front door – 'not there, for pity's sake! By this door – the back entrance.' And snatching the other candles from the table, she led me through the neighbouring room in to the back part of the house. Here was a door opening from a sort of scullery into the orchard. I turned the rusty lock and we passed out and stood in the cool air, beneath the stars. Here my companion gathered her black drapery about her, and stood for a moment, hesitating. I had been infinitely flurried, but my curiosity touching her was uppermost. Agitated, pale, picturesque, she looked, in the early evening light, very beautiful.

'You have been playing all these years a most extraordinary game,' I said.

She looked at me sombrely, and seemed disinclined to reply. 'I came in perfect good faith,' I went on. 'The last time – three months ago – you remember? – you greatly frightened me.'

'Of course it was an extraordinary game,' she answered at last. 'But it was the only way.'

'Had he not forgiven you?'

'So long as he thought me dead, yes. There have been things in my life he could not forgive.'

I hesitated and then – 'And where is your husband?' I asked.

'I have no husband – I have never had a husband.'

She made a gesture which checked further questions, and moved rapidly away. I walked with her round the house to the road, and she kept murmuring – 'It was he – it was he!' When we reached the road she stopped, and asked me which way I was going. I pointed to the road by which I had come, and she said – 'I take the other. You are going to my father's?' she added.

'Directly,' I said.

'Will you let me know tomorrow what you have found?'

'With pleasure. But how shall I communicate with you?'

She seemed at a loss, and looked about her. 'Write a few words,' she said, 'and put them under that stone.' And she pointed to one of the lava slabs that bordered the old well. I gave her my promise to comply, and she turned away. 'I know my road,' she said. 'Everything is arranged. It's an old story.'

She left me with a rapid step, and as she receded into the darkness, resumed, with the dark flowing lines of her drapery, the phantasmal appearance with which she had at first appeared to me. I watched her till she became invisible, and then I took my own leave of the place. I returned to town at a swinging pace, and marched straight to the little yellow house near the river. I took the liberty of entering without a knock, and, encountering no interruption, made my way to Captain Diamond's room. Outside the door, on a low bench, with folded arms, sat the sable Belinda.

'How is he?' I asked.

'He's gone to glory.'

'Dead?' I cried.

She rose with a sort of tragic chuckle.

'He's as big a ghost as any of them now!'

I passed into the room and found the old man lying there irredeemably rigid and still. I wrote that evening a few lines which I proposed on the morrow to place beneath the stone, near the well; but my promise was not destined to be executed. I slept that night very ill – it was natural – and in my restlessness left my bed to walk about the room. As I did so I caught sight, in passing my window, of a red glow in the north-western sky. A house was on fire in the country, and evidently burning fast. It lay in the same direction as the scene of my evening's adventures, and as I stood watching the crimson horizon I was startled by a sharp memory. I had blown out the candle which lighted me, with my companion, to the door through which we escaped, but I had not accounted for the other light, which she had carried into the hall and dropped – heaven knew where – in her consternation. The next day I walked out with my folded letter and turned into the familiar cross-road. The haunted house was a mass of charred beams and smouldering ashes; the well-cover had been pulled off, in quest of water, by the few neighbours who had had the audacity to contest what they must have regarded as a demon-kindled blaze, the loose stones were completely displaced, and the earth had been trampled into puddles.

Markheim

Robert Louis Stevenson

'Yes,' said the dealer, 'our windfalls are of various kinds. Some customers are ignorant, and then I touch a dividend of my superior knowledge. Some are dishonest,' and here he held up the candle so that the light fell strongly on his visitor, 'and in that case,' he continued, 'I profit by my virtue.'

Markheim had but just entered from the daylight streets, and his eyes had not yet grown familiar with the mingled shine and darkness in the shop. At these pointed words, and before the near presence of the flame, he blinked painfully, and looked aside.

The dealer chuckled. 'You come to me on Christmas Day,' he resumed, 'when you know that I am alone in my house, put up my shutters, and make a point of refusing business. Well, you will have to pay for that; you will have to pay for my loss of time, when I should be balancing my books; you will have to pay, besides, for a kind of manner that I remark in you to-day very strongly. I am the essence of discretion, and ask no awkward questions; but when a customer cannot look me in the eye, he has to pay for it.' The dealer once more chuckled; and then, changing to his usual business voice, though still with a note of irony: 'You can give, as usual, a clear account of how you came into the possession of the object?' he continued. 'Still your uncle's cabinet? A remarkable collector, sir!'

And the little pale, round-shouldered dealer stood almost on tiptoe, looking over the top of his gold spectacles, and nodding his head with every mark of disbelief. Markheim returned his gaze with one of infinite pity and a touch of horror.

'This time,' said he, 'you are in error. I have not come to sell, but to buy. I have no curios to dispose of; my uncle's cabinet is bare to the wainscot; even were it still intact, I have done well on the Stock Exchange, and should more likely add to it than otherwise, and my errand to-day is simplicity itself. I seek a Christmas present for a lady,' he continued, waxing more fluent as he struck into the speech he had prepared; 'and certainly I owe you every excuse for thus disturbing you upon so small a matter. But the thing was neglected yesterday; I must produce my little compliment at dinner; and, as you know, a rich marriage is not a thing to be neglected.'

There followed a pause, during which the dealer seemed to weigh this statement incredulously. The ticking of many clocks among the curious lumber of the shop, and the faint rushing of the cabs in a near thoroughfare, filled up the interval of silence.

'Well, sir,' said the dealer, 'be it so. You are an old customer, after all; and if, as you say, you have the chance of a good marriage, far be it from me to be an obstacle. Here is a nice thing for a lady now,' he went on, 'this hand-glass – fifteenth century, warranted; comes from a good collection too: but I reserve the name, in the interests of my customer, who was just like yourself, my dear sir, the nephew and sole heir of a remarkable collector.'

The dealer, while he thus ran on in his dry and biting voice, had stooped to take the object from its place; and, as he had done so, a shock had passed through Markheim, a start both of hand and foot, a sudden leap of many tumultuous passions to the face. It passed as swiftly as it came, and left no trace beyond a certain trembling of the hand that now received the glass.

'A glass,' he said hoarsely, and then paused, and repeated it more clearly. 'A glass? For Christmas? Surely not!'

'And why not?' cried the dealer. 'Why not a glass?'

Markheim was looking upon him with an indefinable

expression. 'You ask me why not?' he said. 'Why look here – look in it – look at yourself! Do you like to see it? No! nor I – nor any man.'

The little man had jumped back when Markheim had so suddenly confronted him with the mirror; but now, perceiving there was nothing worse on hand, he chuckled. 'Your future lady, sir, must be pretty hard-favoured,' said he.

'I ask you,' said Markheim, 'for a Christmas present, and you give me this – this damned reminder of years, and sins, and follies – this hand-conscience! Did you mean it? Had you a thought in your mind? Tell me. It will be better for you if you do. Come, tell me about yourself. I hazard a guess, now, that you are in secret a very charitable man?'

The dealer looked closely at his companion. It was very odd, Markheim did not appear to be laughing; there was something in his face like an eager sparkle of hope, but nothing of mirth.

'What are you driving at?' the dealer asked.

'Not charitable?' returned the other gloomily. 'Not charitable; not pious; not scrupulous; unloving, unbeloved; a hand to get money, a safe to keep it. Is that all? Dear God, man, is that all?'

'I will tell you what it is,' began the dealer, with some sharpness, and then broke off again into a chuckle. 'But I see this is a love-match of yours, and you have been drinking the lady's health.'

'Ah!' cried Markheim, with a strange curiosity. 'Ah, have you been in love? Tell me about that.'

'I,' cried the dealer. 'I in love! I never had the time, nor have I the time to-day for all this nonsense. Will you take the glass?'

'Where is the hurry?' returned Markheim. 'It is very pleasant to stand here talking; and life is so short and insecure that I would not hurry away from any pleasure – no, not even from so mild a one as this. We should rather cling, cling to what little we can get. Like a man at a cliff's edge. Every second is a cliff, if you think upon it – a cliff a mile high – high enough, if we fall, to dash us out of every feature of humanity. Hence it is best to talk pleasantly. Let us talk of each other; why should we wear this mask? Let us be confidential. Who knows, we might become friends?'

'I have just one word to say to you,' said the dealer. 'Either make your purchase, or walk out of my shop.'

'True, true,' said Markheim. 'Enough fooling. To business. Show me something else.'

The dealer stooped once more, this time to replace the glass upon the shelf, his thin blond hair falling over his eyes as he did so. Markheim moved a little nearer, with one hand in the pocket of his greatcoat; he drew himself up and filled his lungs; at the same time many different emotions were depicted together on his face – terror, horror, and resolve, fascination and a physical repulsion; and through a haggard lift of his upper lip his teeth looked out.

'This, perhaps, may suit,' observed the dealer; and then, as he began to re-arise, Markheim bounded from behind upon his victim. The long, skewer-like dagger flashed and fell. The dealer struggled like a hen, striking his temple on the shelf, and then tumbled on the floor in a heap.

Time had some score of small voices in that shop, some stately and slow as was becoming to their great age; others garrulous and hurried. All these tolled out the seconds in an intricate chorus of tickings. Then the passage of a lad's feet, heavily running on the pavement, broke in upon these smaller voices, and startled Markheim into the consciousness of his surroundings. He looked about him awfully. The candle stood on the counter, its flame solemnly wagging in a draught; and by that inconsiderable movement the whole room was filled with noiseless bustle and kept heaving like a sea; the tall shadows nodding, the gross blots of darkness swelling and dwindling as with respiration, the faces of the portraits and the china gods changing and wavering like leaguer of shadows with a long slit of daylight, like a pointing finger.

From these fear-stricken rovings, Markheim's eyes returned to the body of his victim, where it lay both humped and sprawling, incredibly small and strangely meaner than in life.

In these poor, miserly clothes, in that ungainly attitude, the dealer lay like so much sawdust. Markheim had feared to see it, and lo! It was nothing. And yet, as he gazed, this bundle of old clothes and pool of blood began to find eloquent voices. There it must lie; there was none to work the cunning hinges or direct the miracle of locomotion – there it must lie till it was found. Found! Ay, and then? Then would this dead flesh lift up a cry that would ring over England, and fill the world with the echoes of pursuit. Ay, dead or not, this was still the enemy. 'Time was that when the brains were out,' he thought; and the first word struck in to his mind. Time, now that the deed was accomplished – time, which had closed for the victim, had become instant and momentous for the slayer.

The thought was yet in his mind, when, first one and then another, with every variety of pace and voice – one deep as the bell from a cathedral turret, another ringing on its treble notes the prelude of a waltz – the clocks began to strike the hour of three in the afternoon.

The sudden outbreak of so many tongues in that dumb chamber staggered him. He began to bestir himself, going to and fro with the candle, beleaguered by moving shadows, and startled to the soul by chance reflections. In many rich mirrors, some of home designs, some from Venice or Amsterdam, he saw his face repeated and repeated, as it were an army of spies; his own eyes met and detected him; and the sound of his own steps, lightly as they fell, vexed the surrounding quiet. And still, as he continued to fill his pockets, his mind accused him, with a sickening iteration, of the thousand faults of his design. He should have chosen a more quiet hour; he should have been more cautious, and only bound and gagged the dealer, and not killed him; he should have been more bold, and killed the servant also; he should have done all things otherwise; poignant regrets, weary, incessant toiling of the mind to change what was unchangeable, to plan what was now useless, to be the architect of the irrevocable past. Meanwhile, and behind all this activity, brute terrors, like the scurrying of rats in a deserted attic, filled the more remote chambers of his brain with riot; the hand of the constable would fall heavy on his shoulder, and his nerves would jerk like a hooked fish; or he beheld, in galloping defile, the dock, the prison, the gallows, and the black coffin.

Terror of the people in the street sat down before his mind like a besieging army. It was impossible, he thought, but that some rumour of the struggle must have reached their ears and set on edge their curiosity; and now, in all the neighbouring houses, he divined them sitting motionless and with uplifted ear – solitary people, condemned to spend Christmas dwelling alone on memories of the past, and now startlingly recalled from that tender exercise; happy family parties, struck into silence round the table, the mother still with raised finger; every degree and age of humour, but all, by their own hearts, prying and hearkening and weaving the rope that was to hang him. Sometimes it seemed to him he could not move too softly; the clink of the tall Bohemian goblets rang out loudly like a bell; and, alarmed by the bigness of the ticking, he was tempted to stop the clocks. And then, again, with a swift transition of his terrors, the very silence of the place appeared a source of peril, and a thing to strike and freeze the passer-by; and he would step more boldly, and bustle aloud among the contents of the shop, and imitate with elaborate bravado, the movements of a busy man at ease in his own house.

But he was now so pulled about by different alarms that, while one portion of his mind was still alert and cunning, another trembled on the brink of lunacy. One hallucination in particular took a strong hold on his credulity. The neighbour hearkening with white face beside his window, the passer-by arrested by a horrible surmise on the pavement – these could at worst suspect, they could not know; through the brick walls and shuttered windows only sounds could penetrate. But here, within the house, was he alone? He knew he was; he had watched the servant set forth sweethearting in her poor best, 'out for the day' written in every ribbon and smile. Yes, he was alone, of course; and yet, in the bulk of empty house above him, he could surely hear a stir of delicate footing – he was surely conscious, inexplicably conscious of some presence. Ay, surely; to every room and corner of the house his imagination followed it; and now it was a faceless thing, and yet had eyes to see with; and again it was a shadow of himself; and yet again beheld the image of the dead dealer, reinspired with cunning and hatred.

At times, with a strong effort, he would glance at the open door, which still seemed to repel his eyes. The house was tall, the skylight small and dirty, the day blind with fog; and the light that filtered down to the ground storey was exceedingly faint, and showed dimly on the threshold of the shop. And yet, in that strip of doubtful brightness, did there not hang wavering a shadow?

Suddenly, from the street outside, a very jovial gentleman began to beat with a staff on the shop door, accompanying his blows with shouts and railleries in which the dealer was continually called upon by name. Markheim, smitten into ice, glanced at the dead man. But no! he lay quite still; he was fled away far beyond ear-shot of these blows and shoutings; he was sunk beneath seas of silence; and his name, which would once have caught his notice above the howling of a storm, had become an empty sound. And presently the jovial gentleman desisted from his knocking and departed.

Here was a broad hint to hurry what remained to be done, to get forth from this accusing neighbourhood, to plunge into a bath of London multitudes, and to reach, on the other side of day, that haven of safety and apparent innocence – his bed. One visitor had come: at any moment another might follow and be more obstinate. To have done the deed and yet not to reap the profit would be too abhorrent a failure. The money, that was now Markheim's concern; and, as a mean to that, the keys.

He glanced over his shoulder at the open door where the shadow was still lingering and shivering; and with no conscious repugnance of the mind, yet with a tremor of the belly, he drew near the body of his victim. The human character had quite departed. Like a suit half stuffed with bran, the limbs lay scattered, the trunk doubled, on the floor; and yet the thing repelled him. Although so dingy and inconsiderable to the eye, he feared it might have more significance to the touch. He took the body by the shoulders, and turned it on its back. It was strangely light and supple, and the limbs, as if they had been broken, fell into the oddest postures. The face was robbed of all expression; but it was as pale as wax, and shockingly smeared with blood about one temple. That was, for Markheim, the one displeasing circumstance. It carried him back, upon the instant, to a certain fair day in a fishers' village: a grey day, a piping wind, a crowd upon the street, the blare of brasses, the booming of drums, the nasal voice of a ballad-singer; and a boy going to and fro, buried overhead in the crowd and divided between interest and fear, until, coming out upon the chief place of concourse, he beheld a booth and a great screen with pictures, dismally designed, garishly coloured: Brownrigg with her apprentice; the Mannings with their murdered guest; Weare in the death-grip of Thurtell; and a score besides of famous crimes. The thing was as clear as an illusion; he was once again that little boy; he was looking once again, and with the same sense of physical revolt, at these vile pictures; he was still stunned by the thumping of the drums. A bar of that day's music returned upon his memory; and at that, for the first time, a qualm came over him, a breath of nausea, a sudden weakness of the joints, which he must instantly resist and conquer.

He judged it more prudent to confront than to flee from these considerations; looking the more hardily in the dead face, bending his mind to realise the nature and greatness of his crime. So little a while ago that face had moved with every change of sentiment, that pale mouth had spoken, that body had been all on fire with governable energies; and now, and by his act, that piece of life had been arrested, as the horologist, with interjected finger, arrests the beating of the clock. So he reasoned in vain; he could rise to no more remorseful consciousness; the same heart which had shuddered before the painted effigies of crime looked on its reality unmoved. At best, he felt a gleam of pity for one who had been endowed in vain with all those faculties that can make the world a garden of enchantment, one who had never lived and who was now dead. But of penitence, no, not a tremor.

With that, shaking himself clear of these considerations, he found the keys and advanced towards the open door of the shop. Outside, it had begun to rain smartly; and the sound of the shower upon the roof had banished silence. Like some dripping cavern, the chambers of the house were haunted by an incessant echoing, which filled the ear and mingled with the ticking of the clocks. And, as Markheim approached the door, he seemed to hear, in answer to his own cautious tread, the steps of another foot withdrawing up the stair. The shadow still palpitated loosely on the threshold. He threw a ton's weight of resolve upon his muscles, and drew back the door.

The faint, foggy daylight glimmered dimly on the bare floor and stairs; on the bright suit of armour posted, halbert in hand, upon the landing; and on the dark wood-carvings and framed pictures that hung against the yellow panels of the wainscot. So loud was the beating of the rain through all the house that, in Markheim's ears, it began to be distinguished into many different sounds. Footsteps and sighs, the tread of regiments marching in the distance, the chink of money in the counting, and the creaking of doors held stealthily ajar, appeared to mingle with the patter of the drops upon the cupola and the gushing of the water in the pipes. The sense that he was not alone grew upon him to the verge of madness. On every side he was haunted and begirt by presences. He heard them moving in the upper chambers; from the shop, he heard the dead man getting to his legs; and as he began with a great effort to mount the stairs, feet fled quietly before him and followed stealthily behind. If he were but deaf, he thought, how tranquilly he would possess his soul! And then again, and hearkening with ever fresh attention, he blessed himself for that unresting sense which held the outposts and stood a trusty sentinel upon his life. His head turned continually on his neck; his eyes, which seemed starting from their orbits, scouted on every side, and on every side were half rewarded as with the tail of something nameless vanishing. The four-and-twenty steps to the first floor were four-and-twenty agonies.

On that first storey, the doors stood ajar, three of them like three ambushes, shaking his nerves, like the throats of cannon. He could never again, he felt, be sufficiently immured and fortified from men's observing eyes; he longed to be home, girt in by walls, buried among bed-clothes, and invisible to all but God. And at that thought he wondered a little, recollecting tales of other murderers and fear they were said to entertain of heavenly avengers. It was not so, at least, with him. He feared the laws of nature, lest, in their callous and immutable procedure, they should preserve some damning evidence of his crime. He feared tenfold more, with a slavish, superstitious terror, some scission in the continuity of man's experience, some wilful illegality of nature. He played a game of skill, depending on the rules, calculating consequence from cause; and what if nature, as the defeated tyrant overthrew the chess-board, should break the mould of their succession? The like had befallen Napoleon (so writers said) when the winter changed the time of its appearance. The like might befall Markheim: the solid walls might become transparent and reveal his doings like those of bees in a glass hive; the stout plants might yield under his foot like quicksands and detain him in their clutch; ay, and there were soberer accidents that might destroy him; if, for instance, the house should fall and imprison him beside the body of his victim; or the house next door should fly on fire, and the firemen invade him from all sides. These things he feared; and, in a sense, these things might be called the hands of God reached forth against sin. But about God Himself he was at ease; his act was doubtless exceptional, but so were his excuses, which God knew; it was there, and not among men, that he felt sure of justice.

When he had got the safe into the drawing-room, and shut the door behind him, he was aware of a respite from alarms. The room was quite dismantled, uncarpeted besides, and strewn with packing-cases and incongruous furniture; several great pier-glasses, in which he beheld himself at various angles, like an actor on stage; many pictures, framed and unframed, a cabinet of marquetry, and a great old bed, with tapestry hangings. The windows opened to the floor: but by great good fortune the lower part of the shutters had been closed, and this concealed him from the neighbours. Here, then, Markheim drew in a packing-case before the cabinet, and began to search among the keys. It was a long business, for there were many; and it was irksome, besides; for, after all, there might be nothing in the cabinet, and time was on the wing; but the closeness of the occupation sobered him. With the tail of his eye he saw the door – even glanced at it from time to time directly, like a besieged commander pleased to verify the good estate of his defences. But in truth he was at peace. The rain falling in the street sounded natural and pleasant. Presently, on the other side, the notes of a piano were awakened to the music of a hymn, and the voices of many children took up the air and words. How stately, how comfortable was the melody; how fresh the youthful voices; Markheim gave ear to it smilingly, as he sorted out the keys; and his mind was thronged with answerable ideas and images; church-going children and the pealing of the high organ; children afield, bathers by the brookside, ramblers on the brambly common, kite-fliers in the windy and cloud-navigated sky; and then, at another cadence of the hymn, back again to church and the somnolence of summer Sundays, and the high genteel voice of the parson (which he smiled a little to recall) and the painted Jacobean tombs, and the dim lettering of the Ten Commandments in the chancel.

And as he sat thus, at once busy and absent, he was startled to his feet. A flash of ice, a flash of fire, a bursting gush of blood, went over him, and then he stood transfixed and thrilling. A step mounted the stair slowly and steadily, and presently a hand was laid upon the knob, and the lock clicked, and the door opened.

Fear held Markheim in a vice. What to expect he knew not, whether the dead man walking, or the official ministers of human justice, or some chance witness blindly stumbling in to consign him to the gallows. But when a face was thrust into the aperture, glanced round the room, looked at him, nodded and smiled as if in friendly recognition, and then withdrew again, and the door closed behind it, his fear broke loose from his control in a hoarse cry. At the sound of this the visitant returned.

'Did you call me?' he asked pleasantly, and with that he entered the room and closed the door behind him.

Markheim stood and gazed at him with all his eyes. Perhaps there was a film upon his sight, but the outlines of the new-comer seemed to change and waver like those of the idols in the wavering candlelight of the shop; and at times he thought he knew him; and at times he thought he bore a likeness to himself; and always, like a lump of living terror, there lay in his bosom the conviction that this thing was not of the earth and not of God.

And yet the creature had a strange air of the commonplace, as he stood looking on Markheim with a smile; and when he added: 'You are looking for the money, I believe?' it was in the tones of everyday politeness.

Markheim made no answer.

'I should warn you,' resumed the other, 'that the maid has left her sweetheart earlier than usual and will soon be here. If Mr Markheim be found in this house, I need not describe to him the consequences.'

'You know me?' cried the murderer.

The visitor smiled. 'You have long been a favourite of mine,' he said; 'and I have long observed and often sought to help you.'

'What are you?' cried Markheim: 'the devil?'

'What I may be,' returned the other, 'cannot affect the service I propose to render you.'

'It can,' cried Markheim; 'it does! Be helped by you? No, never; not by you! You do not know me yet; thank God, you do not know me!'

'I know you,' replied the visitant, with a sort of kind severity or rather firmness. 'I know you to the soul.'

'Know me!' cried Markheim. 'Who can do so? My life is but a travesty and slander on myself. I have lived to belie by nature. All men do; all men are better than this disguise that grows about and stifles them. You see each dragged away by life, like one whom bravos have seized and muffled in a cloak. If they had their own control – if you could see their faces, they would be altogether different, they would shine out for heroes and saints! I am worse than most; my self is more overlaid; my excuse is known to me and God. But, had I the time, I could disclose myself.'

'To me?' inquired the visitant.

'To you before all,' returned the murderer. 'I suppose you were intelligent. I thought – since you exist – you would prove a reader of the heart. And yet you would propose to judge me by my acts! Think of it; my acts! I was born and I have lived in a land of giants; giants have dragged me by the wrists since I was born out of my mother – the giants of circumstance. And you would judge me by my acts! But can you not look within? Can you not understand that evil is hateful to me? Can you not see within me the clear writing of conscience, never blurred by any wilful sophistry, although too often disregarded? Can you not read me for a thing that surely must be common as humanity – the unwilling sinner?'

'All this is very feelingly expressed,' was the reply, 'but it regards me not. These points of consistency are beyond my province, and I care not in the least by what compulsion you may have been dragged away, so as you are but carried in the right direction. But time flies; the servant delays, looking in the faces of the crowd and at the pictures on the hoardings, but still she keeps moving nearer; and remember, it is as if the gallows itself were striding towards you through the Christmas streets! Shall I help you; I, who know all? Shall I tell you where to find the money?'

'For what price?' asked Markheim.

'I offer you the service for a Christmas gift,' returned the other.

Markheim could not refrain from smiling, with a kind of bitter triumph. 'No,' said he, 'I will take nothing at your hands; if I were dying of thirst, and it was your hand that put the pitcher to my lips, I should find the courage to refuse. It may be credulous, but I will do nothing to commit myself to evil.'

'I have no objection to a death-bed repentance,' observed the visitant.

'Because you disbelieve their efficacy!' Markheim cried.

'I do not say so,' returned the other; 'but I look on these things from a different side, and when the life is done my interest falls. The man has lived to serve me, to spread black looks under colour of religion, or to sow tares in the wheat-field, as you do, in a course of weak compliance with desire. Now that he draws so near to his deliverance, he can add but one act of service – to repent, to die smiling, and thus to build up in confidence and hope that more timorous of my surviving followers. I am not so hard a master. Try me. Accept my help. Please yourself in life as you have done hitherto; please yourself more amply, spread your elbows at the board; and when the night begins to fall and the curtains to be drawn, I tell you, for your greater comfort, that you will find it even easy to compound your quarrel with your conscience, and to make a truckling peace with God. I came but now from such a death-bed, and the room was full of sincere mourners, listening to the man's last words: and when I looked into that face, which had been set as a flint against mercy, I found it smiling with hope.'

'And do you, then, suppose me such a creature?' asked Markheim. 'Do you think I have no more generous aspirations than to sin, and sin, and, at last, sneak into Heaven? My heart rises at the thought. Is this, then, your experience of mankind? Or is it because you find me with red hands that you presume such baseness? And is this crime of murder indeed so impious as to dry up the very springs of good?'

'Murder to me is no special category,' replied the other. 'All sins are murder, even as all life is war. I behold your race, like starving mariners on a raft, plucking crusts out of the hands of famine and feeding on each other's lives. I follow sins beyond the moment of their acting; I find in all that the last consequence is death; and, to my eyes, the pretty maid thwarts her mother with such taking graces on a question of a ball, drips no less visibly with human gore than such a murderer as yourself. Do I say that I follow sins? I follow virtues also; they differ not by the thickness of a nail, they are both scythes for the reaping angel of Death. Evil, for which I live, consists not in action but in character. The bad man is dear to me; not the bad act, whose fruits, if we could follow them far enough down the hurtling cataract of the ages, might yet be found more blessed than those of the rarest virtues. And it is not because you have killed a dealer, but because you are Markheim, that I offered to forward your escape.'

'I will lay my heart open to you,' answered Markheim. 'This crime on which you find me is my last. On the way to it I have learned many lessons; itself is a lesson, a momentous lesson. Hitherto I have been driven with revolt to what I would not; I was a bondslave to poverty, driven and scourged. There are robust virtues that can stand in these temptations; mine was not so; I had a thirst of pleasure. But to-day, and out of this deed, I pluck both warning and riches – both the power and a fresh resolve to be myself. I become in all things a free actor in the world; I begin to see myself all changed, these hands the agents of good, this heart at peace. Something comes over me out of the past; something of what I have dreamed on Sabbath evenings to the sound of the church organ, of what I forecast when I shed tears over noble books, or talked, an innocent child, with my mother. There lies my life; I have wandered a few years, but now I see once more my city of destination.'

'You are to use this money on the Stock Exchange, I think?' remarked the visitor; 'and there, if I mistake not, you have already lost some thousands?'

'Ah,' said Markheim, 'but this time I have a sure thing.'

'This time, again, you will lose,' replied the visitor quietly.

'Ah, but I keep back the half!' cried Markheim.

'That you will also lose,' said the other.

The sweat started upon Markheim's brow. 'Well then, what matter?' he exclaimed. 'Say it be lost, say I am plunged again in poverty, shall one part of me, and that the worst, continue until the end to over-ride the better? Evil and good run strong in me, haling me both ways. I do not love one thing, I love all. I can conceive great deeds, renunciations, martyrdoms; and though I be fallen to such a crime as murder, pity is no stranger to my thoughts. I pity the poor; who knows their trials better than myself? I pity and help them; I prize love, I love honest laughter, there is no good thing nor true thing on earth but I love it from my heart. And are my vices only to direct my life, and my virtues to lie without effect, like some passive lumber of the mind? Not so; good, also, is a spring of acts.'

But the visitant raised a finger. 'For six-and-thirty years that you have been in this world,' said he, 'through many changes of fortune and varieties of humour, I have watched you steadily fall. Fifteen years ago you would have started at a theft. Three years back you would have blenched at the name of murder. Is there any crime, is there any cruelty or meanness, from which you still recoil five years from now? I shall detect you in the fact! Downward, downward, lies your way; nor can anything but death avail to stop you.'

'It is true,' Markheim said huskily. 'I have in some degree complied with evil. But it is so with all: the very saints, in the mere exercise of living, grow less dainty and take on the tone of their surroundings.'

'I will propound to you one simple question,' said the other;

'and, as your answer, I shall read to you your moral horoscope. You have grown in many things more lax; possibly you do right to be so; and, at any account, it is the same with all men. But, granting that, are you in any one particular, however trifling, more difficult to please with your own conduct, or do you go in all things with a looser rein?'

'In any one?' repeated Markheim, with an anguish of consideration. 'No,' he added, with despair, 'in none! I have gone down in all.'

'Then,' said the visitor, 'content yourself with what you are, for you will never change; and the words of your part on this stage are irrevocably written down.'

Markheim stood for a long while silent, and indeed it was the visitor who first broke the silence. 'That being so,' he said, 'shall I show you the money?'

'And grace?' cried Markheim.

'Have you not tried it?' returned the other. 'Two or three years ago, did I not see you on the platform of revival meetings, and was not your voice the loudest in the hymn?'

'It is true,' said Markheim; 'and I see clearly what remains for me by way of duty. I thank you for those lessons from my soul; my eyes are opened, and I behold myself at last for what I am.'

At this moment, the sharp note of the doorbell rang through the house; and the visitant, as though this were some concerted signal for which he had been waiting, changed at once in his demeanour. 'The maid!' he cried. 'She has returned, as I forewarned you, and there is now before you one more difficult passage. Her master, you must say, is ill; you must let her in, with an assured but rather serious countenance – no smiles, no over-acting, and I promise you success! Once the girl is within, and the door closed, the same dexterity that has already rid you of the dealer will relieve you of this last danger in your path. Thenceforward you have the whole evening – the whole night, if needful – to ransack the treasures of the house and to make good your safety. This is help that comes to you with the mask of danger. Up!' he cried: 'up, friend; your life hangs trembling in the scales: up, and act!'

Markheim steadily regarded his counsellor. 'If I be condemned to evil acts,' he said, 'there is still one door of freedom open – I can cease action. If my life be an ill thing, I can lay it down. Though I be, as you say truly, at the beck of every small temptation, I can yet, by one decisive gesture, place myself beyond the reach of all. My love of good is damned to barrenness; it may, and let it be! But I have still my hatred of evil; and from that, to your galling disappointment, you shall see that I can draw both energy and courage.'

The features of the visitor began to undergo a wonderful and lovely change; they brightened and softened with a tender triumph; and, even as they brightened, faded and dislimned. But Markheim did not pause to watch or understand the transformation. He opened the door and went downstairs very slowly, thinking to himself. His past went soberly before him; he beheld it as it was, ugly and strenuous like a dream, random as chance-medley – a scene of defeat. Life, as he thus reviewed it, tempted him no longer; but on the further side he perceived a quiet haven for his barque. He paused in the passage, and looked into the shop, where the candle still burned by the dead body. It was strangely silent. Thoughts of the dealer swarmed into his mind, as he stood gazing. And then the bell once more broke out into impatient clamour.

He confronted the maid upon the threshold with something like a smile.

'You had better go for the police,' said he: 'I have killed your master.'

The Horla

Guy de Maupassant

8th May. What a perfect day! All the morning I lay stretched out on the grass in front of my house, under the towering plane-tree that spreads over the roof, giving protection and shade. I love this countryside, and love to live in this place, for here I am rooted fast by those deep and tender roots that bind a man to the soil where his forefathers lived and died, bind him to ways of thinking and eating, to customs and meat and drink, to the tones of the peasants' voices and turns of phrase, to the smell of the villages, the smell of the earth and of the air itself.

I love this house of mine where I have grown to manhood. From my windows I can see the Seine flowing by my garden, beyond the road, almost past my door – the broad River Seine, which goes from Rouen to Havre, laden with passing boats.

Away to the left lies the city of Rouen, blue-roofed beneath the throng of its pointed Gothic spires; above them all, slender but strong, rises the cathedral's iron shaft. They are innumerable, these spires – filled with bells that ring, under the azure of morning skies, sending forth their distant metallic humming, a brazen song blown by the breeze, stronger now and now fainter, as it rises and falls.

How lovely it was this morning!

Towards eleven, a long line of barges, drawn by a tug the size of a fly, groaning and straining and belching volleys of smoke, filed past my gates.

And after two English schooners, with red flags fluttering to the sky, came a noble Brazilian three-master, gleaming, spotlessly white from stem to stern. I saluted it: I don't know why the sight of this vessel gave me such pleasure.

12 May. For some days I have had a touch of fever; I feel unwell, or rather, I feel depressed.

Whence come these mysterious influences, changing our happiness into gloom, our self-confidence into vague distress? One would thing that the air, the transparent air, was full of unknowable powers, whose mysterious presence affected us. I wake up gay as a bird, feeling as though I must sing. Why? I go for a walk downstream; and suddenly, after strolling a little way, I turn back feeling disheartened, as if some misfortune awaited me at home. Why? Is it some cold shiver, passing over me, that has shaken my nerves, overshadowed my soul? Is it the shape of the clouds, or the colour of the day, the ever-changing hue of things, that has entered my eyes to trouble my thoughts? Who can say? Everything about us, everything we look at but do not see, everything we brush against but do not know, everything we touch but do not feel, has, on ourselves, on our senses, and through them, on our thoughts, on our very heart, effects that are sudden, surprising, inexplicable.

16th May. I am ill, undoubtedly! And I was so well last month! I have a fever, a dreadful fever, or rather a feverish attack of nerves, that afflicts my mind quite as much as my body. I have this constant, horrible feeling of a danger threatening, this apprehension of impending misfortune or approaching death, this presentiment which means no doubt the inroads of some disease, unknown as yet, at work in my blood and my flesh.

18th May. I have been to see my doctor, for I could not sleep any longer. He found that I had a quickened pulse, dilated pupils, and jangling nerves, but no disquieting symptom. I am to have douches and take bromide of potassium.

25th May. No change whatever! My condition is indeed strange. As evening draws on an unaccountable restlessness comes over me, as if the night held some dreadful menace in store for me. I dine quickly, then try to read; but I do not understand the words; I can hardly tell letter from letter. Up and down my room I go, oppressed by a vague and overmastering dread – dread of sleep, dread even of my bed.

Towards two I go to my bedroom. No sooner inside than I turn the key twice in the lock and shoot the bolts. I am frightened … of what? … I who have never been frightened before … I open my cupboards, look under my bed. I listen … listen … for what? Isn't it strange that a mere touch of something, a disturbed circulation, perhaps, some irritation of the network of the nerves, a slight congestion, a tiny interruption in the delicate and very imperfect working of the vital machine, can turn one of the bravest of men into a coward, one of the gayest into a victim of melancholia? Then I go to bed, and I wait for sleep as one might wait for the executioner. I wait in terror of its coming, with beating heart and trembling limbs; and my whole body shudders in the warmth of the blankets, up to the moment when I fall asleep of a sudden, as one would fall into a pit of stagnant water to drown.

I sleep – for some little time – two or three hours – then a dream – no, a nightmare, lays hold on me. I am quite aware that I am in bed and asleep – I feel it and know it – and I also feel that someone is drawing close to me, looking at me, feeling me, getting up on my bed, kneeling on my chest, taking my neck between his hands and squeezing … squeezing with all his strength … trying to strangle me.

And I struggle, bound down by that awful helplessness which paralyses us in dreams; I want to cry out – I cannot; I want to move – I cannot; with fearful efforts, gasping for breath, I try to turn over, to throw off this being who chokes and stifles me – I cannot!

Suddenly I wake, frantic, bathed in sweat. I light a candle. I am alone.

After this attack, which comes every night, I sleep peacefully until dawn.

2nd June. I am worse. What can be the matter with me? The bromide is useless, the douches are useless.

3rd June. An awful night. I am going away for a few days. No doubt a little holiday will set me right.

*

2nd July. Home again. I am quite myself now. And my little holiday has been delightful.

3rd July. Slept badly; clearly there is fever about, for my coachman is suffering from the same complaint as myself. Yesterday, as I came into the house, I noticed how unusually pale he looked.

'What's the matter with you, Jean?' I asked.

'It's like this, sir. I don't sleep now; me nights eat up me days. Ever since master left, it's been like an evil fate over me.'

The other servants are well; but I myself live in dread of a fresh attack.

4th July. A fresh attack, and no mistake! The old nightmares have come back. Last night I felt someone crouching on top of me, who, with his mouth to mine, was drinking my life through my lips. Yes he was draining it out of my throat, as would a leech. Then he got off me, gorged, And I woke up, so battered and bruised and exhausted that I couldn't stir. If this goes on for many more days I shall certainly leave home again.

5th July. Have I lost my reason? What happened last night is so extraordinary that my head feels queer when I think of it!

As is my habit every evening now, I had locked my bedroom door; then, feeling thirsty, I drank half a glass of water, and I happened to notice that my water-bottle was full to the glass stopper.

I then went to bed, dropping off into one of my frightful dreams. After about two hours I was awakened by a seizure more frightful than any before.

Imagine a man who is being assassinated in his sleep, who awakes to find a knife in his lungs, and lies there covered with blood, with the death-rattle in his throat, unable to draw his breath, on the verge of death, understanding nothing at all –

and there you have it.

When at last I recovered my senses, I was again thirsty; I lit a candle and went towards the table where my water-bottle stood. I lifted it, tipping it over my glass; nothing came out. It was empty, entirely empty! At first I was mystified; then, all at once, such a terrible feeling came over me that I had to sit down, or rather, I tumbled into a chair. Then up I jumped again to gaze about me! In a bewilderment of astonishment and fear I sat down once more, before the transparent water-bottle. I stared at it fixedly, trying to solve the riddle. My hands were trembling! Someone, then, had drunk this water! Who? I? I, myself, no doubt! It could only be myself! Well, then, I was a somnambulist; unknown to myself, I was living that strange double life which make us wonder whether there are two creatures in us; or whether an alien creature, unknowable, invisible, quickens our captive limbs at times, when our mind is asleep, and they obey this other creature, just as they would, more faithfully than they would, obey ourselves.

Ah! Who can understand my anguish? Who can understand how a man feels when, wide awake, and wholly reasonable, he stares in terror through the sides of a glass bottle, looking for a pint of water that has disappeared during his sleep! I stayed there until dawn, not daring to go back to bed.

6th July. I am going mad. My water-bottle was drained again last night, or rather, I drained it!

But did I do it? Did I? Who could it be? Who? Ah, God above! I am going mad! Who can save me!

10th July. I have just been making the most remarkable test. Most certainly I am mad! And yet …

On 6th July, before going to bed, I set out on my table wine, milk, water, bread, and strawberries. Someone drank – I drank – all the water and a little milk. The wine was left untouched, also the strawberries.

On 7th July I tried the same test, with the same result.

On 8th July I tried without the water and milk. Nothing was touched.

And on 9th July I replaced the water and milk on my table by themselves, taking care to cover the bottles in white muslin and so tie down the corks. Then I rubbed my lips, beard, and hands, with black lead, and went to bed.

The same inexorable sleep took possession of me, followed soon after by the horrible awakening. I hadn't stirred; the sheets themselves had no stain. I hastened to the table. The muslin covering the bottles remained spotless. I untied the strings, panting with fear. Every drop of water was drunk! Every drop of milk was drunk! Ah God above!

I am leaving for Paris this morning.

*

30th July. I came home yesterday. All is well.

2nd August. Nothing new; beautiful weather. I spend my days watching the Seine flowing by.

4th August. Squabbles among my servants. They say that glasses are being broken in the cupboards at night. The butler accuses the cook, the cook accuses the washerwoman, and she accuses the other two. Who is the culprit? It would take a wise man to say!

6th August. This time I am not mad. I have seen! I have seen! ... Doubts are no longer possible ... I have seen!... I am still cold to the finger-tips, quaking to the marrow of my bones ... I have seen!

At two o'clock, in bright sunlight, I was walking in my rose-garden ... in the autumn rose-walk which is beginning to flower.

As I stopped to look at a *Géant des batailles* that bore three splendid blooms, I saw, I distinctly saw, quite close to me, the stem of one of these roses bend, as if some invisible hand had twisted it, and snap off, as if the hand had plucked it. Then the flower rose in the air, following the curve that an arm would make when carrying it to a mouth. And there it stayed, hanging in the translucent air, all by itself, motionless, a terrifying splash of red, three paces from my eyes.

Aghast, I darted out my hand to snatch it! My hand found nothing; it had vanished. I was seized with a violet fit of anger against myself, for it is not right that a serious-minded, reasonable man should have delusions like this.

But was it really a delusion? I turned round to look for the stem, and found it at once on the rose-tree, just freshly broken off, between the two remaining roses, still on their branch.

At that, I went indoors with my mind in a fearful state. For I am certain now, as certain as that night follows day, that living near to me is an invisible being, who feeds on water and milk, who can touch things, take them and move them about – governed therefore by physical laws unperceived by our senses, and dwelling under my roof …

7th August. A peaceful night. He drank the water in my bottle, but did not disturb my sleep.

I wonder if I am mad? While I was walking just now, in broad sunlight, along the river, doubts of my reason came to me – not vague doubts like those I have had so far; but doubts that were not well defined, real. I have seen madmen; I have known some who remained quite intelligent, clear-headed, far-seeing even in all the things of life, save on one point only. And while they talked on any subject with clearness, penetration, and ease, suddenly their thought, striking on the reef of their madness, was rent in pieces there, scattered and foundered in that wild and terrible ocean, swept by the rushing waves and mists and squalls, that we call insanity.

Certainly I should believe I was mad, quite mad, if I was not conscious of it all, well aware of my mental state, if I was not perfectly clear-headed, when probing down into its causes. Probably, then, I am only subject to delusions, and retain my reason. Some unknown disturbance must have taken place in my brain. Is it not possible that one of the imperceptible keys of the instrument within my brain has refused its work? An accident will sometimes deprive a man of his memory for proper names, or verbs, or figures, or simply dates. And the fact that these divisions of our thought are localized in the brain is well established to-day. What cause for surprise, then, if the faculty that records within me the unreality of certain delusions should be dormant now?

These were my thoughts as I strolled along the river-bank. The sunshine flooded the water, made earth a delight to behold, filled my heart with the love of life – love of the swallows, that rejoiced my eyes with their swiftness; of the sedges that charmed my ear with their rustlings.

Little by little, however, a strange uneasiness came creeping through me. Some power, as it seemed, some occult power was paralysing me, stopping me, restraining me from going farther, was calling me back. I had the uncomfortable feeling that I must return, such as oppresses you when a beloved invalid is left behind at home, and you are seized with the presentiment that a turn for the worse has come.

Back, therefore, I came in spite of myself, sure that I would find bad news at home – a letter or telegram. But there was nothing, and I was left feeling more uneasy and more surprised than if I had again been through some strange experience.

8th August. A frightful evening, last night. He no longer declares himself. But I feel him near me, eyeing me, pervading me, dominating me – and more to be feared, hiding so, than if he was making his continual presence known by supernatural signs.

Yet I slept well.

9th August. Nothing; but I am afraid.

11th August. Still nothing; I cannot stay at home any longer with this fear lodged in my mind; I am going away.

12th August. 10 p.m. All day I have been waiting to leave the house; I couldn't. It was so simple, so easy, the voluntary act that I wished to accomplish – simply to go out, get into my carriage to drive to Rouen. I couldn't. Why?

14th August. I am done for! Someone is master of my mind and controls it! Someone commands my every act, movement, thought. I count for nothing, now, within myself; I am merely a terrified, slave-like witness to my actions. I want to go out. I cannot. He does not wish it; trembling and panic-stricken I stay in the arm-chair where he keeps me. I want to get up, that I may believe I am still my own master. I cannot! I am riveted to my chair, and my chair cleaves so fast to the ground that no power could lift us.

Then, all at once, I must, simply must, go to the end of my garden to pick strawberries and eat them. And I go. I pick the strawberries and I eat them. Ah, God, God, God! Is there a God? If God there be, save me! Oh, what agony! What torture! What terror!

17th August. Ah, what a night! What a night! And yet it seems to me that I really should be rejoicing. I read until one in the morning! Hermann Herestrauss, doctor of philosophy and theogony, has written a book on the history and manifestations of every invisible being that hovers around mankind or is dreamed of in their dreams. He describes their origin, their domain, their powers. But not one of them resembles my familiar. One would say that man, ever since he has been able to think, has had some nervous foreknowledge of a new being – more powerful than himself, his successor in this world, and that, feeling him near but unable to foresee the nature of this over-man, in his terror he has created imaginary occult beings, shifting phantoms which have been born of fear.

After reading till one in the morning I went to sit by my open window to refresh my forehead and my mind with the gentle air of night.

The air was warm and sweet. How I would have enjoyed that night in days gone by!

No moon. The stars flashed and sparkled in the black deeps of the sky. Who dwells in those worlds? What forms, what living creatures, what animals, what plans are yonder? They who think in these far-off worlds, what know they beyond our knowledge? What powers have they transcending our own? What things do they see that are hidden from us? And may not one of their kind, passing one day through space, come down to this earth of ours to conquer it, as the Normans once crossed the sea to conquer weaker races?

We are so weak; so defenceless, so ignorant, so small are we, on this whirling spot of slime mingled with a rain drop!

I dozed off, dreaming in this fashion, in the cool night air.

After sleeping for about forty minutes I opened my eyes awakened by some vague and strange emotion. At first I saw nothing; then, all at once, it seemed to me that a page of the book lying open on my table had turned over of itself. Not a breath of air had passed in through my window. I waited. After about four minutes I saw, I saw – yes, with my eyes I saw one more page rise, then close down on to the one before, as if a finger had turned it over. My arm-chair was empty, *seemed* empty; but I understood that he was there, seated in my chair, and that he was reading. With one wild bound, the bound of an infuriated beast about to disembowel its tamer, I dashed across the room to seize him, throttle him, kill him! … But my chair, before I reached it, topped over as if someone had fled before me – my table rocked, my lamp fell and went out, and windows shut to as if some thief, caught in the act, had darted out in to the night, grasping the frames with both hands.

He had fled then; *he* had been frightened, frightened of me!

Well then … well then … to-morrow … or after … one day or another, I shall be able to seize him with my fingers and crush him. Are not dogs sometimes known to bite, to choke the life out of their masters?

18th August. I have been thinking all day. Ah yes! I shall obey him, follow his suggestions, do everything that he wills, make myself humble, a slave, a craven. He has the upper hand. But the hour will come …

19th August. I know … I know – all! I have just read this in the *Revue du Monde de Scientifique*:

> A curious item of news reaches us from Rio de Janeiro. An epidemic of madness, comparable to those waves of infectious insanity which attacked European peoples in the

Middle Ages, is raging at the moment in the province of San Paulo. The frenzied inhabitants desert their house, villages, and fields, saying that they are pursued, possessed, and controlled, like human cattle, by beings which are invisible though tangible, a kind of vampire which feeds on them during their sleep and also drinks water and milk without appearing to touch any other food.

Professor Don Pedro Henriquez, accompanied by several distinguished doctors, has left for the province of San Paulo, to study *in situ* the causes and symptoms of this extraordinary madness and to propose to the emperor the most fitting measures to restore the raving inhabitants to reason.

Aha, I remember, I remember the lovely Brazilian three-master that passed below my windows on her way up the Seine, last 8th of May! I thought her so beautiful, so white, so pleasant! The Being was on board, coming from the land where his race was born! And he saw me! He saw my white house too; and he leapt from the ship to the shore. Ah, God above!

And now I know, I foresee. Man's reign on earth is over.

HE has come, he that was feared in the innocent, trembling hearts of the early races. He who was exorcised by uneasy priests, whom sorcerers summoned on gloomy nights though invisible as yet to their sight. He whom the forebodings of earth's momentary masters clothed in the monstrous or pleasing shapes of gnomes, spirits, genii, fairies, and hobgoblins. After these first crude picturings of fearful minds, came men with greater insight, who foreshadowed him more clearly. Mesmer guessed at him; and, ten years since, doctors learned the precise nature of his power, before He himself had wielded it. They have toyed with this weapon of the coming Lord, the domination of a mysterious will-power over the enslaved human mind. They have called it magnetism, hypnotism, suggestion … and what not. I have seen them playing like thoughtless children with this horrible power! Woe upon us!

Woe upon Man! He has come, the … the … yes … he is calling it … I am listening! … I can't quite … again … Horla … I heard … the Horla … it is He … the Horla … he has come!

Aha! The vulture has devoured the dove, the wolf has devoured the lamb, and the lion the buffalo with his sharp-pointed horns; man has slain the lion with the arrow, the sword, and the gun; but the Horla will do unto Man what we have done unto the horse and the ox: his chattel, his servant, and his food, by the sole might of his will. Woe upon us!

*

19th August. I shall kill him! I have seen him! I sat down at my table yesterday evening, and I pretended to be writing with concentration. I knew, right well, that he would come roaming round me, close, close, so close that perhaps I could touch him, seize him? And then! Then … I should have the strength of a desperate man. I should have my hands, my knees, my chest, my head, my teeth, to strangle him, crush him, bite him, rend him.

I was watching for him, with every nerve in my body tingling.

I had lit my two lamps and the eight candles over my mantelpiece, as if all this light would help me to make him out.

Facing me was my bed, my old four-poster of oak; to the right, my fireplace; to the left, my door, carefully shut now, after standing open a long time, to attract him; behind me, a great, high wardrobe with a mirror that I used every day for shaving and dressing and always glanced into from habit, to see myself at full length, whenever I passed before it.

So I pretended to be writing, to mislead him, for he was on the watch; and, all of a sudden, I felt, I knew that he was reading over my shoulder, that he was there, touching my ear.

I jumped up, with hands outstretched, wheeling round so quickly that I nearly fell. Well? … my mirror was as bright as in broad daylight, and I could not see myself reflected. It was clear and bright and luminous to its very depth! My reflection did not appear there … yet I was standing right in front! I could see every inch of the clear tall mirror! I stared; and I hadn't the courage to advance one foot or make a single movement, knowing well as I did that he was there, but that he would escape me once more, the invisible-bodied one, who had swallowed up my reflection.

Imagine my fear! And then, behold! All at once I began to see myself in a mist, deep down in the mirror, in a mist as though through a sheet of water; and it seemed to me that the water was slowly gliding from left to right, leaving my reflection clearer with the passing of each second. It was like the end of an eclipse. The thing that shut me out did not seem to have clearly-marked outlines, but a kind of opaque transparence, thinning out by little degrees.

Then at last I was able to see myself perfectly, just as I do every day when I look in the glass.

So, I had seen him! And the terror of it abides, making me shiver yet.

20th August. Kill him, but how? I cannot grasp hold of him. Poison? He would see me mixing it in the water; moreover, would our poisons have any effect on his imperceptible body? They would not, they would certainly not. What then? What then?

21st August. I have sent for a locksmith from Rouen, and have ordered iron shutters for my room, like those that certain private mansions in Paris have, before the lower story windows, for fear of burglars. He is also making me a door to match. I have got the name of a coward, but what do I care!

*

10th September. Rouen, Continental Hotel. It's done … it's done .. but is he dead? My mind is still in a whirl after seeing it all.

Yesterday, then, after the locksmith had fitted my iron shutters and door, I left everything open until midnight, although it was beginning to be cold.

All at once I felt that he was there; and was overjoyed, crazy with joy. I rose in leisurely fashion and sauntered up and down for a long while, to prevent his suspecting a thing; then I took off my boots and put on my slippers with a careless air; then I closed my iron shutters, and, strolling back to the door, shut the door also, turning the key twice. Returning then to the window I made it fast with a padlock and pocketed the key.

Suddenly, I realized that he was following me about excitedly; that he in his turn was afraid, that he was commanding me to open and let him out. I all but gave way; yet did not quite give way. Instead, I stood with my back to the door, opened a crack, just wide enough to let me slip through backwards; and as I am very tall, my head grazed the lintel. I was then certain that he could not have escaped; and I shut him in, alone, alone. Oh, joy, I had him! Then downstairs I went at a run; in the drawing-room below my bedroom I took my two lamps and emptied the oil out over the carpet, over the furniture, and all about; then I set light to it, and escaped, after carefully locking the big front door with two turns of the key.

I went to hide myself at the bottom of the garden, in a clump of laurels. What a time it took! What a time it took! All was dark, silent, motionless; not a breath of air, not a star; mountainous clouds, that I could not see, but which weighed on my mind with a great heavy weight.

I watched my house and waited. What a time it took! I was already beginning to think that the fire had gone out itself, or that *He* had put it out, when one of the lower windows, yielding before the thrust of the fire, fell out with a crash. A flame, a great tongue of flame, yellow and red, long, soft, caressing, climbed up the white wall, licking upwards to the roof. A gleam shot out into the trees, into the branches, into the leaves; and a shiver too – a shiver of fear! The birds were waking; a dog began to howl; I thought day was dawning! Two other windows fell out the next moment, and I saw that the entire lower story of my dwelling was one raging furnace. But a cry, a dreadful cry, the piercing scream of a woman rang out into the night, and two garret windows flew open! I had forgotten my servants! I saw their terrified faces, their arms waving! …

Then, wild with horror, I set off at a run for the village, yelling: 'Help! Help! Fire! Fire!' I met people already on their way from the village, and turned back with them, to see.

But now the house was one vast, awe-inspiring bonfire, a monstrous bonfire that lit up the face of the earth; a bonfire in which human creatures were burning to death; and He, too, burned – He, my prisoner, the New Being, the new master, the Horla!

Suddenly the entire roof fell in, and a volcano of flames shot up sky-high.

Through every window opening into the furnace I could see the cauldron of fire; and thought of him there, in that oven, dead …

Dead? Perhaps? … His body? His body that was transparent to the light of day, could it be destroyed by the means that are deadly to our own?

And if he was not dead? … Time only, perhaps, can lay hands upon that Terrible, Invisible Being. Why this transparent body, this unknowable body – if he too, must fear pain, wounds, sickness, and untimely death?

Untimely death? All human terror lies therein! First Man, then Horla. First comes he that may die on any day, in any hour, at any minute, through any accident; thereafter, he that shall only die when his day and his hour and his minute have come, because he has attained his life's bourne!

No, no, no, no, … there is no room for doubt, no doubt at all!

… He is not dead.

Well then … well then … the only thing left to do is to kill – myself.

The Dream Woman

W. Wilkie Collins

1

I had not been settled much more than six weeks in my country practice, when I was sent for to a neighbouring town to consult with the resident medical man there, on a case of very dangerous illness.

My horse had come down with me, at the end of a long ride that night before, and had hurt himself, luckily, much more than he had hurt his master. Being deprived of the animal's services, I started for my destination by the coach (there were no railways at that time); and I hoped to get back again, towards the afternoon, in the same way.

After the consultation was over I went to the principal inn of the town to wait for the coach. When it came up, it was full inside and out. There was no resource left me, but to get home as cheaply as I could, by hiring a gig. The price asked for this accommodation struck me as being so extortionate, that I determined to look out for an inn of inferior pretensions, and to try if I could not make a better bargain with a less prosperous establishment.

I soon found a likely-looking house, dingy and quiet, with an old-fashioned sign, that had evidently not been repainted for many years past. The landlord, in this case, was not above making a small profit; and as soon as we came to terms, he rang the yard-bell to order the gig.

'Has Robert not come back from that errand?' asked the landlord appealing to the waiter, who answered the bell.

'No, sir, he hasn't.'

'Well, then, you must wake up Isaac.'

'Wake up Isaac?' I repeated; 'that sounds rather odd. Do your ostlers go to bed in the day-time?'

'This one does,' said the landlord, smiling to himself in rather a strange way.

'And dreams, too,' added the waiter.

'Never you mind about that,' retorted his master; 'you go and rouse Isaac up. The gentleman's waiting for his gig.'

The landlord's manner and the waiter's manner expressed a great deal more than they either of them said. I began to suspect that I might be on the trace of something professionally interesting to me, as a medical man; and I thought I should like to look at the ostler, before the waiter awakened him.

'Stop a minute,' I interposed; 'I have rather a fancy for seeing this man before you wake him up. I am a doctor; and if this queer sleeping and dreaming of his comes from anything wrong in his brain, I may be able to tell you what to do with him.'

'I rather think you will find his complaint past all doctoring, sir,' said the landlord. 'But if you would like to see him, you're welcome, I'm sure.'

He led the way across a yard and down a passage to the stables; opened one of the doors; and waiting outside himself, told me to look in.

I found myself in a two-stall stable. In one of the stalls, a horse was munching his corn. In the other, an old man was lying asleep on the litter.

I stooped, and looked at him attentively. It was a withered, woe-begone face. The eyebrows were painfully contracted; the mouth was fast set, and drawn down at the corners. The hollow wrinkled cheeks, and the scanty grizzled hair, told their own tale of past sorrow or suffering. He was drawing his breath convulsively when I first looked at him; and in a moment more he began to talk in his sleep.

'Wake up!' I heard him say, in a quick whisper, through his

clenched teeth. 'Wake up, there! Murder.'

He moved one lean arm slowly till it rested over his throat, shuddered a little, and turned on the straw. Then the arm left his throat, the hand stretched itself out, and clutched at the side towards which he had turned, as if he fancied himself to be grasping at the edge of something. I saw his lips move, and bent lower over him. He was still talking in his sleep.

'Light grey eyes,' he murmured, 'and a droop in the left eyelid – flaxen hair, with a gold-yellow streak in it – all right, mother – fair white arms, with a down on them – little lady's hand, with a reddish look under the finger-nails. The knife – always the cursed knife – first on one side, then on the other. Aha! You she-devil, where's the knife?'

At the last word his voice rose, and he grew restless on a sudden. I saw him shudder on the straw; his withered face became distorted, and he threw up both his hands with a quick hysterical gasp. They struck against the bottom of the manger under which he lay, and the blow awakened him. I had just time to slip through the door, and close it, before his eyes were fairly open, and his senses his own again.

'Do you know anything about that man's past life?' I said to the landlord.

'Yes, sir, I know pretty much well all about it,' was the answer, 'and an uncommon queer story it is. Most people don't believe it. It's true, though, for all that. Why, just look at him,' continued the landlord, opening the stable door again. 'Poor devil! He's so worn out with his restless nights, that he's dropped back into his sleep already.'

'Don't wake him,' I said, 'I'm in no hurry for the gig. Wait till the other man comes back from his errand. And in the meantime, suppose I have some lunch and a bottle of sherry; and suppose you come and help me to get through it.'

The heart of mine host, as I had anticipated, warmed to me over his own wine. He soon became communicative on the subject of the man asleep in the stable; and by little and little, I drew the whole story out of him. Extravagant and incredible as the events must appear to everybody, they are related here just as I heard them, and just as they happened.

2

Some years ago there lived in the suburbs of a large seaport town, on the west coast of England, a man in humble circumstances, by the name of Isaac Scatchard. His means of subsistence were derived from any employment he could get as an ostler, and occasionally, when times went well with him, from temporary engagements in service as stable-helper in private houses. Though a faithful, steady, and honest man, he got on badly in his calling. His ill-luck was proverbial among his neighbours. He was always missing good opportunities by no fault of his own; and always living longest in service with amiable people who were not punctual payers of wages. 'Unlucky Isaac' was his nickname in his own neighbourhood – and no one could say that he did not richly deserve it.

With far more than one man's fair share of adversity to endure, Isaac had but one consolation to support him – and that was of the dreariest and most negative kind. He had no wife and children to increase his anxieties and add to the bitterness of his various failures in life. It might have been from mere insensibility, or it might have been from generous unwillingness to involve another in his own unlucky destiny – but the fact undoubtedly was, that he had arrived at the middle term of life without marrying; and, what is much more remarkable, without once exposing himself, from eighteen to eight-and-thirty, to the genial imputation of ever having had a sweetheart.

When he was out of service, he lived alone with his widowed mother. Mrs Scatchard was a woman above the average in her lowly station, as to capacity and manners. She had seen better days, as the phrase is; but she never referred to them in the presence of curious visitors; and, though perfectly polite to every one who approached her, never cultivated any intimacies among her neighbours. She contrived to provide, hardly enough, for her simple wants, by doing rough work for the tailors; and always managed to keep a decent home for her son to return to, whenever his ill-luck drove him out helpless into the world.

One bleak autumn, when Isaac was getting on fast towards forty, and when he was, as usual, out of place through no fault of his own, he set forth from his mother's cottage on a long walk inland to a gentleman's seat, where he had heard that a stable-helper was required.

It wanted then but two days of his birthday; and Mrs Scatchard, with her usual fondness, made him promise before he started, that he would be back in time to keep that anniversary with her, in as festive a way as their poor means would allow. It was easy for him to comply with this request, even supposing he slept a night each way on the road.

He was to start from home on Monday morning; and whether he got the new place or not, he was to be back for his birthday dinner on Wednesday at two o'clock.

Arriving at his destination too late on the Monday night to make application for the stable-helper's place, he slept at the village inn, and, in good time on the Tuesday morning, presented himself at the gentleman's house, to fill the vacant situation. Here again, his ill-luck pursued him as inexorably as ever. The excellent written testimonials to his character which he was able to produce, availed him nothing; his long walk had been taken in vain – only the day before, the stable-helper's place had been given to another man.

Isaac accepted this new disappointment resignedly, and as a matter of course. Naturally slow in capacity, he had the bluntness of sensibility and phlegmatic patience of disposition which frequently distinguish men with sluggishly-working mental powers. He thanked the gentleman's steward with his usual quiet civility, for granting him an interview, and took his departure with no appearance of unusual depression in his face or manner.

Before starting on his homeward walk, he made some inquiries at the inn, and ascertained that he might save a few miles, on his return, by following a new road. Furnished with full instructions, several times repeated, as to the various turnings he was to take, he set forth on his homeward journey, and walked on all day with only one stoppage for bread and cheese. Just as it was getting towards dark, the rain came on and the wind began to rise; and he found himself, to make matters worse, in a part of the country with which he was entirely unacquainted, though he knew himself to be some fifteen miles from home. The first house he found to inquire at, was a lonely road-side inn, standing on the outskirts of a thick wood. Solitary as the place looked, it was welcome to a lost man who was also hungry, thirsty, footsore, and wet. The landlord was civil and respectable-looking, and the price he asked for a bed was reasonable enough. Isaac therefore decided on stopping comfortably at the inn for that night.

He was constitutionally a temperate man. His supper simply consisted of two rashers of bacon, a slice of homemade bread, and a pint of ale. He did not go to bed immediately after this moderate meal, but sat up with the landlord, talking about his bad prospects and his long run of ill-luck, and diverging from these topics to the subjects of horse-flesh and racing. Nothing was said either by himself, his host, or the few labourers who strayed into the tap-room, which could, in the slightest degree, excite the very small and very dull imaginative faculty which Isaac Scatchard possessed.

At a little after eleven the house was closed. Isaac went round with the landlord, and held the candle while the doors and lower windows were being secured. He noticed with surprise the strength of the bolts, bars, and iron-sheathed shutters.

'You see, we are rather lonely here,' said the landlord. 'We never have had any attempts made to break in yet, but it's always as well to be on the safe side. When nobody is sleeping here I am the only man in the house. My wife and daughter are timid, and the servant-girl takes after her missuses. Another glass of ale, before you turn in? – No? – Well, how such a sober man as you comes to be out of place, is more than I can make out, for one. – Here's where you're to sleep. You're the only lodger to-night, and I think you'll say my missus has done her best to make you comfortable. You're quite sure you won't have another glass of ale? – very well. Good night.'

It was half-past eleven by the clock in the passage as they went upstairs to the bedroom, the window of which looked on to the wood at the back of the house.

Isaac locked the door, set his candle on the chest of drawers, and wearily got ready for bed. The bleak autumn wind was still blowing, and the solemn surging moan of it in the wood was dreary and awful to hear through the night-silence. Isaac felt strangely wakeful. He resolved, as he lay down in bed, to keep the candle alight until he began to grow sleepy; for there was something unendurably depressing in the bare idea of lying awake in the darkness, listening to the dismal, ceaseless moan of the wind in the wood.

Sleep stole on him before he was aware of it. His eyes closed, and he fell off insensibly to rest, without having so much as thought of extinguishing the candle.

The first sensation of which he was conscious, after sinking into a slumber, was a strange shivering that ran through him suddenly from head to foot, and a dreadful sinking pain at the heart, such as he had never felt before. The shivering only disturbed his slumbers – the pain woke him instantly. In one moment he passed from a state of sleep to a state of wakefulness – his eyes wide open – his mental perceptions cleared on a sudden as if by a miracle.

The candle had burnt down nearly to the last morsel of tallow, but the top of the unsnuffed wick had just fallen off, and the light in the little room was, for the moment, fair and full.

Between the foot of the bed and the closed door, there stood a woman with a knife in her hand, looking at him.

He was stricken speechless with terror, but he did not lose

the preternatural clearness of his faculties; and he never took his eyes off the woman. She said not a word as they stared each other in the face; but she began to move slowly towards the left-hand side of the bed.

His eyes followed her. She was a fair fine woman, with yellowish flaxen hair, and light grey eyes, with a droop in the left eyelid. He noticed these things and fixed them on his mind, before she was round at the side of the bed. Speechless, with no expression in her face, with no noise following her footfall, she came closer and closer – stopped – and slowly raised the knife. He laid his right arm over his throat to save it; but, as he saw the knife coming down, threw his hand across the bed to the right side, and jerked his body over that way, just as the knife descended on the mattress within an inch of his shoulder.

His eyes fixed on her arm and hand, as she slowly drew her knife out of the bed. A white, well-shaped arm, with a pretty down lying lightly over the fair skin. A delicate, lady's hand, with the crowning beauty of a pink flush under and round the finger-nails.

She drew the knife out, and passed back again slowly to the foot of the bed; stopped there for a moment looking at him; then came on – still speechless, still with no expression on the beautiful face, still with no sound following the stealthy footfalls – came on to the right side of the bed where he now lay.

As she approached, she raised the knife again, and he drew himself away to the left side. She struck, as before right into the mattress, with a deliberate, perpendicularly downward action of the arm. This time his eyes wandered from her to the knife. It was like the large clasp-knives which he had often seen labouring men use to cut their bread and bacon with. Her delicate little fingers did not conceal more than two-thirds of the handle; he noticed that it was made of buckhorn, clean and shining as the blade was, and looking like new.

For the second time she drew the knife out, concealed it in the wide sleeve of her gown, then stopped by the bedside, watching him. For an instant he saw her standing in that position – then the wick of the spent candle fell over into the socket. The flame diminished to a little blue point, and the room grew dark.

A moment, or less if possible, passed so – and then the wick flamed up, smokily, for the last time. His eyes were still looking eagerly over the right-hand side of the bed when the final flash of light came, but they discerned nothing. The fair woman with the knife was gone.

The conviction that he was alone again, weakened the hold of the terror that had struck him dumb up to this time. The preternatural sharpness which the very intensity of his panic had mysteriously imparted to his faculties, left them suddenly. His brain grew confused – his heart beat wildly – his ears opened for the first time since the appearance of the woman, to a sense of the woeful, ceaseless moaning of the wind among the trees. With the dreadful conviction of the reality of what he had seen still strong within him, he leapt out of bed, and screaming – 'Murder! – Wake up there, wake up!' – dashed headlong through the darkness to the door.

It was fast locked, exactly as he had left it on going to bed.

His cries, on starting up, had alarmed the house. He heard the terrified, confused exclamations of women; he saw the master of the house approaching along the passage, with his burning rush-candle in one hand and his gun in the other.

'What is it?' asked the landlord, breathlessly.

Isaac could only answer in a whisper. 'A woman, with a knife in her hand,' he gasped out. 'In my room – a fair yellow-haired woman; she jabbed at me with the knife, twice over.'

The landlord's pale cheeks grew paler. He looked at Isaac eagerly by the flickering light of his candle; and his face began to get red again – his voice altered, too, as well as his complexion.

'She seems to have missed you twice,' he said.

'I dodged the knife as it came down,' Isaac went on, in the same scared whisper. 'It struck the bed each time.'

The landlord took his candle into the bedroom immediately. In less than a minute he came out again into the passage in a violent passion.

'The devil fly away with you and your woman with the knife! There isn't a mark in the bed-clothes anywhere. What do you mean by coming into a man's place and frightening his family out of their wits by a dream?'

'I'll leave your house,' said Isaac, faintly. 'Better out on the road, in rain and dark, on my way home, than back again in that room, after what I've seen in it. Lend me a light to get my clothes by, and tell me what I'm to pay.'

'Pay!' cried the landlord, leading the way with his light sulkily into the bedroom. 'You'll find your score on the slate when you go downstairs. I wouldn't have taken you in for all the money you've got about you, if I'd known your dreaming, screeching ways beforehand. Look at the bed. Where's the cut of a knife in it? Look at the window – is the lock bursted? Look at the door (which I heard you fasten yourself) – is it broke in? You ought to be ashamed of yourself!'

Isaac answered not a word He huddled on his clothes: and then they went down the stairs together.

'Nigh on twenty minutes past two!' said the landlord, as they passed the clock. 'A nice time in the morning to frighten honest people out of their wits!'

Isaac paid his bill, and the landlord let him out at the front door, asking, with a grin of contempt, as he undid the strong fastenings, whether 'the murdering woman got in that way?'

They parted without a word on either side. The rain had ceased; but the night was dark, and the wind bleaker than ever. Little did the darkness, or the cold, or the uncertainty about the way home matter to Isaac. If he had been turned out into the wilderness in a thunderstorm, it would have been a relief, after what he had suffered in the bedroom of the inn.

What was the fair woman with the knife? The creature of a dream? Or that other creature from the unknown world, called among men by the name of ghost? He could make nothing of the mystery – had made nothing of it, even when it was midday on Wednesday, and when he stood, at last, after many times missing his road, once more on the doorstep of home.

3

His mother came out eagerly to receive him. His face told her in a moment that something was wrong.

'I've lost the place; but that's my luck. I dreamed an ill dream last night, mother – or, maybe, I saw a ghost. Take it either way, it scared me out of my senses, and I'm not my own man again yet.'

'Isaac! Your face frightens me. Come in to the fire. Come in, and tell mother all about it.'

He was as anxious to tell as she was to hear; for it had been his hope, all the way home, that his mother, with her quicker capacity and superior knowledge, might be able to throw some light on the mystery which he could not clear up for himself. His memory of the dream was still mechanically vivid, though his thoughts were entirely confused by it.

His mother's face grew paler and paler as he went on. She never interrupted him by so much as a single word; but when he had done, she moved her chair close to his, put her arm round his neck, and said to him:

'Isaac, you dreamed your ill dream on this Wednesday morning. What time was it when you saw the fair woman with the knife in her hand?'

Isaac reflected on what the landlord had said when they had passed by the clock on his leaving the inn – allowed as nearly as he could for the time that must have elapsed between the unlocking of his bedroom door and the paying of his bill just before going away, and answered:

'Somewhere about two o'clock in the morning.'

His mother suddenly quitted her hold of his neck, and struck her hands together with a gesture of despair.

'This Wednesday is your birthday, Isaac; and two o'clock in

the morning is the time when you were born!'

Isaac's capacities were not quick enough to catch the infection of his mother's superstitious dread. He was amazed, and a little startled also, when she suddenly rose from her chair, opened her old writing-desk, took pen, ink, and paper, and then said to him:

'Your memory is but a poor one, Isaac, and now I'm an old woman, mine's not much better. I want all about this dream of yours to be as well known to both if us, years hence, as it is now. Tell me over again all you told me a minute ago, when you spoke of what the woman with the knife looked like.'

Isaac obeyed, and marvelled much as he saw his mother carefully set down on paper the very words that he was saying.

'Light grey eyes,' she wrote as they came to the descriptive part, 'with a droop in the left eyelid. Flaxen hair, with a gold-yellow streak in it. White arms, with a down upon them. Little lady's hand, with a reddish look about the finger-nails. Clasp-knife with a buckhorn handle, that seemed as good as new.' To these particulars, Mrs Scatchard added the year, month, day of the week, and time in the morning, when the woman of the dream appeared to her son. She then locked up the paper carefully in her writing-desk.

Neither on that day, nor on any day after, could her son induce her to return to the matter of the dream. She obstinately kept her thoughts about it to herself, and even refused to refer again to the paper in her writing-desk. Ere long, Isaac grew weary of attempting to make her break her resolute silence; and time, which sooner or later wears out all things, gradually wore out the impression produced on him by the dream. He began by thinking of it carelessly, and he ended by not thinking of it at all.

This result was the more easily brought about by the advent of some important changes for the better in his prospects, which commenced not long after his terrible night's experience at the inn. He reaped at last the reward of his long and patient suffering under adversity, by getting an excellent place, keeping it for seven years, and leaving it, on the death of his master, not only with an excellent character, but also with a comfortable annuity bequeathed to him as a reward for saving his mistress's life in a carriage accident. Thus it happened that Isaac Scatchard returned to his old mother, seven years after the time of the dream at the inn, with an annual sum of money at his disposal, sufficient to keep them both in ease and independence for the rest of their lives.

The mother, whose health had been bad of late years, profited so much by the care bestowed on her and by freedom from money anxieties, that when Isaac's birthday came round, she was able to sit up comfortably at table and dine with him.

On that day, as the evening drew on, Mrs Scatchard discovered that a bottle of tonic medicine – which she was accustomed to take, and in which she had fancied that a dose or more was still left – happened to be empty. Isaac immediately volunteered to go to the chemist's and get it filled again. It was as rainy and bleak an autumn night as on the memorable past occasion when he lost his way and slept at the road-side inn.

On going into the chemist's shop, he was passed hurriedly by a poorly-dressed woman coming out of it. The glimpse he had of her face struck him, and he looked back after her as she descended the door-steps.

'You're noticing that woman?' said the chemist's apprentice behind the counter. 'It's my opinion there's something wrong with her. She's been asking for laudanum to put to a bad tooth. Master's out for half an hour; and I told her I wasn't allowed to sell poison to strangers in his absence. She laughed in a queer way, and said she would come back in half an hour. If she expects master to serve her, I think she'll be disappointed. It's a case of suicide, sir, if ever there was one yet.'

These words added immeasurably to the sudden interest in the woman which Isaac had felt at the first sight of her face. After he had got the medicine bottle filled, he looked about anxiously for her, as soon as he was out in the street. She was walking slowly up and down on the opposite side of the road.

With his heart, very much to his own surprise, beating fast, Isaac crossed over and spoke to her.

He asked if she was in any distress. She pointed to her torn shawl, her scanty dress, her crushed, dirty bonnet – then moved under a lamp so as to let the light fall on her stern, pale, but still most beautiful face.

'I look like a comfortable, happy woman – don't I?' she said, with a bitter laugh.

She spoke with a purity of intonation which Isaac had never heard before from other than ladies' lips. Her slightest actions seemed to have the easy, negligent grace of a thorough-bred woman. Her skin, for all its poverty-stricken paleness, was as delicate as if her life had been passed in the enjoyment of every social comfort that wealth can purchase. Even her small, finely-shaped hands, gloveless as they were, had not lost their whiteness.

Little by little, in answer to his questions, the sad story of the woman came out. There is no need to relate it here; it is told over and over again in police reports and paragraphs descriptive of attempted suicides.

'My name is Rebecca Murdoch,' said the woman, as she ended.

'I have ninepence left, and I thought of spending it at the chemist's over the way in securing a passage to the other world. Whatever it is, it can't be worse to me than this – so why should I stop here?'

Besides the natural compassion and sadness moved in his heart by what he heard, Isaac felt within him some mysterious influence at work all the time the woman was speaking, which utterly confused his ideas and almost deprived him of his powers of speech. All that he could say in answer to her last reckless words was, that he would prevent her from attempting her own life, if he followed her about all night to do it. His rough, trembling earnestness seemed to impress her.

'I won't occasion you that trouble,' she answered, when he repeated his threat. 'You have given me a fancy for living by speaking kindly to me. No need for the mockery of protestations and promises. You may believe me without them. Come to Fuller's Meadow to-morrow at twelve, and you will find me alive, to answer for myself. No! – no money. My ninepence will do to get me as good a night's lodging as I want.'

She nodded and left him. He made no attempt to follow – he felt no suspicion that she was deceiving him.

'It's strange, but I can't help believing her,' he said to himself, and walked away bewildered towards home.

On entering the house, his mind was still so completely absorbed by its new subject of interest, that he took no notice of what his mother was doing when he came in with the bottle of medicine. She had opened her old writing-desk in his absence, and was now reading a paper attentively that lay inside it. On every birthday of Isaac's since she had written down the particulars of his dream from his own lips, she had been accustomed to read that same paper, and ponder over it in private.

The next day he went to Fuller's Meadow.

He had done only right in believing her so implicitly – she was there, punctual to a minute, to answer for herself. The last-left faint defences in Isaac's heart, against the fascination which a word or look from her began inscrutably to exercise over him, sank down and vanished before her for ever on that memorable morning.

When a man, previously insensible to the influence of women, forms an attachment in middle life, the instances are rare indeed, let the warning circumstances be what they may, in which he is found capable of freeing himself from the tyranny of the new ruling passion. The charm of being spoken to familiarly, fondly, and gratefully by a woman whose language and manners still retained enough of their early refinement to hint at the high social station that she had lost, would have been a dangerous luxury to a man of Isaac's rank at the age of twenty. But it was far more than that – it was certain ruin to him – now that his heart was opening unworthily to a new influence at that middle time of life when strong feelings of all kinds, once implanted, strike root most stubbornly in a man's moral nature. A few more stolen interviews after that first morning in Fuller's Meadow completed his infatuation. In less than a month from the time when he first met her, Isaac Scatchard had consented to give Rebecca Murdoch a new interest in existence, and a chance of recovering the character she had lost, by promising to make her his wife.

She had taken possession not of his passions only, but of his faculties as well. All the mind he had he put into her keeping. She directed him on every point, even instructing him how to break the news of his approaching marriage in the safest manner to his mother.

'If you tell her how you met me and who I am at first,' said the cunning woman, 'she will move heaven and earth to prevent our marriage. Say I am the sister of one of your fellow-servants – ask her to see me before you go into any more particulars – and leave it to me to do the rest. I mean to make her love me next best to you, Isaac, before she knows anything of who I really am.'

The motive of the deceit was sufficient to sanctify it to Isaac. The stratagem proposed relieved him of his one great anxiety, and quieted his uneasy conscience on the subject of his mother. Still, there was something wanting to perfect his happiness, something that he could not realize, something mysteriously untraceable, and yet something that perpetually made itself felt – not when he was absent from Rebecca Murdoch, but, strange to say, when he was actually in her presence! She was kindness itself with him; she never made him feel his inferior capacities and inferior manners – she showed the sweetest anxiety to please him in the smallest trifles; but, in spite of all these attractions, he never could feel quite at his ease with her. At their first meeting, there had mingled with his admiration when he looked in her face, a faint involuntary feeling of doubt whether that face was entirely strange to him. No after-familiarity had the slightest effect on this inexplicable, wearisome uncertainty.

Concealing the truth, as he had been directed, he announced his marriage engagement precipitately and confusedly to his mother, on the day when he contracted it. Poor Mrs Scatchard showed her perfect confidence in her son by flinging her arms round his neck, and giving him joy of having found at last, in the sister of one of his fellow-servants, a woman to comfort and care for him after his mother was gone. She was all eagerness to see the woman of her son's choice; and the next day was fixed for the introduction.

It was a bright sunny morning, and the little cottage parlour was full of light, as Mrs Scatchard, happy and expectant, dressed for the occasion in her Sunday gown, sat waiting for her son and her future daughter-in-law.

Punctual to the appointed time, Isaac hurriedly and nervously led his promised wife into the room. His mother rose to receive her – advanced a few steps, smiling – looking Rebecca full in the eyes – and suddenly stopped. Her face, which had been flushed the moment before, turned white in an instant – her eyes lost their expression of softness and kindness, and assumed a blank look of terror! – her outstretched hands fell to her sides, and she staggered back a few steps with a low cry to her son.

'Isaac!' she whispered, clutching him fast by the arm, when he asked alarmedly if she was taken ill, 'Isaac! Does that woman's face remind you of nothing?'

Before he could answer, before he could look round to where Rebecca stood, astonished and angered by her reception, at the lower end of the room, his mother pointed impatiently to her writing-desk and gave him the key.

'Open it,' she said, in a quick, breathless whisper.

'What does this mean? Why am I treated as if I had no business here? Does your mother want to insult me?' asked Rebecca angrily.

'Open it, and give me the paper in the left-hand drawer. Quick! quick! for heaven's sake!' said Mrs Scatchard, shrinking further back in terror.

Isaac gave her the paper. She looked it over eagerly for a moment – then followed Rebecca, who was now turning away haughtily to leave the room, and caught her by the shoulder – abruptly raised the long, loose sleeve of her gown – and glanced at her hand and arm. Something like fear began to steal over the angry expression of Rebecca's face, as she shook herself free from the old woman's grasp. 'Mad!' she said to herself, 'and Isaac never told me.' With those few words she left the room.

Isaac was hastening after her, when his mother turned and stopped his further progress. It wrung his heart to see the misery and terror in her face as she looked at him.

'Light grey eyes,' she said, in low, mournful, awe-struck tones, pointing towards the open door. 'A droop in the left eyelid; flaxen hair with a gold-yellow streak in it; white arms with a down on them; little, lady's hand, with a reddish look under the finger-nails. *The Dream Woman!* – Isaac, the Dream Woman!'

That faint cleaving doubt which he had never been able to shake off in Rebecca Murdoch's presence, was fatally set at rest for ever. He *had* seen her face, then, before – seven years before, on his birthday, in the bedroom of the lonely inn.

'Be warned! Oh, my son, be warned! Isaac! Isaac! Let her go, and do you stop with me!'

Something darkened the parlour window as those words were said. A sudden chill ran through him, and he glanced sidelong at the shadow. Rebecca Murdoch had come back. She was peering in curiously at them over the low window-blind.

'I have promised to marry, mother,' he said, 'and marry, I must.'

The tears came into his eyes as he spoke, and dimmed his sight; but he could just discern the fatal face outside, moving away from the window.

His mother's head sank lower.

'Are you faint?' he whispered.

'Broken-hearted, Isaac.'

He stooped down and kissed her. The shadow, as he did so, returned to the window; and the fatal face peered in curiously once more.

4

Three weeks after that day Isaac and Rebecca were man and wife. All that was hopelessly dogged and stubborn in the man's moral nature, seemed to have closed round his fatal passion, and to have fixed it unassailably in his heart.

After that first interview in the cottage parlour, no consideration could induce Mrs Scatchard to see her son's wife again, or even to talk of her when Isaac tried hard to plead her cause after their marriage.

This course of conduct was not in any degree occasioned by a discovery of the degradation in which Rebecca had lived. There was no question of that between mother and son. There was no question of anything but the fearfully exact resemblance between the living, breathing woman, and the spectre-woman of Isaac's dream.

Rebecca on her side, neither felt nor expressed the slightest sorrow at the estrangement between herself and her mother-in-law. Isaac, for the sake of peace, had never contradicted her first idea that age and long illness had affected Mrs Scatchard's mind. He even allowed his wife to upbraid him for not having confessed this to her at the time of their marriage engagement, rather than risk anything by hinting at the truth. The sacrifice of his integrity before his one all-mastering delusion, seemed but a small thing, and cost his conscience but little, after the sacrifices he had already made.

The time of waking from his delusion – the cruel and the rueful time – was not far off. After some quiet months of married life, as the summer was ending, and the year was getting on towards the month of his birthday, Isaac found his wife altering towards him. She grew sullen and contemptuous;

she formed acquaintances of the most dangerous kind, in defiance of his objections, his entreaties, and his commands; and, worst of all, she learnt, ere long, after every fresh difference with her husband, to seek the deadly self-oblivion of drink. Little by little, after the first miserable discovery that his wife was keeping company with drunkards, the shocking certainty forced itself on Isaac that she had grown to be a drunkard herself.

He had been in a sadly desponding state for some time before the occurrence of these domestic calamities. His mother's health, as he could but too plainly discern every time he went out to see her at the cottage, was failing fast; and he upbraided himself in secret as the cause of the bodily and mental suffering she endured. When to his remorse on his mother's account was added the shame and misery occasioned by the discovery of his wife's degradation, he sank under the double trial, his face began to alter fast, and he looked, what he was, a spirit-broken man.

His mother, still struggling bravely against the illness that was hurrying her to the grave, was the first to notice the sad alteration in him, and the first to hear of his last, worst trouble with his wife. She could only weep bitterly, on the day when he made his humiliating confession; but on the next occasion when he went to see her, she had taken a resolution, in reference to his domestic afflictions, which astonished, and even alarmed him. He found her dressed to go out, and on asking the reason, received the answer:

'I am not long for this world, Isaac,' she said; 'and I shall not feel easy on my death-bed, unless I have done my best to the last to make my son happy. I mean to put my own fears and my own feelings out of the question, and to go with you to your wife, and try what I can do to reclaim her. Give me your arm, Isaac and let me do the last thing I can in this world to help my son, before it is too late.'

He could not disobey her; and they walked together slowly towards his miserable home.

It was only one o'clock in the afternoon when they reached the cottage where he lived. It was their dinner hour, and Rebecca was in the kitchen. He was thus able to take his mother quietly into the parlour, and then prepare his wife for the interview. She had fortunately drank but little at that early hour, and she was less sullen and capricious than usual.

He returned to his mother, with his mind tolerably at ease. His wife soon followed him into the parlour, and the meeting between her and Mrs Scatchard passed off better than he had ventured to anticipate; though he observed with secret apprehension that his mother, resolutely as she controlled herself in other respects, could not look his wife in the face when she spoke to her. It was a relief to him, therefore, when Rebecca began to lay the cloth.

She laid the cloth, brought in the bread-tray, and cut a slice from the loaf for her husband, then returned to the kitchen. At that moment, Isaac, still anxiously watching his mother, was startled by seeing the same ghastly change pass over her face which had altered it so awfully on the morning when Rebecca and she first met. Before he could say a word, she whispered with a look of horror:

'Take me back! – home, home again, Isaac! Come with me, and never go back again!'

He was afraid to ask for an explanation; he could only sign her to be silent, and help her quickly to the door. As they passed the bread-tray on the table, she stopped and pointed to it.

'Did you see what your wife cut your bread with?' she asked in a low whisper.

'No, mother; I was not noticing. What was it?'

'Look!'

He did look. A new clasp-knife, with a buckhorn handle, lay with the loaf in the bread-tray. He stretched out his hand, shudderingly, to possess himself of it; but at the same time, there was a noise in the kitchen, and his mother caught at his arm.

'The knife of the dream! Isaac, I'm faint with fear – take me away, before she comes back!'

He was hardly able to support her. The visible, tangible reality of the knife struck him with a panic, and utterly destroyed any faint doubts he might have entertained up to this time, in relation to the mysterious dream-warning of nearly eight years before. By a last desperate effort, he summoned self-possession enough to help his mother out of the house – so quietly, that the 'Dream Woman' (he thought of her by that name now) did not hear their departure.

'Don't go back, Isaac, don't go back!' implored Mrs Scatchard, as he turned to go away, after seeing her safely seated again in her own room.

'I must get the knife,' he answered under his breath. His mother tried to stop him; but he hurried out without another word.

On his return, he found that his wife had discovered their secret departure from the house. She had been drinking, and was in a fury of passion. The dinner in the kitchen was flung under the grate; the cloth was off the parlour table. Where was the knife?

Unwisely, he asked for it. She was only too glad of the opportunity of irritating him, which the request afforded her. 'He wanted the knife, did he? Could he give her a reason why? – No? Then he should not have it – not if he went down on his knees to ask for it.' Further recriminations elicited the fact that she bought it a bargain, and that she considered it her own especial property. Isaac saw the uselessness of attempting to get the knife by fair means, and determined to search for it, later in the day, in secret. The search was unsuccessful. Night came on, and he left the house to walk about the streets. He was afraid now to sleep in the same room as her.

Three weeks passed. Still sullenly enraged with him, she would not give up the knife; and still that fear of sleeping in the same room with her possessed him. He walked about at night, or dozed in the parlour, or sat watching by his mother's bed-side. Before the expiration of the first week in the new month his mother died. It wanted then but ten days of her son's birthday. She had longed to live till that anniversary. Isaac was present at her death; and her last words in this world were addressed to him:

'Don't go back, my son – don't go back!'

He was obliged to go back, if it were only to watch his wife. Exasperated to the last degree by his distrust of her, she had revengefully sought to add a sting to his grief, during the last days of his mother's illness, by declaring that she would assert her right to attend the funeral. In spite of all that he could do or say, she held with wicked pertinacity to her words and, on the day appointed for the burial, forced herself – inflamed and shameless with drink – into her husband's presence, and declared that she would walk in the funeral procession to his mother's grave.

This last worst outrage, accompanied by all that was most insulting in word and look, maddened him for the moment. He struck her.

The instant the blow was dealt, he repented it. She crouched down, silent, in a corner of the room, and eyed him steadily; it was a look that cooled his hot blood, and made him tremble. But there was no time now to think of a means of making atonement. Nothing remained, but to risk the worst till the funeral was over. There was but one way of making sure of her. He locked her into the bed-room.

When he came back, some hours after, he found her sitting, very much altered in look and bearing, by the bedside, with a bundle on her lap. She rose, and faced him quietly, and spoke with a strange stillness in her voice, a strange repose in her eyes, a strange composure in her manner.

'No man has ever struck me twice,' she said; 'and my husband shall have no second opportunity. Set the door open and let me go. From this day forth we see each other no more.'

Before he could answer she passed him, and left the room. He saw her walk away up the street.

Would she return?

All that night he watched and waited; but no footstep came near the house. The next night, overcome by fatigue, he lay down in bed in his clothes, with the door locked, the key on the table, and the candle burning. His slumber was not disturbed. The third night, the fourth, the fifth, the sixth passed and nothing happened. He lay down on the seventh, still in his clothes, still with the door locked, the key on the table, and the candle burning; but easier in his mind.

Easier in his mind, and in perfect health of body, when he fell off to sleep. But his rest was disturbed. He woke twice, without any sensation of uneasiness. But the third time it was that never-be-forgotten shivering of the night at the lonely inn, that dreadful sinking pain at the heart, which once more aroused him in an instant.

His eyes opened towards the left-hand side of the bed, and there stood –

The Dream Woman again? No! His wife; the living reality, with the dream-spectre's face – in the dream-spectre's attitude: the fair arm up; the knife clasped in the delicate white hand.

He sprang upon her, almost at the instant of seeing her, and yet not quickly enough to prevent her from hiding the knife. Without a word from him, without a cry from her, he pinioned her in the chair. With one hand he felt up her sleeve; and there, where the Dream Woman had hidden the knife, his wife had hidden it – the knife with the buckhorn handle, that looked like new.

In despair of that fearful moment his brain was steady, his heart was calm. He looked at her fixedly, with the knife in his hand, and said these last words:

'You told me we should see each other no more, and you have come back. It is my turn now to go, and to go for ever. I say that we shall see each other no more; and my word shall not be broken.'

He left her, and set forth into the night. There was a bleak wind abroad, and the smell of recent rain was in the air. The distant church clocks chimed the quarter as he walked rapidly beyond the last houses in the suburb. He asked the first policeman he met, what hour that was, of which the quarter past had just struck.

The man referred sleepily to his watch, and answered, 'Two o'clock.' Two in the morning. What day of the month was this day that had just begun? He reckoned it up from the date of his mother's funeral. The fatal parallel was complete – it was his birthday!

As the ominous doubt forced itself on his mind, he stopped, reflected, and turned back again towards the city. He was still resolute to hold his word, and never to let her see him more; but there was a thought now in his mind of having her watched and followed. The knife was in his possession; the world was before him; but a new distrust of her – a vague, unspeakable, superstitious dread – had overcome him.

'I must know where she goes, now she thinks I have left her,' he said to himself, as he stole back wearily to the precincts of his house.

It was still dark. He had left the candle burning in the bed-chamber; but when he looked up to the window of the room now, there was no light in it. He crept cautiously to the house door. On going away, he remembered to have closed it; on trying it now, he found it open.

He waited outside, never losing sight of the house till day-light. Then he ventured indoors – listened, and heard nothing – looked into the kitchen, scullery, parlour; and found nothing: went up at last into the bedroom – it was empty. A picklock lay on the floor, betraying how she had gained entrance in the night, and that was the only trace of her.

Whither had she gone? No mortal tongue could tell him. The darkness had covered her flight; and when the day broke, no man could say where the light found her.

Before leaving the house and the town for ever, he gave instructions to a friend and neighbour to sell his furniture for anything it would fetch, and to apply the proceeds towards employing the police to trace her. The directions were honestly followed, and the money was all spent; but the inquiries led to nothing. The picklock on the bedroom floor remained the last useless trace of the Dream Woman.

At this part of the narrative the landlord paused; and, turning towards the window of the room in which we were sitting, looked in the direction of the stable-yard.

'So far,' he said, 'I tell you what was told to me. The little that remains to be added, lies within my own experience. Between two and three months after the events I have just been relating, Isaac Scatchard came to me, withered and old-looking before his time, just as you see him today. He had his testimonials to character with him, and he asked me for employment here. Knowing that my wife and he were distantly related, I gave him a trial, in consideration of that relationship, and liked him in spite of his queer habits. He is as sober, honest, and willing a man as there is in England. As for his restlessness at night, and his sleeping away his leisure time in the day, who can wonder at it after hearing his story? Besides, he never objects to being roused up, when he's wanted, so there's not much inconvenience to complain of, after all.'

'I suppose he is afraid of a return of that dreadful dream, and of waking out of it in the dark?'

'No,' returned the landlord. 'The dream comes back to him so often, that he has got to bear with it by this time resignedly enough. It's his wife keeps him waking at night, as he often told me.'

'What! Has she never been heard of yet?'

'Never. Isaac himself has the one perpetual thought, that she is alive and looking for him. I believe he wouldn't let himself drop off to sleep towards two in the morning, for a king's ransom. Two in the morning, he says, is the time she will find him, one of these days. Two in the morning is the time, all the year round, when he likes to be most certain that he has got the clasp-knife safe about him. He does not mind being alone, as long as he is awake, except on the night before his birthday, when he firmly believes himself to be in peril of his life. The birthday has only come round once since he has been here, and then he sat up along with the night-porter. "She's looking for me," is all he says, when anybody speaks to him about the one anxiety of his life; "she's looking for me." He may be right. She *may* be looking for him. Who can tell?'

'Who can tell?' said I.

A Confession Found in a Prison in the Time of Charles the Second

Charles Dickens

I held a lieutenant's commission in His Majesty's army and served abroad in the campaigns of 1677 and 1678. The treaty of Nimeguen being concluded, I returned home, and retiring from the service withdrew to a small estate lying a few miles east of London, which I had recently acquired in right of my wife.

This is the last night I have to live, and I will set down the naked truth without disguise. I was never a brave man, and had always been from my childhood of a secret, sullen, distrustful nature. I speak of myself as if I had passed from the world, for while I write this my grave is digging and my name is written in the black book of death.

Soon after my return to England, my only brother was seized with mortal illness. This circumstance gave me slight or no pain, for since we had been men we had associated but very little together. He was open-hearted and generous, handsomer than I, more accomplished, and generally beloved. Those who sought my acquaintance abroad or at home because they were friends of his, seldom attached themselves to me long, and would usually say in our first conversation that they were surprised to find two brothers so unlike in their manners and appearance. It was my habit to lead them on to this avowal, for I knew what comparisons they must draw between us, and having a rankling envy in my heart, I sought to justify it to myself.

We had married two sisters. This additional tie between us, as it may appear to some, only estranged us the more. His wife knew me well. I never struggled with any secret jealousy or gall when she was present but that woman knew it as well as I did. I never raised my eyes at such times but I found hers fixed upon me; I never bent them on the ground or looked another way, but I felt that she overlooked me always. It was an inexpressible relief to me when we quarrelled, and a greater relief still when I heard abroad that she was dead. It seems to me now as if some strange and terrible foreshadowing of what has happened since, must have hung over us then. I was afraid of her, she haunted me, her fixed and steady look comes back upon me now like the memory of a dark dream and makes my blood run cold.

She died shortly after giving birth to a child – a boy. When my brother knew that all hope of his own recovery was past, he called my wife to his bed-side and confided this orphan, a child of four years old, to her protection. He bequeathed to him all the property he had, and willed that in case of the child's death it should pass to my wife as the only acknowledgement he could make her for her care and love. He exchanged a few brotherly words with me deploring our long separation, and being exhausted, fell into a slumber from which he never awoke.

We had no children, and as there had been a strong affection between the sisters, and my wife had almost supplied the place of a mother to this boy, she loved him as if he had been her own. The child was ardently attached to her; but he was his mother's image in face and spirit and always mistrusted me.

I can scarcely fix the date when the feelings first came upon me, but I soon began to be uneasy when this child was by. I never roused myself from some moody train of thought but I marked him looking at me: not with mere childish wonder, but with something of the purpose and meaning that I had so often noted in his mother. It was no effort of my fancy, founded on close resemblance of feature and expression. I never could look the boy down. He feared me, but seemed by some instinct to despise me while he did so; and even when he drew back beneath my gaze – as he would when we were alone, to get nearer to the door – he would keep his bright eyes upon me still.

Perhaps I hide the truth from myself, but I do not think that when this began, I meditated to do him any wrong. I may have thought how serviceable his inheritance would be to us, and may have wished him dead, but I believe I had no thought of compassing his death. Neither did the idea come upon me at once, but by very slow degrees, presenting itself at first in dim shapes at a very great distance, as men may think of an earthquake or the last day – then drawing nearer and nearer and losing something of its horror and improbability – then coming to be part and parcel, nay nearly the whole sum and substance of my daily thoughts, and resolving itself into a question of means and safety; not of doing or abstaining from the deed.

While this was going on within me, I never could bear that the child should see me looking at him, and yet I was under a fascination which made it a kind of business with me to contemplate his slight and fragile figure and think how easily it might be done. Sometimes I would steal upstairs and watch him as he slept, but usually I hovered in the garden near the window of the room in which he learnt his little tasks, and there as he sat upon a low seat beside my wife, I would peer at him for hours together from behind a tree: starting like the guilty wretch I was at every rustling of a leaf, and still gliding back to look and start again.

Hard by our cottage, but quite out of sight, and (if there were any wind astir) of hearing too, was a deep sheet of water. I spent days in shaping with my pocket-knife a rough model of a boat, which I finished at last and dropped in the child's way. Then I withdrew to a secret place which he must pass if he stole away alone to swim this bauble, and lurked there for his coming. He came neither that day nor the next, though I waited from noon till nightfall. I was sure that I had him in my net for I heard him prattling of the toy, and knew that in his infant pleasure he kept it by his side in bed. I felt no weariness or fatigue, but waited patiently, and on the third day he passed me, running joyously along, with his silken hair streaming in the wind and he singing – God have mercy upon me! – singing a merry ballad – who could hardly lisp the words.

I stole down after him, creeping under certain shrubs which grow in that place, and none but devils know with what terror, I, a full-grown man, tracked the footsteps of that baby as he approached the water's brink. I was close upon him, had sunk upon my knee and raised my hand to thrust him in, when he saw my shadow in the stream and turned him round.

His mother's ghost was looking from his eyes. The sun burst forth from behind a cloud: it shone in the bright sky, the glistening earth, the clear water, the sparkling drops of rain upon the leaves. There were eyes in everything. The whole great universe of light was there to see murder done. I know not what he said; he came of bold and manly blood, and child as he was, he did not crouch or fawn upon me. I heard him cry that he would try to love me – not that he did – and then I saw him running back towards the house. The next I saw my own sword naked in my hand and he lying at my feet stark dead – dabbled here and there with blood but otherwise no different from what I had seen him in his sleep – in the same attitude too, with his cheek resting upon his little hand.

I took him in my arms and laid him – very gently now that he was dead – in a thicket. My wife was from home that day and would not return until the next. Our bed-room window, the only sleeping room on that side of the house, was but a few feet from the ground, and I resolved to descend from it at night and bury him in the garden. I had no thought that I had failed in my design, no thought that the water would be dragged and nothing found, that the money must now lie waste since I must encourage the idea that the child was lost or stolen. All my thoughts were bound up and knotted together, in the one absorbing necessity of hiding what I had done.

How I felt when they came to tell me that the child was

missing, when I ordered scouts in all directions, when I gasped and trembled at everyone's approach, no tongue can tell or mind of man conceive. I buried him that night. When I parted the boughs and looked into the dark thicket, there was a glow-worm shining like the visible spirit of God upon the murdered child. I glanced down into his grave when I had placed him there and still it gleamed upon his breast: an eye of fire looking up to Heaven to supplication to the stars that watched me at my work.

I had to meet my wife, and break the news, and give her hope that the child would soon be found. All this I did – with some appearance, I suppose, of being sincere, for I was the object of no suspicion. This done, I sat at the bed-room window all day long and watched the spot where the dreadful secret lay.

It was in a piece of ground which had been dug up to be newly turfed, and which I had chosen on that account as the traces of my spade were less likely to attract attention. The men who laid down the grass must have thought me mad. I called to them continually to expedite their work, ran out and worked beside them, trod down the turf with my feet, and hurried them with frantic eagerness. They had finished their task before night, and then I thought myself comparatively safe.

I slept – not as men do who wake refreshed and cheerful, but I did sleep, passing from vague and shadowy dreams of being hunted down, to visions of the plot of grass, through which now a hand and now a foot and now the head itself was starting out. At this point I always woke and stole to the window to make sure that it was not really so. That done I crept to bed again, and thus I spent the night in fits and starts, getting up and lying down full twenty times and dreaming the same dream over and over again – which was far worse than lying awake, for every dream had a whole night's suffering of its own. Once I thought the child was alive and that I had never tried to kill him. To wake from that dream was the most dreadful agony of all.

The next day I sat at the window and again, never once taking my eyes from the place, which, although it was covered by the grass, was as plain to me – its shape, its size, its depth, its jagged sides, and all – as if it had been open to the light of day. When a servant walked across it, I felt as if he must sink in; when he had passed I looked to see that his feet had not worn the edges. If a bird lighted there, I was in terror lest by some tremendous interposition it should be instrumental in the discovery; if a breath of air sighed across it, to me it whispered murder. There was not a sight or sound how ordinary, mean or unimportant soever, but was fraught with fear. And in this state of ceaseless watching I spent three days.

On the fourth, there came to the gate one who had served with me abroad, accompanied by a brother officer of his whom I had never seen. I felt that I could not bear to be out of sight of the place. It was a summer evening, and I bade my people take a table and a flask of wine into the garden. Then I sat down *with my chair upon the grave*, and being assured that nobody could disturb it now, without my knowledge, tried to drink and talk.

They hoped that my wife was well – that she was not obliged to keep her chamber – that they had not frightened her away. What could I do but tell them with a faltering tongue about the child? The officer whom I did not know was a down-looking man and kept his eyes upon the ground while I was speaking. Even that terrified me! I could not divest myself of the idea that he saw something there which caused him to suspect the truth. I asked him hurriedly if he supposed that – and stopped. 'That the child had been murdered?' said he, looking mildly at me. 'Oh no! what could a man gain by murdering a poor child?' I could have told him what a man gained by such a deed, no one better, but I held my peace and shivered as with an ague.

Mistaking my emotion they were endeavouring to cheer me with the hope that the boy would certainly be found – great cheer that was for me – when we heard a low deep howl, and presently there sprung over the wall two great dogs, who bounding into the garden repeated the baying sound we had heard before.

'Blood-hounds!' cried my visitors.

What need to tell me that! I had never seen one of that kind in all my life, but I knew what they were and for what purpose they had come. I grasped the elbows of my chair, and neither spoke nor moved.

'They are of the genuine breed,' said the man whom I had known abroad, 'and being out for exercise have no doubt escaped from their keeper.'

Both he and his friend turned to look at the dogs, who with their noses to the ground moved restlessly about, running to and fro, and up and down, and across, and round in circles, careering about like wild things, and all this time taking no notice of us, but ever and again lifting their heads and repeating the yell we had heard already, then dropping their noses to the ground again and tracking earnestly here and there. They now began to snuff the earth more eagerly than they had done yet, and although they were still very restless, no longer beat about in such wide circuits, but kept near to one spot, and constantly diminished the distance between themselves and me.

At last they came up close to the great chair on which I sat, and raising their frightful howl once more, tried to tear away the wooden rails that kept them from the ground beneath. I saw how I looked, in the faces of the two who were with me.

'They scent some prey,' said they, both together.

'They scent no prey!' cried I.

'In heaven's name move,' said the one I knew, very earnestly, 'or you will be torn to pieces.'

'Let them tear me limb from limb, I'll never leave this place!' cried I. 'Are dogs to hurry men to shameful deaths? Hew them down, cut them in pieces.'

'There is some foul mystery here!' said the officer whom I

did not know, drawing his sword. 'In King Charles's name assist me to secure this man.'

They both set upon me and forced me away, though I fought and bit and caught at them like a madman. After a struggle they got me quietly between them, and then, my God! I saw the angry dogs tearing at the earth and throwing it up into the air like water.

What more have I to tell? That I fell upon my knees and with chattering teeth confessed the truth and prayed to be forgiven. That I have since denied and now confess to it again. That I have been tried for the crime, found guilty, and sentenced. That I have not the courage to anticipate my doom or to bear up manfully against it. That I have no compassion, no consolation, no hope, no friend. That my wife has happily lost for the time those faculties which would enable her to know my misery or hers. That I am alone in this stone dungeon with my evil spirit, and that I die to-morrow!

Silence

Leonid Andreyev

One moonlit night in May, while the nightingales sang, Father Ignatius's wife entered his chamber. Her countenance expressed suffering, and the little lamp she held in her hand trembled. Approaching her husband, she touched his shoulder, and managed to say between her sobs:

'Father, let us go to Verochka.'

Without turning his head, Father Ignatius glanced severely at his wife over the rims of his spectacles, and looked long and intently, till she waved her unoccupied hand and dropped on a low divan.

'That one toward the other be so pitiless!' she pronounced slowly, with emphasis on the final syllables, and her good plump face was distorted with a grimace of pain and exasperation, as if in this manner she wished to express what stern people they were – her husband and daughter.

Father Ignatius smiled and arose. Closing his book, he removed his spectacles, placed them in the case and meditated. His long, black beard, inwoven with silver threads, lay dignified on his breast, and it slowly heaved at every breath.

'Well, let us go!' said he.

Olga Stepanovna quickly arose and entered in an appealing, timid voice:

'Only don't revile her, father! You know the sort she is.'

Vera's chamber was in the attic, and the narrow, wooden stair bent and creaked under the heavy tread of Father Ignatius. Tall and ponderous, he lowered his head to avoid striking the floor of the upper story, and frowned disdainfully when the white jacket of his wife brushed his face. Well he knew that nothing would come of their talk with Vera.

'Why do you come?' asked Vera, raising a bared arm to her eyes. The other arm lay on top of a white summer blanket hardly distinguishable from the fabric, so white, translucent and cold was its aspect.

'Verochka!' began her mother, but sobbing, she grew silent.

'Vera!' said her father, making an effort to soften his dry and hard voice, 'Vera, tell us, what troubles you?'

Vera was silent.

'Vera, do not we, your mother and I, deserve your confidence? Do we not love you? And is there someone nearer to you than we? Tell us about your sorrow, and believe me you'll feel better for it. And we too. Look at your aged mother, how much she suffers!'

'Verochka!'

'And I …' The dry voice trembled, truly something had broken in it. 'And I … do you think I find it easy? And if I did not see that some sorrow is gnawing at you – and what is it? And I, your father, do not know what it is. Is it right that it should be so?'

Vera was silent. Father Ignatius very cautiously stroked his beard, as if afraid that his fingers would enmesh themselves involuntarily in it, and continued:

'Against my wish you went to St. Petersburg – did I pronounce a curse upon you, you who disobeyed me? Or did I not give you money? Or, you'll say, I have not been kind? Well, why then are you silent? There, you've had your St. Petersburg!'

Father Ignatius became silent, and an image arose before him of something huge, of granite, and terrible, full of invisible dangers and strange and indifferent people. And there, alone and weak, was his Vera and there they had lost her. An awful hatred against that terrible and mysterious city grew in the soul of Father Ignatius, and an anger against his daughter who was silent, obstinately silent.

'St. Petersburg has nothing to do with it,' said Vera morosely, and closed her eyes. 'And nothing is the matter with me. Better go to bed, it is late.'

'Verochka,' whimpered her mother. 'Little daughter, do confess to me.'

'Akh, mama!' impatiently Vera interrupted her.

Father Ignatius sat down on a chair and laughed.

'Well, then it's nothing?' he inquired ironically.

'Father,' sharply put in Vera, raising herself from the pillow, 'you know that I love you and mother. Well, I do feel a little weary. But that will pass. Do go to sleep, and I also wish to sleep. And to-morrow, or some other time, we'll have a chat.'

Father Ignatius impetuously arose so that the chair hit the wall, and took his wife's hand.

'Let us go.'

'Verochka!'

'Let us go, I tell you!' shouted Father Ignatius. 'If she has forgotten God, shall we …'

Almost forcibly he led Olga Stepanovna out of the room, and when they descended the stairs, his wife, decreasing her gait, said in a harsh whisper:

'It was you, priest, who have made her such. From you she learned her ways. And you'll never answer for it. Akh, unhappy creature that I am!'

And she wept, and as her eyes filled with tears, her foot, missing a step, would descend with a sudden jolt, as if she were eager to fall into some existent abyss below.

From that day Father Ignatius ceased to speak with his daughter, but she seemed not to notice it. As before she lay in her room, or walked about, continually wiping her eyes with the palms of her hands as if they contained some irritating foreign substance. And crushed between these two silent people, the jolly, fun-loving wife of the priest quailed and seemed lost not knowing what to say or do.

Occasionally Vera took a stroll. A week following the interview she went out in the evening, as was her habit. She was not seen alive again, as on this evening she threw herself under the train, which cut her in two.

Father Ignatius himself directed the funeral. His wife was not present in church, as at the news of Vera's death she was prostrated by a stroke. She lost control of her feet, hands and tongue, and she lay motionless in the semi-darkened room when the church bells rang out. She heard the people, as they issued out of church and passed the house, intone the chants, and she made an effort to raise her hand, and to make a sign of the cross, but her hand refused to obey; she wished to say: 'Farewell, Vera!' but the tongue lay in her mouth huge and heavy. And her attitude was so calm, that it gave one an impression of restfulness or sleep. Only her eyes remained open.

At the funeral, in church, were many people who knew Father Ignatius, and many strangers, and all bewailed Vera's terrible death, and tried to find in the movements and voice of Father Ignatius because of his severity and proud manners, his scorn of sinners, for his unforgiving spirit, his envy and covetousness, his habit of utilizing every opportunity to extort money from his parishioners. They all wished to see him suffer, to see his spirit broken, to see him conscious in his two-fold guilt for the death of his daughter – as a cruel father and a bad priest – incapable of preserving his own flesh from sin. They cast searching glances at him, and he, feeling these glances directed toward his back, made efforts to hold erect its broad and strong expanse, and his thoughts were not concerning his dead daughter, but concerning his own dignity.

'A hardened priest!' said, with a shake of his head, Karzenoff, a carpenter, to whom Father Ignatius owed five rubles for frames.

And thus, hard and erect, Father Ignatius reached the burial ground, and in the same manner he returned. Only at the door of his wife's chamber did his spine relax a little, but this may have been due to the fact that the height of the door was inadequate to admit his tall figure. The change from broad daylight made it difficult for him to distinguish the face of his wife, but, after scrutiny, he was astonished at its calmness and because the eyes showed no tears. And there was neither anger, nor sorrow in the eyes – they were dumb, and they kept silent with difficulty, reluctantly, as did the entire plump and helpless body, pressing against the feather bedding.

'Well, how do you feel?' inquired Father Ignatius.

The lips, however, were dumb; the eyes also were silent. Father Ignatius laid his hand on her forehead; it was cold and moist, and Olga Stepanovna did not show in any way that she had felt the hand's contact. When Father Ignatius removed his hand there gazed at him, immobile, two grey eyes, seeming almost entirely dark from the dilated pupils, and there was neither sadness in them, nor anger.

'I am going into my own room,' said Father Ignatius, who began to feel cold and terror.

He passed through the drawing-room, where everything appeared neat and in order, as usual, and where, attired in white covers, stood tall chairs, like corpses in their shrouds. Over one window hung an empty wire cage, with the door open.

'Nastasya!' shouted Father Ignatius, and his voice seemed to him coarse, and he felt ill at ease because he raised his voice so high in these silent rooms, so soon after his daughter's funeral. 'Nastasya!' he called out in a lower tone of voice, 'where is the canary?'

'She flew away, to be sure.'

'Why did you let it out?'

Nastasya began to weep, and wiping her face with the edges of her calico handkerchief, said through her tears:

'It was my young mistress's soul. Was it right to hold it?'

And it seemed to Father Ignatius that the yellow, happy little canary, always singing with inclined head, was really the soul of Vera, and if it had not flown away it wouldn't have been possible to say that Vera had died. He became even more incensed at the maidservant and shouted:

'Off with you!'

And when Nastasya did not find the door at once he added:

'Fool!'

From the day of the funeral silence reigned in the little house. It was not stillness, for stillness is merely the absence of sounds; it was silence, because it seemed that they who were silent could say something but would not. So thought Father Ignatius each time he entered his wife's chamber and met that obstinate gaze, so heavy in its aspect that it seemed to transform the very air into lead, which bore down one's head and spine. So thought he, examining his daughter's music sheets, which bore imprints of her voice, as well as her books and her portrait, which she brought with her from St. Petersburg. Father Ignatius was accustomed to scrutinize the portrait in established order: First, he would gaze on the cheek upon which a strong light was thrown by the painter; in his fancy he would see upon it a slight wound, which he had noticed on Vera's cheek in death, and the source of which he could not understand. Each time he would meditate upon causes; he reasoned that if it was made by the train the entire head would have been crushed, whereas the head of Vera remained wholly untouched. It was possible that someone did it with his foot when the corpse was removed, or accidentally with a finger nail.

To contemplate at length upon the details of Vera's death taxed the strength of Father Ignatius, so that he would pass on to the eyes. These were dark, handsome, with long lashes, which cast deep shadows beneath, causing the whites to seem particularly luminous, both eyes appearing to be enclosed in black, mourning frames. A strange expression was given them by the unknown but talented artist; it seemed as if in the space between the eyes and the object upon which they gazed there lay a thin, transparent film. It resembled somewhat the effect obtained by an imperceptible layer of dust on the black top of a piano, softening the shine of polished wood. And no matter how Father Ignatius placed the portrait, the eyes insistently followed him, but there was no speech in them, only silence; and this silence was so clear that it seemed it could be heard. And gradually Father Ignatius began to think that he heard silence.

Every morning after breakfast Father Ignatius would enter the drawing-room, throw a rapid glance at the empty cage and the other familiar objects, and seating himself in the armchair would close his eyes and listen to the silence of the house. There was something grotesque about this. The cage kept silence, stilly and tenderly, and in this silence were felt sorrow and tears, and distant dead laughter. The silence of his wife, softened by the walls, continued insistent, heavy as lead, and terrible, so terrible that on the hottest day Father Ignatius would be seized by cold shivers. Continuous and cold as the grave, and mysterious as death, was the silence of his daughter. The silence itself seemed to share this suffering and struggled as it were, with the terrible desire to pass into speech; however, something strong and cumbersome, as a machine, held it motionless and stretched it out as a wire. And somewhere at the distant end, the wire would begin to agitate and resound subduedly, feebly and plaintively. With joy, yet with terror, Father Ignatius would seize upon this engendered sound, and resting with his arms upon the arms of the chair, would lean his head forward, awaiting the sound to reach him. But the sound would break and pass into silence.

'How stupid!' muttered Father Ignatius, angrily, arising from the chair, still erect and tall. Through the window he saw, suffused with sunlight, the street, which was paved with round, even-sized stones, and directly across, the stone wall of a long, windowless shed. On the corner stood a cab-driver, resembling a clay statue, and it was difficult to understand why he stood there, when for hours there was not a single passer-by.

Father Ignatius had occasion for considerable speech outside his house. There was talking to be done with the clergy, with the members of his flock, while officiating at ceremonies, sometimes with acquaintances at social evenings; yet, upon his return he would feel invariably that the entire day he had been silent. This was due to the fact that with none of those people could he talk upon that matter which concerned him most, and upon which he would contemplate each night: Why did Vera die?

Father Ignatius did not seem to understand that now this could not be known, and still thought it was possible to know. Each night – all his nights had become sleepless – he would picture that minute when he and his wife in dead midnight, stood near Vera's bed, and he entreated her: 'Tell us!' And when in his recollection, he would reach these words, the rest appeared to him not as it was in reality. His closed eyes, preserving in their darkness a live and undimmed picture of that night, saw how Vera raised herself in her bed, smiled and tried to say something. And what was that she tried to say? That unuttered word of Vera's, which should have solved all, seemed so near, that if one only had bent his ear and suppressed the beats of his heart, one could have heard it, and at the same time it was so infinitely, so hopelessly distant. Father Ignatius would arise from his bed, stretch forth his joined hands and, wringing them would exclaim:

'Vera!'

And he would be answered by silence.

One evening Father Ignatius entered the chamber of Olga Stepanovna, whom he had not come to see for a week, seated himself at her head, and turning away from that insistent heavy gaze, said:

'Mother! I wish to talk to you about Vera. Do you hear?'

Her eyes were silent, and Father Ignatius raising his voice, spoke sternly and powerfully, as he was accustomed to speak with penitents.

'I am aware that you are under the impression that I have been the cause of Vera's death. Reflect, however, did I love her less than you loved her? You reason absurdly. I have been stern; did that prevent her from doing as she wished? I have forfeited the dignity of a father, I humbly bent my neck, when she defied my malediction and departed – hence. And you – did you not entreat her to remain, until I commanded you to be silent? Did I beget cruelty in her? Did I not teach her about

God, about humility, above love?'

Father Ignatius quickly glanced into the eyes of his wife, and turned away.

'What was there for me to do when she did not wish to reveal her sorrow? Did I not command her? Did I not entreat her? I suppose, in your opinion, I should have dropped on my knees before the maid, and cried like an old woman! How should I know what was going on in her head! Cruel, heartless daughter!'

Father Ignatius hit his knees with his fist.

'There was no love in her – that's what! As far as I'm concerned, that's settled, of course – I am a tyrant! Perhaps she loved you – you, who wept and humbled yourself?'

Father Ignatius gave a hollow laugh.

'There's love for you! And as a solace for you, what a death she chose! A cruel, ignominious death. She died in the dust, in the dirt – as a d-dog who is kicked in the jaw.'

The voice of Father Ignatius sounded low and hoarse:

'I feel ashamed! Ashamed to go out in the street! Ashamed before the alter! Ashamed before God! Cruel, undeserving daughter! Accurst in thy grave!'

When Father Ignatius glanced at his wife she was unconscious, and revived only after several hours. When she regained consciousness her eyes were silent, and it was impossible to tell whether or not she remembered what Father Ignatius had said.

That very night – it was a moonlit, calm, warm and deathly still night in May – Father Ignatius, proceeding on his tiptoes, so as not to be overheard by his wife and the sick-nurse, climbed the stairs and entered Vera's room. The window in the attic had remained closed since the death of Vera, and the atmosphere was dry and warm, with a light odour of burning that comes from heat generated during the day in the iron roof. The air of lifelessness and abandonment permeated the apartment, which for a long time had remained unvisited, and where the timber of the walls, the furniture and other objects gave forth a slight odour of continued putrescence. A bright streak of moonlight fell on the window-sill, and on the floor, and, reflected by the white, carefully washed boards, cast a dim light into the room's corners, while the white, clean bed, with two pillows, one large and one small, seemed phantom-like and aerial. Father Ignatius opened the window, causing to pour into the room a considerable current of fresh air, smelling of dust, of the nearby river and the blooming linden. An indistinct sound as of voices in chorus also entered occasionally; evidently young people rowed and sang.

Quietly treading with naked feet, resembling a white phantom, Father Ignatius made his way to the vacant bed, bent his knees and fell down on the pillows, embracing them – on that spot where should have been Vera's face. Long he lay there thus; the song grew louder, then died out; but he still lay there, while his long, black hair spread over his shoulders and the bed.

The moon had changed its position, and the room grew darker, when Father Ignatius raised his head and murmured, putting into his voice the entire strength of his long-suppressed and unconscious love and hearkening to his own words, as if it were not he who was listening, but Vera.

'Vera, daughter mine! Do you understand what you are to me, daughter? Little daughter! My heart, my blood and my life. Your father – your old father – is already grey, and is also feeble.'

The shoulders of Father Ignatius shook and the entire burdened figure became agitated. Suppressing his agitation, Father Ignatius murmured tenderly, as to an infant:

'Your old father entreats you. No, little Vera, he supplicates. He weeps. He never has wept before. Your sorrow, little child, your sufferings – they are also mine. Greater than mine.'

Father Ignatius shook his head.

'Greater, Verochka. What is death to an old man like me? But you – if you only knew how delicate and weak and timid you are! Do you recall how you bruised your finger once and the blood trickled and you cried a little? My child! I know that you love me, love me intensely. Every morning you kiss my hand. Tell me, do tell me, what grief troubles your little head, and I – with these hands – shall smother your grief. They are still strong, Vera, these hands.'

The hair of Father Ignatius shook.

'Tell me!'

Father Ignatius fixed his eyes on the wall, and wrung his hands.

'Tell me!'

Stillness prevailed in the room, and from afar was heard the prolonged and broken whistle of a locomotive.

Father Ignatius, gazing out of his dilated eyes, as if there had arisen suddenly before him the frightful phantom of the mutilated corpse, slowly raised himself from his knees, and with a credulous motion reached for his head with his hand, with spread and tensely stiffening fingers. Making a step toward the door, Father Ignatius whispered brokenly:

'Tell me!'

And he was answered by silence.

The next day, after an early and lonely dinner, Father Ignatius went to the graveyard, the first time since his daughter's death. It was warm, deserted and still; it seemed more like an illuminated night. Following habit, Father Ignatius, with effort, straightened his spine, looked severely about him and thought that he was the same as formerly; he was conscious neither of the new, terrible weakness in his legs, nor that his long beard had become entirely white as if a hard frost had hit it. The road to the graveyard led through a long, direct street, slightly on an upward incline, and at its termination loomed the arch of the graveyard gate, resembling a dark, perpetually open mouth, edged with glistening teeth.

Vera's grave was situated in the depth of the grounds, where the sandy little pathways terminated and Father Ignatius, for a considerable time, was obliged to blunder along the narrow footpaths, which led in a broken line between green mounds, by all forgotten and abandoned. Here and there appeared, green with age, sloping tombstones, broken railings and large, heavy stones planted in the ground, and seemingly crushing it with some cruel, ancient spite. Near one such stone was the grave of Vera. It was covered with fresh turf, turned yellow; around, however, all was in bloom. Ash embraced maple tree; and the widely spread hazel bush stretched out over the grave its bending branches with their downy, shaggy foliage. Sitting down on a neighbouring grave and catching his breath, Father Ignatius looked around him, throwing a glance upon the cloudless, desert sky, where in complete immovability, hung the glowing sun disk – and here he only felt that deep, incomparable stillness which reigns in graveyards, when the wind is absent and the slumbering foliage has ceased its rustling. And anew the thought came to Father Ignatius that this was not a stillness but a silence. It extended to the very brick walls of the graveyard, crept over them and occupied the city. And it terminated only – in those grey, obstinate and reluctantly silent eyes.

Father Ignatius' shoulders shivered, and he lowered his eyes upon the grave of Vera. He gazed long upon the little tufts of grass uprooted together with the earth from some open, windswept field and not successful in adapting themselves to a strange soil; he could not imagine that there, under this grass, only a few feet from him, lay Vera. And this nearness seemed incomprehensible and brought confusion into the soul and a strange agitation. She, of whom Father Ignatius was accustomed to think as one passed away forever into the dark depths of eternity, was here, close by – and it was hard to understand that she, nevertheless, was no more and never again would be. And in the mind's fancy of Father Ignatius it seemed that if he could only utter some word, which was almost upon his lips, or if he could make some sort of movement, Vera would issue forth from her grave and arise to the same height and beauty that was once hers. And not alone would she arise, but all corpses, intensely sensitive in their solemnly cold silence.

Father Ignatius removed his wide-brimmed black hat, smoothed down his disarranged hair and whispered:

'Vera!'

Father Ignatius felt ill at ease, fearing to be overheard by a stranger, and stepping on the grave he gazed around him. No one was present, and this time he repeated loudly:

'Vera!'

It was the voice of an aged man, sharp and demanding, and it was strange that a so-powerfully expressed desire should remain without answer.

'Vera!'

Loudly and insistently the voice called, and when it relapsed into silence, it seemed for a moment that somewhere from underneath came an incoherent answer. And Father Ignatius, clearing his ear of his long hair, pressed it to the rough prickly turf.

'Vera, tell me!'

With terror, Father Ignatius felt pouring into his ear something cold as of the grave, which froze his marrow; Vera seemed to be speaking – speaking, however, with the same unbroken silence. This feeling became more racking and terrible, and when Father Ignatius forced himself finally to tear away his head, his face was pale as that of a corpse, and he fancied that the entire atmosphere trembled and palpitated from a resounding silence, and that this terrible sea was being swept by a wild hurricane. The silence strangled him; with icy waves it rolled through his head and agitated the hair; it smote against his breast, which groaned under the blows. Trembling from head to foot, casting around him sharp and sudden glances, Father Ignatius slowly raised himself and with a prolonged and tortuous effort attempted to straighten his spine and to give proud dignity to his trembling body. He succeeded in this. With measured protractiveness, Father Ignatius shook the dirt from his knees, put on his hat, made the sign of the cross three times over the grave, and walked away with an even and firm gait, not recognizing, however, the familiar burial ground and losing his way.

'Well, here I've gone astray!' smiled Father Ignatius, halting at the branching of the footpaths.

He stood there for a moment, and unreflecting, turned to the left, because it was impossible to stand and to wait. The silence drove him on. It arose from the green graves; it was the breath issuing from the grey, melancholy crosses; in thin, stifling currents it came from all pores of the earth, satiated with the dead. Father Ignatius increased his stride. Dizzy, he circled the same paths, jumped over graves, stumbled across railings, clutching with his hands the prickly, metallic garlands, and turning the soft material of his dress to tatters. His sole thought was to escape. He fled from one place to another, and finally broke into a dead run, seeming very tall and unusual in the flowing cassock, and his hair streaming in the wind. A corpse arisen from the grave, could not have frightened a passer-by more than this wild figure of a man, running and leaping, and waving his arms, his face distorted and insane, and the open mouth breathing with a dull, hoarse sound. With one long leap, Father Ignatius landed on a little street, at one end of which appeared the small church, attached to the graveyard. At the entrance on a low bench, dozed an old man, seemingly a distant pilgrim, and near him, assailing each other, were two quarrelling old beggar women, filling the air with their oaths.

When Father Ignatius reached his home, it was already dusk, and there was light in Olga Stepanovna's chamber. Not undressing and without removing his hat, dusty and tattered, Father Ignatius approached his wife and fell on his knees.

'Mother … Olga … have pity on me!' he wept. 'I shall go mad.'

He dashed his head against the edge of the table and wept with anguish, as one who was weeping for the first time. Then he raised his head, confident that a miracle would come to pass, that his wife would speak and would pity him.

'My love!'

With his entire body he drew himself towards his wife – and met the gaze of those grey eyes. There was neither compassion in them, nor anger. It was possible his wife had forgiven him, but in her eyes there was neither pity, nor anger. They were dumb and silent.

And silent was the entire dark, deserted house.

The Withered Arm

Thomas Hardy

I. A Lorn Milkmaid

It was an eighty-cow dairy, and the troop of milkers, regular and supernumerary, were all at work; for, though the time of year was as yet but early April, the feed lay entirely in water-meadows, and the cows were 'in full pail'. The hour was about six in the evening, and three-fourths of the large, red, rectangular animals having been finished off, there was opportunity for a little conversation.

'He do bring home his bride to-morrow, I hear. They've come as far as Anglebury to-day.'

The voice seemed to proceed from the belly of the cow called Cherry, but the speaker was a milking-woman, whose face was buried in the flank of that motionless beast.

'Hav' anybody seen her?' said another.

There was negative response from the first. 'Though they say she's a rosy-cheeked, tisty-tosty little body enough,' she added; and as the milk-maid spoke she turned her face so that she could glance past her cow's tail to the other side of the barton, where a thin, fading woman of thirty milked somewhat apart from the rest.

'Years younger than he, they say,' continued the second, with also a glance of reflectiveness in the same direction.

'How old do you call him, then?'

'Thirty or so.'

'More like forty,' broke in an old milkman near, in a long white pinafore or 'wropper', and with the brim of his hat tied down, so that he looked like a woman. 'A was born before our Great Weir was builded, and I hadn't man's wages when I laved water there.'

The discussion waxed so warm that the purr of the milk-streams became jerky, till a voice from another cow's belly cried with authority, 'Now then, what the Turk do it matter to us about Farmer Lodge's age, or Farmer Lodge's new mis'ess? I shall have to pay him nine pound a year for the rent of every one of these milchers, whatever his age or hers. Get on with your work, or 'twill be dark afore we have done. The evening is pinking in a'ready.' This speaker was the dairyman himself, by whom the milkmaids and men were employed.

Nothing more was said publicly about Farmer Lodge's wedding, but the first woman murmured under her cow to her next neighbour, 'Tis hard for *she*,' signifying the thin worn milkmaid aforesaid.

'O no,' said the second. 'He ha'n't spoke to Rhoda Brook for years.'

When the milking was done they washed their pails and hung them on a many-forked stand made as usual of the peeled limb of an oak-tree, set upright in the earth, and resembling a colossal antlered horn. The majority then dispersed in various directions homeward. The thin woman who had not spoken was joined by a boy of twelve or thereabout, and the twain went away up the field also.

Their course lay apart from that of the others, to a lonely spot high above the water-meads, and not far from the border of Egdon Heath, whose dark countenance was visible in the distance as they drew nigh to their home.

'They've just been saying down in barton that your father brings his young wife home from Anglebury to-morrow,' the woman observed. 'I shall want to send you for a few things to market, and you'll be pretty sure to meet 'em.'

'Yes, mother,' said the boy. 'Is father married then?'

'Yes ... You can give her a look, and tell me what she's like, if you do see her.'

'Yes, mother.'

'If she's dark or fair, and if she's tall – as tall as I. And if she seems like a woman who has ever worked for a living, or one that has been always well off, and has never done anything, and shows marks of the lady on her, as I expect she do.'

'Yes.'

They crept up the hill in the twilight and entered the cottage. It was built of mud-walls, the surface of which had been washed by many rains into channels and depressions that left none of the original flat face visible; while here and there in the thatch above a rafter showed like a bone protruding through the skin.

She was kneeling down in the chimney-corner, before two pieces of turf laid together with the heather inwards, blowing at the red-hot ashes with her breath till the turves flamed. The radiance lit her pale cheek, and made her dark eyes, that had once been handsome, seem handsome anew. 'Yes,' she resumed, 'see if she is dark or fair, and if you can, notice if her hands be white; if not, see if they look as though she had ever done housework, or are milker's hands like mine.'

The boy again promised, inattentively this time, his mother not observing that he was cutting a notch with his pocket-knife in the beech-backed chair.

II. The Young Wife

The road from Anglebury to Holmstoke is in general level; but there is one place where a sharp ascent breaks its monotony. Farmers homeward-bound from the former market-town, who trot all the rest of the way, walk their horses up this short incline.

The next evening while the sun was yet bright a handsome new gig, with a lemon-coloured body and red wheels, was spinning westward along the level highway at the heels of a powerful mare. The driver was a yeoman in the prime of life, cleanly shaven like an actor, his face being toned to that bluish-vermillion hue which so often graces a thriving farmer's features when returning home after successful dealings in the town. Beside him sat a woman, many years his junior – almost, indeed, a girl. Her face too was fresh in colour, but it was of a totally different quality – soft and evanescent, like the light under a heap of rose-petals.

Few people travelled this way, for it was not a main road, and the long white riband of gravel that stretched before them was empty, save of one small scarce-moving speck, which presently resolved itself into the figure of a boy, who was creeping on at a snail's pace, and continually looking behind him – the heavy bundle he carried being some excuse for, if not the reason of, his dilatoriness. When the bouncing gig-party slowed at the bottom of the incline above mentioned, the pedestrian was only a few yards in front. Supporting the large bundle by putting one hand on his hip, he turned and looked straight at the farmer's wife as though he would read her through and through, pacing along abreast of the horse.

The low sun was full in her face, rendering every feature, shade, and contour distinct, from the curve of her little nostril to the colour of her eyes. The farmer, though he seemed annoyed at the boy's persistent presence, did not order him to get out of the way; and thus the lad preceded them, his hard gaze never leaving her, till they reached the top of the ascent, when the farmer trotted on with relief in his lineaments – having taken no outward notice of the boy whatever.

'How that poor lad stared at me!' said the young wife.

'Yes dear; I saw that he did.'

'He is one of the village, I suppose?'

'One of the neighbourhood. I think he lives with his mother a mile or two off.'

'He knows who we are, no doubt?'

'O yes. You must expect to be stared at just at first, my pretty Gertrude.'

'I do – though I think the poor boy may have looked at us

in the hope we might relieve him of his heavy load, rather than from curiosity.'

'Oh no,' said her husband off-handedly. 'These country lads will carry a hundredweight once they get it on their backs; beside, his pack had more size than weight in it. Now then, another mile and I shall be able to show you our house in the distance – if it is not too dark before we get there.' The wheels spun round, and particles flew from their periphery as before, till a white house of ample dimensions revealed itself, with farm-buildings and ricks at the back.

Meanwhile the boy had quickened his pace, and turning up a by-lane some mile and a half short of the white farmstead, ascended towards the leaner pastures, and so on to the cottage of his mother.

She had reached home after her day's milking at the outlying dairy, and was washing cabbage at the doorway in the declining light. 'Hold up the net a moment,' she said, without preface, as the boy came up.

He flung down his bundle, held the edge of the cabbage-net, and as she filled its meshes with the dripping leaves she went on. 'Well, did you see her?'

'Yes; quite plain.'

'Is she ladylike?'

'Yes, and more. A lady complete.'

'Is she young?'

'Well, she's growed up, and her ways be quite a woman's.'

'Of course. What colour is her hair and face?'

'Her hair is lightish, and her face as comely as a live doll's.'

'Her eyes, then, are not dark like mine?'

'No – of a bluish turn, and her mouth is very nice and red; and when she smiles, her teeth show white.'

'Is she tall?' said the woman sharply.

'I couldn't see. She was sitting down.'

'Then do you go to Holmstoke church to-morrow morning: she's sure to be there. Go early and notice her walking in, and come home and tell me if she's taller than I.'

'Very well, mother. But why don't you go and see for yourself?'

'*I* go to see her! I wouldn't look up at her if she were to pass my window this instant. She was with Mr Lodge, of course. What did he say or do?'

'Just the same as usual.'

'Took no notice of you?'

'None.'

Next day the mother put a clean shirt on the boy, and started him off for Holmstoke church. He reached the ancient little pile when the door was just being opened and he was the first to enter. Taking his seat by the front, he watched all the parishioners file in. The well-to-do Farmer Lodge came nearly last, and his young wife, who accompanied him, walked up the aisle with the shyness natural to a modest woman who had appeared thus for the first time. As all other eyes were fixed upon her, the youth's stare was not noticed now.

When he reached home his mother said, 'Well?' before he had entered the room.

'She is not tall. She is rather short,' he replied.

'Ah!' said his mother, with satisfaction.

'But she's very pretty – very. In fact, she's lovely.' The youthful freshness of the yeoman's wife had evidently made an impression even on the somewhat hard nature of the boy.

'That's all I want to hear,' said his mother quickly. 'Now, spread the tablecloth. The hare you wired is very tender; but mind that nobody catches you. – You've never told me what sort of hands she had.'

'I have never seen 'em. She never took off her gloves.'

'What did she wear this morning?'

'A white bonnet and a silver-coloured gownd. It whewed and whistled so loud when it rubbed against the pews that the lady coloured up more than ever for very shame at the noise, and pulled it in to keep it from touching; but when she pushed into her seat, it whewed more than ever. Mr Lodge, he seemed pleased, and his waistcoat stuck out, and his great golden seals hunt like a lord's; but she seemed to wish her noisy gownd anywhere but on her.'

'Not she! However, that will do now.'

These descriptions of the newly-married couple were continued from time to time by the boy at his mother's request, after any chance encounter he had had with them. But Rhoda Brook, though she might easily have seen Mrs Lodge for herself by walking a couple of miles, would never attempt an excursion towards the quarter where the farmhouse lay. Neither did she, at the daily milking in the dairyman's yard on Lodge's outlying second farm, ever speak on the subject of the recent marriage. The dairyman, who rented the cows of Lodge, and knew perfectly the tall milkmaid's history, with manly kindliness always kept the gossip in the cow-barton from annoying Rhoda. But the atmosphere thereabout was full of the subject during the first days of Mrs Lodge's arrival, and from her boy's description and the casual words of the other milkers, Rhoda Brook could raise a mental image of the unconscious Mrs Lodge that was realistic as a photograph.

III. A Vision

One night, two or three weeks after the bridal return, when the boy was gone to bed, Rhoda sat a long time over the turf ashes that she had raked out in front of her to extinguish them. She contemplated so intently the new wife, as presented to her in her mind's eye over the embers, that she forgot the lapse of time. At last, wearied with her day's work, she too retired.

But the figure which had occupied her so much during this and the previous days was not to be banished at night. For the first time Gertrude Lodge visited the supplanted woman in her dreams. Rhoda Brook dreamed – since her assertion that she really saw, before falling asleep, was not to be believed – that the young wife, in the pale silk dress and white bonnet, but with features shockingly distorted, and wrinkled as by age, was sitting upon her chest as she lay. The pressure of Mrs Lodge's person grew heavier; the blue eyes peered cruelly into her face, and then the figure thrust forward its left hand mockingly, so as to make the wedding-ring it wore glitter in Rhoda's eyes. Maddened mentally, and nearly suffocated by pressure, the sleeper struggled; the incubus, still regarding her, withdrew to the foot of the bed, only, however, to come forward by degrees, resume her seat, and flash her left hand as before.

Gasping for breath, Rhoda, in a last desperate effort, swung out her right hand, seized the confronting spectre by its obtrusive left arm, and whirled it backward to the floor, starting up herself as she did so with a low cry.

'O merciful heaven!' she cried, sitting on the edge of the bed in a cold sweat; 'that was not a dream – she was here!'

She could feel her antagonist's arm within her grasp even now – the very flesh and bone of it, as it seemed. She looked on the floor whither she had whirled the spectre, but there was nothing to be seen.

Rhoda Brook slept no more that night, and when she went milking at the next dawn they noticed how pale and haggard she looked. The milk that she drew quivered into the pail: her hand had not calmed even yet, and still retained the feel of the arm. She came home to breakfast as wearily as if it had been supper-time.

'What was that noise in your chimmer, mother, last night?' said her son. 'You fell off the bed, surely?'

'Did you hear anything fall? At what time?'

'Just when the clock struck two.'

She could not explain, and when the meal was done went silently about her household work, the boy assisting her, for he hated going afield on the farms, and she indulged his reluctance. Between eleven and twelve the garden-gate clicked, and she lifted her eyes to the window. At the bottom of the garden, within the gate, stood the woman of her vision. Rhoda seemed transfixed.

'Ah, she said she would come!' exclaimed the boy, also

observing her.

'Said so – when? How does she know us?'

'I have seen and spoken to her. I talked to her yesterday.'

'I told you,' said the mother, flushing indignantly, 'never to speak to anybody in that house, or go near the place.'

'I did not speak to her till she spoke to me. And I did not go near the place. I met her in the road.'

'What did you tell her?'

'Nothing. She said, "Are you the poor boy who had to bring the heavy load from market?" And she looked at my boots, and said they would not keep my feet dry if it came on wet, because they were so cracked. I told her I lived with my mother, and we had enough to do to keep ourselves, and that's how it was; and she said then, "I'll come and bring you some better boots, and see your mother." She gives away things to other folks in the meads besides us.'

Mrs Lodge was by this time close to the door – not in her silk, as Rhoda had dreamt of in the bed-chamber, but in a morning hat, and gown of common light material, which became her better than silk. On her arm she carried a basket.

The impression remaining from the night's experience was still strong. Brook had almost expected to see the wrinkles, the scorn, and the cruelty on her visitor's face. She would have escaped an interview had escape been possible. There was, however, no backdoor to the cottage, and in an instant the boy had lifted the latch to Mrs Lodge's gentle knock.

'I see I have come to the right house,' said she, glancing at the lad, and smiling. 'But I was not sure till you opened the door.'

The figure and action were those of the phantom; but her voice was so indescribably sweet, her glance so winning, her smile so tender, so unlike that of Rhoda's midnight visitant, that the latter could hardly believe the evidence of her senses. She was truly glad that she had not hidden away in sheer aversion, as she had been inclined to do. In her basket Mrs Lodge brought the pair of boots that she had promised to the boy, and other useful articles.

At these proofs of kindly feeling towards her and hers Rhoda's heart reproached her bitterly. This innocent young thing should have her blessing and not her curse. When she left them a light seemed gone from the dwelling. Two days later she came again to know if the boots fitted, and less than a fortnight after that paid Rhoda another call. On this occasion the boy was absent.

'I walk a good deal,' said Mrs Lodge, 'and your house is the nearest outside our own parish. I hope you are well. You don't look quite well.'

Rhoda said she was well enough, and, indeed, though the paler of the two, there was more of the strength that endures in her well-defined features and large frame than in the soft-cheeked young woman before her. The conversation became quite confidential as regarded their powers and weaknesses; and when Mrs Lodge was leaving, Rhoda said, 'I hope you will find this air agree with you, ma'am, and not suffer from the damp of the water-meads.'

The younger one replied that there was not much doubt of it, her general health being usually good. 'Though, now you remind me,' she added, 'I have one little ailment which puzzles me. It is nothing serious but I cannot make it out.'

She uncovered her left hand and arm, and their outline confronted Rhoda's gaze as the exact original of the limb she had beheld and seized in her dream. Upon the pink round surface of the arm were faint marks of an unhealthy colour, as if produced by a rough grasp. Rhoda's eyes became riveted on the discolourations; she fancied that she discerned in them the shape of her own four fingers.

'How did it happen?' she said mechanically.

'I cannot tell,' replied Mrs Lodge, shaking her head. 'One night when I was sound asleep, dreaming I was away in some strange place, a pain suddenly shot into my arm there, and was so keen as to awaken me. I must have struck it in the daytime, I suppose, though I don't remember doing so.' She added, laughing, 'I tell my dear husband that it looks just as if he had flown into a rage and struck me there. O, I daresay it will soon disappear.'

'Ha, ha! Yes … On what night did it come?'

Mrs Lodge considered, and said it would be a fortnight ago on the morrow. 'When I awoke I could not remember where I was,' she added, 'till the clock striking two reminded me.'

She had named the night and the hour of Rhoda's spectral encounter, and Brook felt like a guilty thing. The artless disclosure startled her; she did not reason on the freaks of coincidence, and all the scenery of that ghastly night returned with double vividness to her mind.

'O, can it be,' she said to herself, when her visitor had departed, 'that I exercise a malignant power over people against my own will?' She knew that she had been slyly called a witch since her fall; but never having understood why that particular stigma had been attached to her, it had passed disregarded. Could this be the explanation, and had such things as this ever happened before?

IV. A Suggestion

The summer drew on, and Rhoda Brook almost dreaded to meet Mrs Lodge again, notwithstanding that her feeling for the young wife amounted wellnigh to affection. Something in her own individuality seemed to convict Rhoda of crime. Yet a fatality sometimes would direct the steps of the latter to the outskirts of Holmstoke whenever she left her house for any other purpose than her daily work, and hence it happened that their next encounter was out of doors. Rhoda could not avoid the subject which had so mystified her, and after the first few words she stammered, 'I hope your – arm is well again, ma'am?' She had perceived with consternation that Gertrude Lodge carried her left arm stiffly.

'No; it is not quite well. Indeed, it is no better at all; it is rather worse. It pains me dreadfully sometimes.'

'Perhaps you had better go to a doctor, ma'am.'

She replied that she had already seen a doctor. Her husband had insisted upon her going to one. But the surgeon had not seemed to understand the afflicted limb at all; he had told her to bathe it in hot water, and she had bathed it, but the treatment had done no good.

'Will you let me see it?' said the milkwoman.

Mrs Lodge pushed up her sleeve and disclosed the place, which was a few inches above the wrist. As soon as Rhoda Brook saw it, she could hardly preserve her composure. There was nothing of the nature of a wound, but the arm at that point had a shrivelled look, and the outline of the four fingers appeared more distinct than at the former time. Moreover, she fancied that they were imprinted in precisely the relative position of her clutch upon the arm in the trance: the first finger towards Gertrude's wrist, and the fourth towards her elbow.

What the impress resembled seemed to have struck Gertrude herself since their last meeting. 'It looks almost like finger-marks,' she said; adding with a faint laugh, 'My husband says it is as if some witch, or the devil himself, had taken hold of me there, and blasted the flesh.'

Rhoda shivered. 'That's fancy,' she said hurriedly. 'I wouldn't mind it, if I were you.'

'I shouldn't so much mind it,' said the younger, with hesitation, 'if – if I hadn't a notion that it makes my husband – dislike me – no, love me less. Men think so much of personal appearance.'

'Some do – he for one.'

'Yes; and he was very proud of mine, at first.'

'Keep your arm covered from his sight.'

'Ah – he knows the disfigurement is there!' She tried to hide the tears that filled her eyes.

'Well, ma'am, I earnestly hope it will go away soon.'

And so the milkwoman's mind was chained anew to the subject by a horrid sort of spell as she returned home. The sense of having been guilty of an act of malignity increased, affect as she might to ridicule her superstition. In her secret heart Rhoda did not altogether object to a slight diminution of her successor's beauty, by whatever means it had come about; but she did not wish to inflict upon her physical pain. For though this pretty young woman had rendered impossible any reparation which Lodge might have made Rhoda for his past conduct, everything like resentment at the unconscious usurpation had quite passed away from the elder's mind.

If the sweet and kindly Gertrude Lodge only knew of the dream-scene in the bed-chamber, what would she think? Not to inform her of it seemed treachery in the presence of her friendliness; but tell she could not of her own accord – neither could she devise a remedy.

She mused upon the matter the greater part of the night, and the next day, after the morning milking, set out to obtain another glimpse of Gertrude Lodge if she could, being held to her by a gruesome fascination. By watching the house from a distance the milkmaid was presently able to discern the farmer's wife in a ride she taking alone – probably to join her husband in some distant field. Mrs Lodge perceived her, and cantered in her direction.

'Good morning, Rhoda!' Gertrude said, when she had come up. 'I was going to call.'

Rhoda noticed that Mrs Lodge held the reins with some difficulty.

'I hope – the bad arm,' said Rhoda.

'They tell me there is possibly one way by which I might be able to find out the cause, and so perhaps the cure, of it,' replied the other anxiously. 'It is by going to some clever man over in Egdon Heath. They did not know if he was still alive – and I cannot remember his name at this moment; but they said that you knew more of his movements than anybody else hereabout, and could tell me if he were still to be consulted. Dear me – what was his name? But you know.'

'Not Conjuror Trendle?' said her thin companion, turning pale.

'Trendle – yes. Is he alive?'

'I believe so,' said Rhoda, with reluctance.

'Why do you call him conjuror?'

'Well – they say – they used to say he was a – he had powers other folks have not.'

'O, how could my people be so superstitious as to recommend a man of that sort! I thought they meant some medical man. I shall think no more of him.'

Rhoda looked relieved, and Mrs Lodge rode on. The milk-woman had inwardly seen, from the moment she heard of her having been mentioned as a reference for this man, that there must exist a sarcastic feeling among the workfolk that a sorceress would know the whereabouts of the exorcist. They suspected her, then. A short time ago this would have given no concern to a woman of her common sense. But she had a haunting reason to be superstitious now; and she had been seized with sudden dread that this Conjour Trendle might name her as the malignant influence which was blasting the fair person of Gertrude and so lead her friend to hate her for ever, and to treat her as some fiend in human shape.

But all was not over. Two days after, a shadow intruded into the window-pattern thrown on Rhoda Brook's floor by the afternoon sun. The woman opened the door at once, almost breathlessly.

'Are you alone?' said Gertrude. She seemed to be no less harassed and anxious than Brook herself.

'Yes,' said Rhoda.

'The place on my arm seems worse, and troubles me!' the young farmer's wife went on. 'It is so mysterious! I do hope it will not be an incurable wound. I have again been thinking of what they said about Conjour Trendle. I don't really believe in such men, but I should not mind just visiting him, from curiosity – though on no account must my husband know. Is it far to where he lives?'

'Yes – five miles,' said Rhoda backwardly. 'In the heart of Egdon.'

'Well, I should have to walk. Could not you go with me to show me the way – say to-morrow afternoon?'

'O, not I – that is,' the milkwoman murmured, with a start of dismay. Again the dread seized her that something to do with her fierce act in the dream might be revealed, and her character in the eyes of the most useful friend she had ever had be ruined irretrievably.

Mrs Lodge urged, and Rhoda finally assented, though with much misgiving. Sad as the journey would be to her, she could not conscientiously stand in the way of a possible remedy for her patron's strange affliction. It was agreed that, to escape suspicion of their mystic intent, they should meet at the edge of the heath at the corner of a plantation which was visible from the spot where they now stood.

V. Conjuror Trendle

By the next afternoon Rhoda would have done anything to escape this inquiry. But she had promised to go. Moreover, there was a horrid fascination at times in becoming instrumental in throwing such possible light on her own character as would reveal her to be something greater in the occult world than she had ever herself suspected.

She started just before the time of day mentioned between them, and half-an-hour's brisk walking brought her to the south-eastern extension of the Egdon tract of country, where the fir plantation was. A slight figure, cloaked and veiled, was already there. Rhoda recognized, almost with a shudder, that Mrs Lodge bore her left arm in a sling.

They hardly spoke to each other, immediately set out on their climb into the interior of this solemn country, which stood high above the rich alluvial soil they had left half-an-hour before. It was a long walk; thick clouds made the atmosphere dark, though it was as yet only early afternoon; and the wind howled dismally over the slopes of the heath – not improbably the same heath which had witnessed the agony of the Wessex King Ina, presented to after-ages as Lear. Gertrude Lodge talked most, Rhoda replying with monosyllabic preoccupation. She had a strange dislike to walking on the side of her companion where hung the afflicted arm, moving round to the other when inadvertently near it. Much heather had been brushed by their feet when they descended upon a cart-track, beside which stood the house of the man they sought.

He did not profess his remedial practices openly, or care anything about their continuance, his direct interest being those of a dealer in furze, turf, 'sharp sand', and other local products. Indeed, he affected not to believe largely in his own powers, and when warts that had been shown him for the core miraculously disappeared – which it must be owned they infallibly did – he would say lightly, 'O, I only drink a glass of grog upon 'em at your expense – perhaps it's all chance,' and immediately turn the subject.

He was at home when they arrived, having in fact seen them descending into his valley. He was a grey-bearded man, with a reddish face, and he looked singularly at Rhoda the first moment he beheld her. Mrs Lodge told him her errand; and then with words of self-disparagement he examined her arm.

'Medicine can't cure it,' he said promptly. 'Tis the work of an enemy.'

Rhoda shrank into herself, and drew back.

'An enemy? What enemy?' asked Mrs Lodge.

He shook his head. 'That's best known to yourself,' he said. 'If you like, I can show the person to you, though I shall not myself know who it is. I can do no more; and don't wish to do that.'

She pressed him; on which he told Rhoda to wait outside where she stood, and took Mrs Lodge into the room. It opened immediately from the door; and, as the latter remained ajar, Rhoda Brook could see the proceedings without taking part in them. He brought a tumbler from the dresser, nearly filled it with water, and fetching an egg, prepared it in some private way; after which he broke it on the edge of the glass, so that the white went in and the yolk remained. As it was getting gloomy, he took the glass and its contents to the window, and told Gertrude to watch the mixture closely. They leant over the table together, and the milkwoman could see the opaline hue of the egg-fluid changing form as it sank in the water, but she was not near enough to define the shape that it assumed.

'Do you catch the likeness of any face or figure as you look?' demanded the conjurer of the young woman.

She murmured a reply, in tones so low as to be inaudible to Rhoda, and continued to gaze intently into the glass. Rhoda turned, and walked a few steps away.

When Mrs Lodge came out, and her face was met by the light, it appeared exceedingly pale – as pale as Rhoda's – against the sad dun shades of the upland's garniture. Trendle shut the door behind her and they at once started homeward together. But Rhoda perceived that her companion had quite changed.

'Did he charge much?' she asked tentatively.

'O no – nothing. He would not take a farthing,' said Gertrude.

'And what did you see?' inquired Rhoda.

'Nothing I – care to speak of.' The constraint in her manner was remarkable; her face was so rigid as to wear an oldened aspect, faintly suggestive of the face in Rhoda's bed-chamber.

'Was it you who first proposed coming here?' Mrs Lodge suddenly inquired, after a long pause. 'How very odd, if you did!'

'No. But I am not sorry we have come all things considered,' she replied. For the first time a sense of triumph possessed her, and she did not altogether deplore that the young thing at her side should learn that their lives had been antagonized by other influences than their own.

The subject was no more alluded to during the long and dreary walk home. But in some way or other a story was whispered about the many-dairied lowland that winter that Mrs

Lodge's gradual loss of the use of her left arm was owing to her being 'overlooked' by Rhoda Brook. The latter kept her own counsel about the incubus, but her face grew sadder and thinner; and in the spring she and her boy disappeared from the neighbourhood of Holmstoke.

VI. A Second Attempt

Half a dozen years passed away, and Mr and Mrs Lodge's married experience sank into prosiness, and worse. The farmer was usually gloomy and silent; the woman whom he had wooed for her grace and beauty was contorted and disfigured in the left limb; moreover, she had brought him no child, which rendered it likely that he would be the last of a family who had occupied that valley for some two hundred years. He thought of Rhoda Brook and her son; and feared this might be a judgement from heaven upon him.

The once blithe-hearted and enlightened Gertrude was changing into an irritable, superstitious woman, whose whole time was given to experimenting upon her ailment with every quack remedy she came across. She was honestly attached to her husband, and was ever secretly hoping against hope to win back his heart again by regaining some at least of her personal beauty. Hence it arose that her closet was lined with bottles, packets, and ointment-pots of every description – nay, bunches of mystic herbs, charms, and books of necromancy, which in her schoolgirl time she would have ridiculed as folly.

'Damned if you won't poison yourself with these apothecary messes and witch mixtures some time or other,' said her husband, when his eye chanced to fall upon the multitudinous array.

She did not reply, but turned her sad, soft glance upon him in such heart-swollen reproach that he looked sorry for his words. And added, 'I only meant it for your good, you know, Gertrude.'

'I'll clear out the whole lot, and destroy them,' said she huskily,' and try such remedies no more!'

'You want somebody to cheer you,' he observed. 'I once thought of adopting a boy; but he is too old now. And he is gone away I don't know where.'

She guessed to whom he alluded; for Rhoda Brook's story had in the course of years become known to her; though not a word had ever passed between her husband and herself on the subject. Neither had she ever spoken to him of her visit to Conjurer Trendle, and of what was revealed to her, or she thought was revealed to her, by that solitary heathman.

She was now five-and-twenty; but she seemed older. 'Six years of marriage, and only a few months of love,' she sometimes whispered to herself. And then she thought of the apparent cause, and said, with a tragic glance at her withering limb, 'If I could only again be as I was when he first saw me!'

She obediently destroyed her nostrums and charms; but there remained a hankering wish to try something else – some other sort of cure altogether. She had never revisited Trendle since she had been conducted to the house of the solitary by Rhoda against her will; but it now suddenly occurred to Gertrude that she would, in a last desperate effort at deliverance from this seeming curse, again seek out the man, if he yet lived. He was entitled to a certain credence, for the indistinct form he had raised in the glass had undoubtedly resembled the only woman in the world who – as she now knew, though not then – could have a reason for bearing her ill-will. The visit should be paid.

This time she went alone, though she nearly got lost on the heath, and roamed a considerable distance out of her way. Trendle's house was reached at last, however; he was not indoors, and instead of waiting at the cottage, she went to where his bent figure was pointed out to her at work a long way off. Trendle remembered her, and laying down the handful of furze-roots which he was gathering and throwing into a heap, he offered to accompany her in her homeward direction, as the distance was considerable and the days were short. So they walked together, his head bowed nearly to the earth, and his form a colour with it.

'You can send away warts and other excrescences, I know,' she said; 'why can't you send away this?' and the arm was uncovered.

'You think too much of my powers!' said Trendle; 'and I am old and weak now, too. No, no; it is too much for me to attempt in my own person. What have you tried?'

She named to him some of the hundred medicaments and counter-spells which she had adopted from time to time. He shook his head.

'Some were good enough,' he said approvingly; 'but not many of them for such as this. This is of the nature of a blight, not of the nature of a wound, and if you ever do throw it off, it will be all at once.'

'If I only could!'

'There is only one chance of doing it known to me. It has never failed in kindred afflictions – that I can declare. But it is hard to carry out, and especially for a woman.'

'Tell me!' said she.

'You must touch with the limb the neck of a man who's been hanged.'

She started a little at the image he had raised.

'Before he's cold – just after he's cut down,' continued the conjuror impassively.

'How can that do good?'

'It will turn the blood and change the constitution. But, as I say, to do it is hard. You must go to the jail when there's a hanging, and wait for him when he's brought off the gallows. Lots have done it, though perhaps not such pretty women as you. I used to send dozens for skin complaints. But that was in former times. The last I sent was in '13 – near twelve years ago.'

He had no more to tell her, and, when he had put her into a straight track homeward, turned and left her, refusing all money as at first.

VII. A Ride

The communication sank deep into Gertrude's mind. Her nature was rather a timid one; and probably of all remedies that the white wizard could have suggested there was not one which would have filled her with so much aversion as this, not to speak of the immense obstacles in the way of its adoption.

Casterbridge, the county-town, was a dozen or fifteen miles off; and though in those days, when men were executed for horse-stealing, arson, and burglary, an assize seldom passed without a hanging, it was not likely that she could get access to the body of the criminal unaided. And the fear of her husband's anger made her reluctant to breathe a word of Trendle's suggestion to him or to anybody about him.

She did nothing for months, and patiently bore her disfigurement as before. But her woman's nature, craving for renewed love, through the medium of renewed beauty (she was but twenty-five), was ever stimulating her to try what, at any rate, could hardly do her any harm. 'What came by a spell will go by a spell surely,' she would say. Whenever her imagination pictured the act she shrank in terror from the possibility of it; then the words of the conjuror, 'It will turn your blood', were seen to be capable of a scientific no less than a ghastly interpretation; the mastering desire returned, and urged her on again.

There was at this time but one county paper, and that her husband only occasionally borrowed. But old-fashioned days had old-fashioned means, and news was extensively conveyed by word of mouth from market to market, or from fair to fair, so that, whenever such an event as an execution was about to take place, few within a radius of twenty miles were ignorant of the coming sight; and, so far as Holmstoke was concerned, some enthusiasts had been known to walk all the way to Casterbridge and back in one day, solely to witness the spectacle. The next assizes were in March; and when Gertrude Lodge heard that they had been held, she inquired stealthily at the inn as to the result, as soon as she could find opportunity.

She was, however, too late. The time at which the sentences were to be carried out had arrived, and to make the journey and obtain admission at such short notice required at least her husband's assistance. She dared not tell him, for she had found by delicate experiment that these smouldering village beliefs made him furious if mentioned, partly because he half entertained them himself. It was therefore necessary to wait for another opportunity.

Her determination received a fillip from learning that two epileptic children had attended from this very village of Holmstoke many years before with beneficial results, though the experiment had been strongly condemned by the neighbouring clergy. April, May, June passed; and it is no overstatement to say that by the end of the last-named month Gertrude wellnigh longed for the death of a fellow-creature. Instead of her formal prayers each night, her unconscious prayer was, 'O Lord, hang some guilty or innocent person soon!'

This time she made earlier inquiries, and was altogether more systematic in her proceedings. Moreover, the season was summer, between the haymaking and the harvest, and in the leisure thus afforded him her husband had been holiday-taking away from home.

The assizes were in July, and she went to the inn as before. There was to be one execution – only one – for arson.

Her greatest problem was not how to get to Casterbridge, but what means she should adopt for obtaining admission to the jail. Though access for such purposes had formerly never been denied, the custom had fallen into desuetude; and in contemplating her possible difficulties, she was again almost driven to fall back upon her husband. But, on sounding him about the assizes, he was so uncommunicative, so more than usually cold, that she did not proceed, and decided that whatever she did she would do alone.

Fortune, obdurate hitherto, showed her unexpected favour. On the Thursday before the Saturday fixed for the execution,

Lodge remarked to her that he was going away from home for another day or two on business at a fair, and that he was sorry he could not take her with him.

She exhibited on this occasion so much readiness to stay at home that he looked at her in surprise. Time had been when she would have shown deep disappointment at the loss of such a jaunt. However, he lapsed into his usual taciturnity, and on the day named left Holmstoke.

It was now her turn. She at first had thought of driving, but on reflection held that driving would not do, since it would necessitate her keeping to the turnpike-road, and so increase by tenfold the risk of her ghastly errand being found out. She decided to ride, and avoid the beaten track, notwithstanding that in her husband's stables there was no animal just at present which by any stretch of imagination could be considered a lady's mount, in spite of his promise before marriage to always keep a mare for her. He had, however, many cart-horses, fine ones of their kind; and among the rest was a serviceable creature, an equine Amazon, with a back as broad as a sofa, on which Gertrude had occasionally taken an airing when unwell. This horse she chose.

On Friday afternoon one of the men brought it round. She was dressed, and before going down looked at her shrivelled arm. 'Ah!' she said to it, 'if it had not been for you this terrible ordeal would have been saved me!'

When strapping up the bundle in which she carried a few articles of clothing, she took occasion to say to the servant, 'I take these in case I should not get back to-night from the person I am going to visit. Don't be alarmed if I am not in by ten, and close up the house as usual. I shall be at home to-morrow for certain.' She meant then to tell her husband privately; the deed accomplished was not like the deed projected. He would almost certainly forgive her.

And then the pretty palpitating Gertrude Lodge went from her husband's homestead; but though her goal was Casterbridge she did not take the direct route thither through

Stickleford. Her cunning course at first was in precisely the opposite direction. As soon as she was out of sight, however, she turned left, by a road which led into Egdon, and on entering the heath wheeled round, and set out in the true course, due westerly. A more private way down the county could not be imagined; and as to direction, she had merely to keep her horse's head to a point a little to the right of the sun. She knew that she would light upon a furze-cutter or cottager of some sort from time to time, from whom she might correct her bearing.

Though the date was comparatively recent, Egdon was much less fragmentary in character than now. The attempts – successful and otherwise – at cultivation on the lower slopes, which intrude and break up the original heath into small detached heaths, had not been carried far; Enclosure Acts had not taken effect, and the banks and fences which now exclude the cattle of those villagers who formerly enjoyed rights of commonage thereon, and the carts of those who had turbary privileges which kept them in firing all the year round, were not erected. Gertrude, therefore, rode along with no other obstacles than the prickly furze-bushes, the mats of heather, the white water-courses, and the natural steeps and declivities of the ground.

Her horse was sure, if heavy-footed and slow, and though a draught animal, was easy-paced; had it been otherwise, she was not a country woman who could have ventured to ride over such a bit of country with a half-dead arm. It was therefore nearly eight o'clock when she drew rein to breathe her bearer on the last outlying high point of heath-land towards Casterbridge, previous to leaving Egdon for the cultivated valleys.

She halted before a pool called Rushy-pond, flanked by the ends of two hedges; a railing ran through the centre of the pond, dividing it in half. Over the railing she saw the low green country; over the green trees the roofs of the town; over the roofs a white flat façade, denoting the entrance to the country jail. On the roof of this front specks were moving about; they seemed to be workmen erecting something. Her flesh crept. She descended slowly, and was soon amid corn-fields and pastures. In another half-hour, when it was almost dusk, Gertrude reached the White Hart, the first inn of the town on that side.

Little surprise was excited by her arrival; farmers' wives rode on horseback then more than they do now; though, for that matter, Mrs Lodge was not imagined to be a wife at all; the innkeeper supposed her some harum-skarum young woman who had come to attend 'hang-fair' next day. Neither her husband nor herself ever dealt in Casterbridge market, so that she was unknown. While dismounting she beheld a crowd of boys standing at the door of a harness-maker's shop just above the inn, looking inside it with deep interest.

'What is going on there?' she asked the ostler.

'Making the rope for to-morrow.'

She throbbed responsively, and contracted her arm.

'Tis sold by the inch afterwards,' the man continued. 'I could get you a bit, miss, for nothing, if you'd like?'

She hastily repudiated any such wish, all the more from a curious creeping feeling that the condemned wretch's destiny was becoming interwoven with her own; and having engaged a room for the night, sat down to think.

Up to this time she had formed but the vaguest notions about her means of obtaining access to the prison. The words of the cunning-man returned to her mind. He had implied that she should use her beauty, impaired though it was, as a pass-key. In her experience she knew little about jail functionaries; she had heard of a high-sheriff and an under-sheriff, but dimly only. She knew, however, that there must be a hangman, and to the hangman she determined to apply.

VIII. A Water-side Hermit

At this date, and for several years after, there was a hangman to almost every jail. Gertrude found, on enquiry, that the Casterbridge official dwelt in a lonely cottage by a deep slow river flowing under the cliff on which the prison buildings were situate – the stream being the self-same one, though she did not know it, which watered the Stickleford and Holmstoke meads lower down in its course.

Having changed her dress, and before she had eaten or drunk – for she could not take her ease till she had ascertained some particulars – Gertrude pursued her way by a path along the water-side to the cottage indicated. Passing thus the outskirts of the jail, she discerned on the level roof over the gateway three rectangular lines against the sky, where the specks had been moving in her distant view; she recognized what the erection was, and passed quickly on. Another hundred yards brought her to the executioner's house, which a boy pointed out. It stood close to the same stream, and was hard by a weir, the waters of which emitted a steady roar.

While she stood hesitating the door opened, and an old man came forth, shading a candle with one hand. Locking the door on the outside, he turned to a flight of wooden steps fixed against the end of the cottage, and began to ascend them, this being evidently the staircase to his bedroom. Gertrude hastened forward, but by the time she reached the foot of the ladder he was at the top. She called to him loudly enough to be heard above the road of the weir; he looked down and said, 'What d'ye want here?'

'To speak to you a minute.'

The candlelight, such as it was, fell upon her imploring, pale, upturned face, and Davies (as the hangman was called) backed down the ladder. 'I was just going to bed,' he said. "Early to bed and early to rise", but I don't mind stopping a minute for such a one as you. Come into the house.' He opened the door, and preceded her to the room within.

The implements of his daily work, which was that of a jobbing gardener, stood in a corner, and seeing probably that she looked rural, he said, 'If you want me to undertake country work I can't come, for I never leave Casterbridge for gentle nor simple – not I . My real calling is officer of justice,' he added formally.

'Yes, yes! That's it. To-morrow!'

'Ah! I thought so. Well, what's the matter about that? 'Tis no use to come here about the knot – folks do come continually, but I tell 'em one knot is as merciful as another if ye keep it under the ear. Is the unfortunate man a relation; or, I should say, perhaps' (looking at her dress) 'a person who's been in your employ?'

'No. What time is the execution?'

'The same as usual – twelve o'clock, or as soon after as the London mail-coach gets in. We always wait for that, in case of a reprieve.'

'O – a reprieve – I hope not!' she said involuntarily.

'Well, - hee, hee! – as a matter of business, so do I! But still, if ever a young fellow deserved to be let off, this one does; only just turned eighteen, and only present by chance when the rick was fired. Howsomever, there's not much risk of it, as they are obliged to make an example of him, there having been so much destruction of property that way lately.'

'I mean,' she exclaimed, 'that I want to touch him for a charm, a cure of an affliction, by the advice of a man who has proved the virtue of the remedy.'

'O yes, miss! Now I understand. I've had such people come in past years. But it didn't strike me that you looked of a sort to require blood-turning. What's the complaint? The wrong kind for this, I'll be bound.'

'My arm.' She reluctantly showed the withered skin.

'Ah! – 'tis all a-scram!' said the hangman examining it.

'Yes,' said she.

'Well,' he continued, with interest, 'that *is* the class o' subject, I'm bound to admit! I like the look of the wownd; it is truly as suitable for the cure as any I ever saw. 'Twas a knowing-man that sent 'ee, whoever he was.'

'You can contrive for me all that's necessary?' she said breathlessly.

'You should really have gone to the governor of the jail, and your doctor with 'ee, and given your name and address – that's how it used to be done, if I recollect. Still, perhaps, I can manage it for a trifling fee.'

'O, thank you! I would rather do it this way, as I should like it kept private.'

'Lover not to know, eh?'

'No – husband.'

'Aha! Very well. I'll get 'ee a touch of the corpse.'

'Where is it now?' she said shuddering.

'It? – *he*, you mean; he's living yet. Just inside that little small winder up there in the glum.' He signified the jail on the cliff above.

She thought of her husband and her friends. 'Yes, of course,' she said; 'and how am I to proceed?'

He took her to the door. 'Now, do you be waiting at the little wicket in the wall, that you'll find up there in the lane, not later than one o'clock. I will open it from the inside, as I shan't come home to dinner till he's cut down. Good-night. Be punctual; and if you don't want anybody to know 'ee, wear a veil. Ah – once I had such a daughter as you!'

She went away, and climbed the path above, to assure herself that she would be able to find the wicket next day. Its outline was soon visible to her – a narrow opening in the outer wall of the prison precincts. The steep was so great that, having reached the wicket, she stopped a moment to breathe; and, looking back upon the water-side cot, saw the hangman again ascending his outdoor staircase. He entered the loft or chamber to which it led, and in a few minutes extinguished his light.

The town clock struck ten, and she returned to the White Hart as she had come.

IX. A Rencounter

It was one o'clock on Saturday. Gertrude Lodge, having been admitted to the jail as above described, was sitting in a waiting-room within the second gate, which stood under a classic archway of ashlar, then comparatively modern, and bearing the inscription COVNTY JAIL: 1793. This had been the façade she saw from the heath the day before. Near at hand was a passage to the roof on which the gallows stood.

The town was thronged, and the market suspended; but Gertrude had seen scarcely a soul. Having kept to her room till the hour of the appointment, she had proceeded to the spot by a way which avoided the open space below the cliff where the spectators had gathered; but she could, even now, hear the multitudinous babble of their voices, out of which rose at intervals the hoarse croak of a single voice uttering the words, 'Last dying speech and confession!' There had been no reprieve, and the execution was over; but the crowd still waited to see the body taken down.

Soon the persistent woman heard a trampling overhead, then a hand beckoned to her, and, following directions, she went out and crossed the inner paved court beyond the gatehouse, her knees trembling so that she could scarcely walk. One of her arms was out of its sleeve, and only covered by her shawl.

On the spot at which she had now arrived were two trestles, and before she could think of their purpose she heard heavy feet descending stairs somewhere at her back. Turn her head she would not, or could not, and, rigid in this position, she was conscious of a rough coffin passing her shoulder, borne by four men. It was open, and in it lay the body of a young man, wearing the smockfrock of a rustic, and fustian breeches. The corpse had been thrown into the coffin so hastily that the skirt of the smockfrock was hanging over. The burden was temporarily deposited on the trestles.

By this time the young woman's state was such that a grey

mist seemed to float before her eyes, on account of which, and the veil she wore, she could scarcely discern anything: it was as though she had nearly died, but was held up by a sort of galvanism.

'Now!' said a voice close at hand, and she was just conscious that the word had been addressed to her.

By a last strenuous effort she advanced, at the same time hearing persons approaching behind her. She bared the poor curst arm; and Davies, uncovering the face of the corpse, took Gertrude's hand, and held it so that her arm lay across the dead man's neck, upon a line the colour of an unripe blackberry, which surrounded it.

Gertrude shrieked: 'the turn o' the blood', predicted by the conjuror, had taken place. But at that moment a second shriek rent the air of the enclosure: it was not Gertrude's, and its effect upon her was to make her start round.

Immediately behind her stood Rhoda Brook, her face drawn, and her eyes red with weeping. Behind Rhoda stood Gertrude's own husband; his countenance lined, his eyes dim, but without a tear.

'D–n you! What are you doing here?' he said hoarsely.

'Hussy – to come between us and our child now!' cried Rhoda. 'This is the meaning of what Satan showed me in the vision! You are like her at last!' And clutching the bare arm of the younger woman, she pulled her unresistingly back against the wall. Immediately Brook had loosened her hold the fragile young Gertrude slid down against the feet of her husband. When he lifted her up she was unconscious.

The mere sight of the twain had been enough to suggest to her that the dead young man was Rhoda's son. At that time the relatives of an executed convict had the privilege of claiming the body for burial, if they chose to do so; and it was for this purpose that Lodge was awaiting the inquest with Rhoda. He had been summoned by her as soon as the young man was taken in the crime, and at different times since; and he had attended in court during the trial. This was the 'holiday' he had been indulging in of late. The two wretched parents had wished to avoid exposure; and hence had come themselves for the body, a wagon and sheet for its conveyance and covering being in waiting outside.

Gertrude's case was so serious that it was deemed advisable to call her the surgeon who was at hand. She was taken out of the jail into the town; but she never reached home alive. Her delicate vitality, sapped perhaps by the paralyzed arm, collapsed under the double shock that followed the severe strain, physical and mental, to which she had subjected herself during the previous twenty-four hours. Her blood had been 'turned' indeed – too far. Her death took place in the town three days after.

Her husband was never seen in Casterbridge again; once only in the old market-place at Anglebury, which he had so much frequented, and very seldom in public anywhere. Burdened at first with moodiness and remorse, he eventually changed for the better, and appeared as a chastened and thoughtful man. Soon after attending the funeral of his poor young wife he took steps towards giving up the farms in Holmstoke and the adjoining parish, and, having sold every head of his stock, he went away to Port-Bredy, at the other end of the county, living there in solitary lodgings till his death two years later of a painless decline. It was then found that he had bequeathed the whole of his not inconsiderable property to a reformatory for boys, subject to the payment of a small annuity to Rhoda Brook, if she could be found to claim it.

For some time she could not be found; but eventually she reappeared in her old parish, – absolutely refusing, however, to have anything to do with the provision made for her. Her monotonous milking at the dairy was resumed, and followed for many long years, till her form became bent, and her once abundant dark hair white and worn away at the forehead – perhaps by long pressure against the cows. Here, sometimes, those who knew her experiences would stand and observe her, and wonder what sombre thoughts were beating inside that impassive, wrinkled brow, to the rhythm of the alternating milk-streams.

The Mysterious Mansion

Honoré De Balzac

About a hundred yards from the town of Vendôme, on the borders of the Loire, there is an old grey house, surmounted by very high gables, and so completely isolated that neither tanyard nor shabby hostelry, such as you may find at the entrance to all small towns, exists in its immediate neighbourhood.

In front of this building, overlooking the river, is a garden, where the once well-trimmed box borders that used to define the walks now grow wild as they list. Several willows that spring from the Loire have grown as rapidly as the hedge that encloses it, and half conceal the house. The rich vegetation of those weeds that we call foul adorns the sloping shore. Fruit trees, neglected from the last ten years, no longer yield their harvest, and their shoots form coppices. The wall-fruit grows like hedges against the walls. Paths once gravelled are overgrown with moss, but, to tell the truth, there is no trace of a path. From the height of the hill, to which cling the ruins of the old castle of the Dukes of Vendôme, the only spot whence the eye can plunge into this enclosure, it strikes you that, at a time not easy to determine, this plot of land was the delight of a country gentleman, who cultivated roses and tulips and horticulture in general, and who was besides a lover of fine fruit. An arbour is still visible, or rather the débris of an arbour, where there is a table that time has not quite destroyed. The aspect of this garden of bygone days suggests the negative joys of peaceful, provincial life, as one might reconstruct the life of a worthy tradesman by reading the epitaph on his tombstone. As if to completed the sweetness and sadness of the ideas that possess one's soul, one of the walls displays a sun-dial decorated with the following commonplace Christian inscription: 'Ultimam cogita!' The roof of this house is horribly dilapidated, the shutters are always closed, the balconies are covered with swallows' nests, the doors are perpetually shut, weeds have drawn green lines in the cracks of the flights of steps, the locks and bolts are rusty. Sun, moon, winter, summer, and snow have worn the panelling, warped the boards, gnawed the paint. The lugubrious silence which reigns there is only broken by birds, cats, martins, rats and mice, free to course to and fro, to fight and to eat each other. Everywhere an invisible hand has graven the word *mystery*.

Should your curiosity lead you to glance at this house from the side that points to the road, you would perceive a great door which the children of the place have riddled with holes. I afterward heard that this door had been closed for the last ten years. Through the holes broken by the boys you would have observed the perfect harmony that existed between the façades of both garden and courtyard. In both the same disorder prevails. Tufts of weed encircle the paving stones. Enormous cracks furrow the walls, round whose blackened crests twine the thousand garlands of the pellitory. The steps are out of joint, the wire of the bell is rusted, the spouts are cracked. What fire from heaven has fallen here? What tribunal has decreed that salt should be strewn on this dwelling? Has God been blasphemed, has France been betrayed? These are the questions we ask ourselves, but get no answer from the crawling things that haunt the place. The empty and deserted house is a gigantic enigma, of which the key is lost. In bygone times it was a small fief, and bears the name of the Grande Bretêche.

I inferred that I was not the only person to whom my good landlady had communicated the secret of which I was to be the sole recipient, and I prepared to listen.

'Sir,' she said, 'when the Emperor sent the Spanish prisoners of war and others here, the Government quartered on me a young Spaniard who had been sent to Vendôme on parole. Parole notwithstanding he went out every day to show himself to the sous-préfect. He was a Spanish grandee! Nothing less! His name ended in os and dia, something like Burgos de Férédia. I have his name on my books; you can read it if you like. Oh! but he was a handsome young man for a Spaniard; they are all said to be ugly. He was only five feet and a few inches high, but he was well-grown; he had small hands that he took such care of; ah! you should have seen! He had as many brushes for his hands as a woman for her whole dressing apparatus! He had thick black hair, a fiery eye, his skin was rather bronzed, but I liked the look of it. He wore the finest linen I have ever seen on any one, although I have had princesses staying here, and, among others, General Bertrand, the Duke and Duchess d'Abrantés, Monsieur Decazes, and the King of Spain. He didn't eat much; but his manners were so polite, so amiable, that one could not owe him a grudge. Oh! I was very fond of him, although he didn't open his lips four times in the day, and it was impossible to keep up a conversation with him, for if you spoke to him, he did not answer. It was a fad, a mania with them all, I heard say. He read his breviary like a priest, he went to Mass and to all the services regularly. Where did he sit? Two steps from the chapel of Madame de Merret. As he took his place there the first time he went to church, nobody suspected him of any intention in so doing. Besides, he never raised his eyes from his prayer-book, poor young man! After that, sir, in the evening he would walk on the mountains, among the castle ruins. It was the poor man's only amusement, it reminded him of his country. They say that Spain is all mountains! From the commencement of his imprisonment he stayed out late. I was anxious when I found that he did not come home before midnight; but we got accustomed to this fancy of his. He took the key of the door, and we left off sitting up for him. He lodged in a house of ours in the Rue des Casernes. After that, one of our stable-men told us that in the evening when he led the horses to the water, he thought he had seen the Spanish grandee swimming far down the river like a live fish. When he returned, I told him to take care of the rushes; he appeared vexed to have been seen in the water. At last, one day, or rather one morning, we did not find him in his room; he had not returned. After searching everywhere, I found some writing in the drawer of a table, where there were fifty gold pieces of Spain that are called doubloons and were worth about five thousand francs; and ten thousand francs' worth of diamonds in a small sealed box. The writing said, that in case he did not return, he left us the money and the diamonds, on condition of paying for Masses to thank God for his escape, and for his salvation. In those days my husband had not been taken from me; he hastened to seek him everywhere.

'And now for the strange part of the story. He brought home the Spaniard's clothes, that he had discovered under a big stone, in a sort of pilework by the river-side near the castle, nearly opposite to the Grande Bretêche. My husband had gone there so early that no one had seen him. After reading the letter, he burned the clothes, and according to Count Férédia's desire we declared that he had escaped. The sous-préfect sent all the gendarmerie in pursuit of him; but brust! they never caught him. Lepas believed that the Spaniard had drowned himself. I, sir, don't think so; I am more inclined to believe that he had something to do with the affair of Madame de Merret, seeing that Rosalie told me that the crucifix that her mistress thought so much of, that she had it buried with her, was of ebony and silver. Now in the beginning of his stay here, Monsieur de Férédia had one in ebony and silver, that I never saw him with later. Now, sir, don't you consider that I need have no scruples about the Spaniard's fifteen thousand francs, and that I have a right to them?'

'Certainly; but you haven't tried to question Rosalie?' I said.

'Oh, yes, indeed, sir; but to no purpose! The girl's like a wall. She knows something, but is impossible to get her to talk.'

After exchanging a few more words with me, my landlady

left me a prey to vague and gloomy thoughts, to a romantic curiosity, and a religious terror not unlike the profound impression produced on us when by night, on entering a dark church, we perceive a faint light under high arches; a vague figure glides by – the rustle of a robe or cassock is heard, and we shudder.

Suddenly the Grande Bretêche and its tall weeds, its barred windows, its rusty ironwork, its closed doors, its deserted apartments, appeared like a fantastic apparition before me. I essayed to penetrate the mysterious dwelling, and to find the knot of its dark story – the drama that had killed three persons. In my eyes Rosalie became the most interesting person in Vendôme. As I studied her, I discovered the traces of secret care, despite the radiant health that shone in her plump countenance. There was in her the germ of remorse or hope; her attitude revealed a secret, like the attitude of a bigot who prays to excess, or of the infanticide who ever hears the last cry of her child. Yet her manners were rough and ingenuous – her silly smile was not that of a criminal, and could you but have seen the great kerchief that encompassed her portly bust, framed and laced in by a lilac and blue cotton gown, you would have dubbed her innocent. No, I thought, I will not leave Vendôme without learning the history of the Grande Bretêche. To gain my ends I will strike up a friendship with Rosalie, if needs be.

'Rosalie,' said I, one evening.

'Sir?'

'You are not married?'

She started slightly.

'Oh, I can find plenty of men, when the fancy takes me to be made miserable,' she said, laughing

She soon recovered from the effects of her emotion, for all women, from the great lady to the maid of the inn, possess a composure that is peculiar to them.

'You are too good-looking and well favoured to be short of lovers. But tell me, Rosalie, why did you take service in an inn after leaving Madame de Merret? Did she leave you nothing to live on?'

'Oh, yes! But sir, my place is the best in all Vendôme.'

The reply was one of those that judges and lawyers would call evasive. Rosalie appeared to me to be situated in this romantic history like the square in the midst of a chessboard. She was at the heart of the truth and chief interest; she seemed to me to be bound in the very knot of it. The conquest of Rosalie was no longer to be an ordinary siege – in this girl was centred the last chapter of a novel, therefore from this moment Rosalie became the object of my preference.

One morning I said to Rosalie: 'Tell me all you know about Madame de Merret.'

'Oh!' she replied in terror, 'do not ask that of me, Monsieur Horace.'

Her pretty face fell – her clear, bright colour faded – and her eyes lost their innocent brightness.

'Well, then,' she said, at last, 'if you must have it so, I will tell you about it; but promise to keep my secret!'

'Done! my dear girl, I must keep your secret with the honour of a thief, which is the most loyal in the world.'

Were I to transcribe Rosalie's diffuse eloquence faithfully, an entire volume would scarcely contain it; so I shall abridge.

The room occupied by Madame de Merret at the Bretêche was on the ground floor. A little closet about four feet deep, built in the thickness of the wall, served as her wardrobe. Three months before the eventful evening of which I am about to speak, Madame de Merret had been so seriously indisposed that her husband had left her to herself in her own apartment, while he occupied another on the first floor. By one of those chances that it is impossible to foresee, he returned home from the club (where he was accustomed to read the papers and discuss politics with the inhabitants of the place) two hours later than usual. His wife supposed him to be at home, in bed and asleep. But the invasion of France had been the subject of a most animated discussion; the billiard-match had been exciting, he had lost forty francs, an enormous sum for Vendôme, where every one hoards, and where manners are restricted within the limits of a praiseworthy modesty, which perhaps is the source of the true happiness that no Parisian covets. For some time past Monsieur de Merret had been satisfied to ask Rosalie if his wife had gone to bed; and on her reply, which was always in the affirmative, had immediately gained his own room with the good temper engendered by habit and confidence. On entering his house, he took it into his head to go and tell his wife of his misadventure, perhaps by way of consolation. At dinner he found Madame de Merret most coquettishly attired. On his way to the club it had occurred to him that his wife was restored to health, and that her convalescence had added to her beauty. He was, as husbands are wont to be, somewhat slow in making this discovery. Instead of calling Rosalie, who was occupied just then in watching the cook and coachman play a difficult hand at brisque, Monsieur de Merret went to his wife's room by the light of a lantern that he deposited on the first step of the staircase. His unmistakable step resounded under the vaulted corridor. At the moment that the Count turned the handle of his wife's door, he fancied he could hear the door of the closet I spoke of close; but when he entered Madame de Merret was alone before the fireplace. The husband thought ingenuously that Rosalie was in the closet, yet a suspicion that jangled in his ear put him on his guard. He looked at his wife and saw in her eyes I know not what wild and hunted expression.

'You are very late,' she said. Her habitually pure, sweet voice seemed changed to him.

Monsieur de Merret did not reply, for at that moment Rosalie entered. It was a thunderbolt for him. He strode about the room, passing from one window to the other, with a mechanical motion and folded arms.

'Have you heard bad news, or are you unwell?' inquired his wife, timidly, while Rosalie undressed her.

He kept silent.

'You can leave me,' said Madame de Merret to her maid; 'I will put my hair in curl papers myself.'

From the expression of her husband's face she foresaw trouble, and wished to be alone with him. When Rosalie had gone, or was supposed to have gone (for she stayed in the corridor a few minutes), Monsieur de Merret came and stood in front of his wife, and said coldly to her:

'Madame, there is someone in your closet!' She looked calmly at her husband and replied simply:

'No, sir.'

This answer was heartening to Monsieur de Merret; he did not believe it. Yet his wife had never appeared to him purer or more saintly than at that moment. He rose to open the closet door; Madame de Merret took his hand, looked at him with an expression of melancholy, and said in a voice that betrayed singular emotion:

'If you find no one there, remember this, all will be over between us!' The extraordinary dignity of his wife's manner restored the Count's profound esteem for her, and inspired him with one of those resolutions that only lack a vaster stage to become immortal.

'No,' said he, 'Josephine, I will not go there. In either case it would separate us forever. Hear me, I know how pure you are at heart, and that you life is a holy one. You would not commit a mortal sin to save your life.'

At these words Madame de Merret turned a haggard gaze upon her husband.

'Here, take your crucifix,' he added. 'Swear to me before God that there is no one in there; I will believe you, I will never open that door.'

Madame de Merret took the crucifix and said:

'I swear.'

'Louder,' said the husband,' and repeat "I swear before God that there is no one in that closet." '

She repeated the sentence calmly.

'That will do,' said Monsieur de Merret, coldly.

After a moment of silence:

'I never saw this pretty toy before,' he said, examining the ebony crucifix inlaid with silver, and most artistically chiselled.

'I found it at Duvivier's, who bought it off a Spanish monk when the prisoners passed through Vendôme last year.'

'Ah!' said Monsieur de Merret, as he replaced the crucifix on the nail, and he rang. Rosalie did not keep him waiting. Monsieur de Merret went quickly to meet her, led her to the bay window that opened on to the garden and whispered to her:

'Listen! I know that Gorenflot wishes to marry you, poverty is the only drawback, and you told him that you would be his wife if he found the means to establish himself as a master mason. Well! go and fetch him, tell him to come here with his trowel and tools. Manage not to awaken any one in his house but himself; his fortune will be more than your desires. Above all, leave this room without babbling, otherwise – ' He frowned. Rosalie went away, he recalled her.

'Here, take my latchkey,' he said. 'Jean!' then cried Monsieur de Merret, in tones of thunder in the corridor. Jean, who was at the same time his coachman and his confidential servant, left his game of cards and came.

'Go to bed, all of you,' said his master, signing to him to approach; and the Count added, under his breath: 'When they are all asleep – *asleep*, d'ye hear? – you will come down and tell me.' Monsieur de Merret, who had not lost sight of his wife all the time he was giving his orders, returned quietly to her at the fireside and began to tell her of the game of billiards and the talk of the club. When Rosalie returned she found Monsieur and Madame de Merret conversing very amicably.

The Count had lately had all the ceilings of his reception rooms on the ground floor repaired. Plaster of Paris is difficult to obtain in Vendôme; the carriage raises its price. The Count had therefore bought a good deal, being well aware that he could find plenty of purchasers for whatever might remain over. This circumstance inspired him with the design he was about to execute.

'Sir, Gorenflot has arrived,' said Rosalie in low tones.

'Show him in,' replied the Count in loud tones.

Madame de Merret turned rather pale when she saw the mason.

'Gorenflot,' said her husband, 'go and fetch bricks from the coach-house and bring sufficient to wall up the door of this closet; you will use the plaster I have over to coat the wall with.' Then calling Rosalie and the workman aside:

'Listen, Gorenflot,' he said in an undertone, 'you will sleep here to-night. But to-morrow you will have a passport to a foreign country, to a town to which I will direct you. I shall give you six thousand francs for your journey. You will stay ten years in that town; if you do not like it, you may establish yourself in another, provided it be in the same country. You will pass through Paris, where you will await me. There will be paid to you on your return, provided you have fulfilled the conditions of our bargain. This is the price for your absolute silence as to what you are about to do tonight. As to you, Rosalie, I will give you ten thousand francs on the day of your wedding, on condition of your marrying Gorenflot; but if you wish to marry, you must hold your tongues; or – no dowry.'

'Rosalie,' said Madame de Merret, 'do my hair.'

The husband walked calmly up and down, watching the door, the mason, and his wife, but without betraying any insulting doubts. Madame de Merret chose a moment when the workman was unloading bricks and her husband was at the other end of the room to say to Rosalie: ' a thousand francs a year for you, my child, if you can tell Gorenflot to leave a chink at the bottom.' Then out loud, she added coolly:

'Go and help him!'

Monsieur and Madame de Merret were silent all the time that Gorenflot took to brick up the door. This silence, on the part of the husband, who did not choose to furnish his wife with a pretext for saying things of a double meaning, had its purpose; on the part of Madame de Merret it was either pride or prudence. When the wall was about half-way up, the sly workman took advantage of a moment when the Count's back was turned, to strike a blow with his trowel in one of the glass panes of the closet door. This act informed Madame de Merret that Rosalie had spoken to Gorenflot.

All three then saw a man's face; it was dark and gloomy with black hair and eyes of flame. Before her husband turned, the poor woman had time to make a sign to the stranger that signified: Hope!

At four o'clock, toward dawn, for it was the month of September, the construction was finished. The mason was handed over to the care of Jean, and Monsieur de Merret went to bed in his wife's room.

On the following morning, he said carelessly:

'The deuce! I must go to the Mairie for the passport.' He put his hat on his head, advanced three steps towards the door, altered his mind and took the crucifix.

His wife trembled for joy. 'He is going to Duvivier,' she thought. As soon as the Count had left, Madame de Merret rang for Rosalie; then in a terrible voice:

'The trowel, the trowel!' she cried, 'and quick to work! I saw how Gorenflot did it; we shall have time to make a hole and to mend it again.'

In the twinkling of an eye, Rosalie brought a sort of mattock to her mistress, who with unparalled ardour set about demolishing the wall. She had already knocked out several bricks and was preparing to strike a more decisive blow when she perceived Monsieur de Merret behind her. She fainted.

'Lay Madame on her bed,' said the Count coldly. He had foreseen what would happen in his absence and had set a trap for his wife; he had simply written to the mayor, and had sent for Duvivier. The jeweller arrived just as the room had been put in order.

'Duvivier,' inquired the Count, 'did you buy crucifixes off the Spaniards who passed through here?'

'No, sir?'

'That will do, thank you,' he said looking at his wife like a tiger. 'Jean,' he added, 'you will see that my meals are served in the Countess's room; she is ill, and I shall not leave her until she has recovered.'

The cruel gentleman stayed with his wife for twenty days. In the beginning, when there were sounds in the walled closet, and Josephine attempted to implore his pity for the dying stranger, he replied, without permitting her to say a word:

'You have sworn on the cross that there is no one there.'

Transformation

Mary Shelley

Forthwith this frame of mine was wrench'd
With a woful agony,
Which forced me to begin my tale,
And then it set me free.
Since then, at an uncertain hour,
That agony returns;
And till my ghastly tale is told
This heart within me burns.
Coleridge's *Ancient Mariner*

I have heard it said, that when any strange, supernatural, and necromantic adventure has occurred to a human being, that being, however desirous he may be to conceal the same, feels at certain periods torn up as it were by an intellectual earthquake, and is forced to bare the inner depths of his spirit to another. I am a witness of the truth of this. I have dearly sworn to myself never to reveal to human ears the horrors to which I once, in excess of fiendly pride, delivered myself over. The holy man who heard my confession, and reconciled me to the church, is dead. None knows that once –

Why should it not be thus? Why tell a tale of impious tempting of Providence, and soul-subduing humiliation? Why? answer me, ye who are wise in the secrets of human nature! I only know that so it is: and in spite of strong resolve – of a pride that too much masters me – of shame, and even of fear, so to render myself odious to my species – I must speak.

Genoa! My birth-place – proud city! Looking upon the blue

waves of the Mediterranean sea – dost thou remember me in my boyhood, when thy cliffs and promontories, thy bright sky and gay vineyards, were my world? Happy time! When to the young heart the narrow-bounded universe, which leaves by its very limitation, free scope to the imagination, enchains our physical energies, and, sole period in our lives, innocence and enjoyment are united. Yet, who can look back to childhood, and not remember its sorrows and its harrowing fears? I was born with the most imperious, haughty, tameless spirit, with which ever mortal was gifted. I quailed before my father only: and he, generous and noble, but capricious and tyrannical, at once fostered and checked the wild impetuosity of my character, making obedience necessary, but inspiring no respect for the motives which guided his commands. To be a man, free, independent; or, in better words, insolent and domineering, was the hope and prayer of my rebel heart.

My father had one friend, a wealthy Genoese noble, who in a political tumult was suddenly sentenced to banishment, and his property confiscated. The Marchese Torella went into exile alone. Like my father, he was a widower: he had one child, the almost infant Juliet, who was left under my father's guardianship. I should certainly have been an unkind master to the lovely girl, but that I was forced by my position to become her protector. A variety of childish incidents all tended to one point, – to make Juliet see in me a rock of refuge; I in her, one who must perish through the soft sensibility of her nature too rudely visited, but for my guardian care. We grew up together. The opening rose in May was not more sweet than this dear girl. An irradiation of beauty was spread over her face. Her form, her step, her voice – my heart weeps even now, to think of all of relying, gentle, loving, and pure, that was enshrined in that celestial tenement. When I was eleven and Juliet eight years of age, a cousin of mine, much older than either – he seemed to us a man – took great notice of my playmate; he called her his bride, and asked her to marry him. She refused, and he insisted, drawing her unwillingly towards him. With the countenance and emotions of a maniac I threw myself on him – I strove to draw his sword – I clung to his neck with the ferocious resolve to strangle him: he was obliged to call for assistance to disengage himself from me. On that night I led Juliet to the chapel of our house: I made her touch the sacred relics – I harrowed her child's heart, and profaned her child's lips with an oath, that she would be mine, and mine only.

Well, those days passed away. Torella returned in a few years, and became wealthier and more prosperous than ever. When I was seventeen, my father died; he had been magnificent to prodigality; Torella rejoiced that my minority would afford an opportunity for repairing my fortunes. Juliet and I had been affianced beside my father's deathbed – Torella was to be a second parent to me.

I desired to see the world, and I was indulged. I went to Florence, to Rome, to Naples; thence I passed to Toulon, and at length reached what had long been the bourne of my wishes, Paris. There was wild work in Paris then. The poor king, Charles the Sixth, now sane, now mad, now a monarch, now an abject slave, was the very mockery of humanity. The queen, the dauphin, the Duke of Burgundy, alternately friends and foes – now meeting in prodigal feasts, now shedding blood in rivalry – were blind to the miserable state of their country, and the dangers that impended over it, and gave themselves wholly up to dissolute enjoyment or savage strife. My character still followed me. I was arrogant and self-willed; I loved display, and above all, I threw all control far from me. Who could control me in Paris? My young friends were eager to foster passions which furnished them with pleasures. I was deemed handsome – I was master of every knightly accomplishment. I was disconnected with any political party. I grew a favourite with all: my presumption and arrogance were pardoned in one so young: I became a spoiled child. Who could control me? – not the letters and advice of Torella – only strong necessity visiting me in the abhorred shape of an empty purse. But there were means to refill this void. Acre after acre, estate after estate, I sold. My dress, my jewels, my horses and their caparisons, were almost unrivalled in gorgeous Paris, while the lands of my inheritance passed into possession of others.

The Duke of Orleans was waylaid and murdered by the Duke of Burgundy. Fear and terror possessed all Paris. The dauphin and the queen shut themselves up; every pleasure was suspended. I grew weary of this state of things, and my heart yearned for my boyhood's haunts. I was nearly a beggar, yet still I would go there, claim my bride, and rebuild my fortunes. A few happy ventures as a merchant would make me rich again. Nevertheless, I would not return in humble guise. My last act was to dispose of my remaining estate near Albaro for half its worth, for ready money. Then I dispatched all kinds of artificers, arras, furniture of regal splendour, to fit up the last relic of my inheritance, my palace in Genoa. I lingered a little longer yet, ashamed at the part of the prodigal returned, which I feared I should play. I sent my horses. One matchless Spanish jennet I despatched to my promised bride; its caparisons flamed with jewels and cloth of gold. In every part I caused to be entwined the initials of Juliet and her Guido. My present found favour in hers and in her father's eyes.

Still to return a proclaimed spendthrift, the mark of impertinent wonder, perhaps of scorn, and to encounter singly the reproaches or taunts of my fellow-citizens, was no alluring prospect. As a shield between me and censure, I invited some few of the most reckless of my comrades to accompany me; thus I went armed against the world, hiding a rankling feeling, half fear and half penitence, by bravado and in insolent display of satisfied vanity.

I arrived in Genoa. I trod the pavement of my ancestral palace. My proud step was no interpreter of my heart, for I deeply felt that, though surrounded by every luxury. I was a beggar. The first step I took in claiming Juliet must widely declare me such. I read contempt or pity in the looks of all. I fancied, so apt is conscience to imagine what it deserves, that rich and poor, young and old, all regarded me with derision.

Torella came not near me. No wonder that my second father should expect a son's deference from me in waiting first on him. But, galled and stung by a sense of my follies and demerit, I strove to throw the blame on others. We kept nightly orgies in Palazzo Carega. To sleepless, riotous nights, followed listless, supine mornings. At the Ave Maria we showed our dainty persons in the streets, scoffing at the sober citizens, casting insolent glances on the shrinking women. Juliet was not among them – no, no; if she had been there, shame would have driven me away, if love had not brought me to her feet.

I grew tired of this. Suddenly I paid the Marchese a visit. He was at his villa, one among the many which deck the suburb of San Pietro d'Arena. It was the month of May – a month of May in that garden of the world – the blossoms of the fruit trees were fading among thick, green foliage; the vines were shooting forth; the ground strewed with the fallen olive blooms; the fire-fly was in the myrtle hedge; heaven and earth wore a mantle of surpassing beauty. Torella welcomed me kindly, though seriously; and even his shade of displeasure soon wore away. Some resemblance to my father – some look and tone of youthful ingenuousness, lurking still in spite of my misdeeds, softened the good old man's heart. He sent for his daughter – he presented me to her as her betrothed. The chamber became hallowed by a holy light as she entered. Hers was that cherub look, those large, soft eyes, full dimpled cheeks, and mouth of infantine sweetness, that expresses the rare union of happiness and love. Admiration first possessed me; she is mine! was the second proud emotion, and my lips curled with haughty triumph. I had not been the *enfant gâté* of the beauties of France not to have learnt the art of pleasing the soft heart of woman. If towards men I was overbearing, the deference I paid to them was the more in contrast. I commenced my courtship by the display of a thousand gallantries to Juliet, who, vowed to me from infancy, had never admitted the devotion of admiration, was uninitiated in the language of lovers.

For a few days all went well. Torella never alluded to my extravagance; he treated me as a favourite son. But the time came, as we discussed the preliminaries to my union with his daughter, when this fair face of things should be overcast. A contract had been drawn up in my father's lifetime. I had rendered this, in fact, void, by having squandered the whole of the wealth which was to have been shared by Juliet and myself. Torella, in consequence, chose to consider this bond as cancelled, and proposed another, in which, though the wealth he bestowed was immeasurably increased, there were so many restrictions as to the mode of spending it, that I, who saw independence only in free career being given to my own impetuous will, taunted him as taking advantage of my situation, and refused utterly to subscribe to his condition. The old man mildly strove to recall me to reason. Roused pride became the tyrant of my thought: I listened with indignation – I repelled him with disdain.

'Juliet, thou art mine! Did we not interchange vows in our innocent childhood? Are we not one in the sight of God? And shall thy cold-hearted, cold-blooded father divide us? Be generous, my love, be just; take not away a gift, last treasure of thy Guido – retract not they vows – let us defy the world, and setting at nought the calculations of age, find in our mutual affection a refuge from every ill.'

Fiend I must have been, with such sophistry to endeavour to poison that sanctuary of holy thought and tender love. Juliet shrank from me affrighted. Her father was the best and kindest of men, and she strove to show me how, in obeying him, every good would follow. He would receive my tardy submission with warm affection; and generous pardon would follow my repentance. Profitless words for a young and gentle daughter to use to a man accustomed to make his will, law; and to feel in his own heart a despot so terrible and stern, that he could yield obedience to nought save his own imperious desires! My resentment grew with resistance; my wild companions were ready to add fuel to the flame. We laid a plan to carry off Juliet.

At first it appeared to be crowned with success. Midway, on our return, we were overtaken by the agonized father and his attendants. A conflict ensued. Before the city guard came to decide the victory in favour of our antagonists, two of Torella's servitors were dangerously wounded.

This portion of my history weighs most heavily with me. Changed man as I am, I abhor myself in the recollection. May none who hear this tale ever have felt as I. A horse driven to fury by a rider armed with barbed spurs, was not more a slave than I, to the violent tyranny of my temper. A fiend possessed my soul, irritating it to madness. I felt the voice of conscience within me; but if I yielded to it for a brief interval, it was only to be a moment after torn, as by a whirlwind, away – borne along on the stream of desperate rage – the plaything of the storms engendered by pride. I was imprisoned, and, at the instance of Torella, set free. Again I returned to carry off both him and his child to France; which hapless county, then preyed on by freebooters and gangs of lawless soldiery, offered a grateful refuge to a criminal like me. Our plots were discovered. I was sentenced to banishment; and, as my debts were already enormous, my remaining property was put in the hands of commissioners for their payment. Torella again offered his mediation, requiring only my promise not to renew my abortive attempts on himself and his daughter. I spurned his offers, and fancied that I triumphed when I was thrust out from Genoa, a solitary and penniless exile. My companions were gone; they had been dismissed the city some weeks before, and were already in France. I was alone – friendless; with nor sword at my side, not ducat in my purse.

I wandered along the sea-shore, a whirlwind of passion possessing and tearing my soul. It was as if a love coal had been set burning in my breast. At first I meditated on what *I should do*. I would join a band of freebooters. Revenge! – the word seemed balm to me: – I hugged it – caressed it – till, like a serpent, it stung me. Then again I would abjure and despise Genoa, that little corner of the world. I would return to Paris, where so many of my friends swarmed; where my services would be eagerly accepted; where I would carve out fortune with my sword, and might, through success, make my paltry birth-place, and the false Torella, rue the day when they drove me, a new Coriolanus, from her walls. I would return to Paris – thus, on foot – a beggar – and present myself in my poverty to those I had formerly entertained sumptuously? There was gall in the mere thought of it.

The reality of things began to dawn upon my mind, bringing despair in its train. For several months I had been a prisoner: the evils of my dungeon had whipped my soul to madness, but they had subdued my corporeal frame. I was weak and wan. Torella had used a thousand artifices to administer to my comfort; I had detected and scorned them all – and I reaped the harvest of my obduracy. What was to be done? – Should I crouch before my foe, and sue for forgiveness? – Die rather ten thousand deaths! – Never should they obtain that victory! Hate – I swore eternal hate! Hate from whom? – to whom? – from a wandering outcast – to a mighty noble. I and my feelings were nothing to them: already had they forgotten one so unworthy. And Juliet! – her angel-face and sylph-like form gleamed among the clouds of my despair with vain beauty: for I had lost her – the glory and flower of the world! Another will call her his! – that smile of paradise will bless another!

Even now my heart fails within me when I recur to this rout of grim-visaged ideas. Now subdued almost to tears, now raving in my agony, still I wandered along the rocky shore, which grew at each step wilder and more desolate. Hanging rocks and hoar precipices overlooked the tideless ocean; black caverns yawned; and for ever, among the seaworn recesses, murmured and dashed the unfruitful waters. Now my way was almost barred by an abrupt promontory, now rendered nearly impracticable by fragments fallen from the cliff. Evening was at hand, when, seaward, arose, as if on the waving of a wizard's wand, a murky web of clouds, blotting the late azure sky, and darkening and disturbing the till now placid deep. The clouds had strange fantastic shapes; and they changed, and mingled, and seemed to be driven about by a mighty spell. The waves raised their white crests; the thunder first muttered, then roared from across the waste of waters, which took a deep purple dye, flecked with foam. The spot where I stood, looked, on one side, to the wide-spread ocean; on the other, it was barred by a rugged promontory. Round this cape suddenly came, driven by the wind, a vessel. In vain the mariners tried to force a path for her to the open sea – the gale drove her on the rocks. It will perish! – all on board will perish! – Would I were among them! And to my young heart the idea of death came for the first time blended with that of joy. It was an awful sight to behold that vessel struggling with her fate. Hardly could I discern the sailors, but I heard them. It was soon all over! – A rock, just covered by the tossing waves, and so unperceived, lay in wait for its prey. A crash of thunder broke over my head at the moment that, with a frightful shock, the skiff dashed upon her unseen enemy. In a brief space of time she went to pieces. There I stood in safety; and there were my fellow-creatures, battling, how hopelessly, with annihilation. Methought I saw them struggling – too truly did I hear their shrieks, conquering the barking surges in their shrill agony. The dark breakers threw hither and thither the fragments of the wreck: soon it disappeared. I had been fascinated to gaze till the end: at last I sank on my knees – I covered my face with my hands: I again looked up: something was floating on the billows towards the shore. It neared and neared. Was that a human form? – It grew more distinct: and at last a mighty wave, lifting the whole freight, lodged it upon a rock. A human being bestriding a sea-chest! – A Human being! – Yet was it one? Surely never such had existed before – a misshapen dwarf, with squinting eyes, distorted features, and body deformed till it became a horror to behold. My blood, lately warming towards a fellow-being so snatched from a watery tomb, froze in my heart. The dwarf got off his chest; he tossed his straight, straggling hair from his odious visage:

'By St. Beelzebub!' he exclaimed, 'I have been well bested.' He looked round and saw me. 'Oh, by the fiend! Here is another ally of the mighty one. To what saint did you offer prayers, friend – if not to mine? Yet I remember you not on board.'

I shrank from the monster and his blasphemy. Again he questioned me, and I muttered some inaudible reply. He continued:

'Your voice is drowned by this dissonant roar. What a noise the big ocean makes! Schoolboys bursting from their prison are not louder than these waves set free to play. They disturb me. I will no more of their ill-timed brawling – Silence, hoary One! – Winds, avaunt! – to your homes! – Clouds, fly to the antipodes, and leave our heaven clear!'

As he spoke, he stretched out his two long lank arms, that looked like spider's claws, and seemed to embrace with them the expanse before him. Was it a miracle? The clouds became broken, and fled: the azure sky first peeped out, and then was spread a calm field of blue above us; the stormy gale was exchanged to the softly breathing west; the sea grew calm; the waves dwindled to riplets.

'I like obedience even in these stupid elements,' said the dwarf. 'How much more in the tameless mind of man! It was a well got up storm, you must allow – and all of my own making.'

It was tempting Providence to interchange talk with this magician. But *Power*, in all its shapes, is venerable to man. Awe, curiosity, a clinging fascination, drew me towards him.

'Come, don't be frightened, friend,' said the wretch: 'I am good-humoured when pleased; and something does please me in your well-proportioned body and handsome face, though you look a little woebegone. You suffered a land – I, a sea wreck. Perhaps I can allay the tempest of your fortunes as I did my own. Shall we be friends?' – And he held out his hand; I could not touch it. 'Well, then, companions – that will do as well. And now, while I rest after the buffeting I underwent just now, tell me why, young and gallant as you seem, you wander thus alone and downcast on this wild sea-shore.'

The voice of the wretch was screeching and horrid, and his contortions as he spoke were frightful to behold. Yet he did gain a kind of influence over me, which I could not master, and I told him my tale. When it was ended, he laughed long and loud: the rocks echoed back the sound: hell seemed yelling around me.

'Oh, thou cousin of Lucifer!' said he; 'so thou too hast fallen through thy pride; and, though bright as the son of Morning, thou art ready to give up thy good looks, thy bride, and thy well-being, rather than submit thee to the tyranny of good. I honour thy choice, by my soul! – So thou hast fled, and yield the day; and mean to starve on these rocks, and to let the birds peck out thy dead eyes, while thy enemy and thy betrothed rejoice in thy ruin. Thy pride is strangely akin to humility, methinks.'

As he spoke, a thousand fanged thoughts stung me to the heart.

'What would you that I should do?' I cried.

'I! – Oh, nothing, but lie down and say your prayers before you die. But, were I you, I know the deed that should be done.'

I drew near him. His supernatural powers made him an oracle in my eyes; yet a strange unearthly thrill quivered through my frame as I said – 'Speak! – teach me – what act do you advise?'

'Revenge thyself, man! – humble thy enemies! – set thy foot on the old man's neck, and possess thyself of his daughter!'

'To the east and west I turn,' cried I, 'and see no means! Had I gold, much could I achieve; but, poor and single, I am powerless.'

The dwarf had been seated on his chest as he listened to my story. Now he got off; he touched a spring; it flew open! – What a mine of wealth – of blazing jewels, beaming gold, and pale silver – was displayed therein. A mad desire to possess this treasure was born within me.

'Doubtless,' I said, 'one so powerful as you could do all things.'

'Nay,' said the monster, humbly, 'I am less omnipotent than I seem. Some things I possess which you may covet; but I would give them all for a small share, or even a loan of what is yours.'

'As nothing is my sole inheritance, what besides nothing would you have?'

'Your comely face and well-made limbs.'

I shivered. Would this all-powerful monster murder me? I had no dagger. I forgot to pray – but I grew pale.

'I ask for a loan, not a gift,' said the frightful thing: 'lend me your body for three days – you shall have mine to cage your soul the while, and, in payment, my chest. What say you to the bargain? – Three short days.'

We are told that it is dangerous to hold unlawful talk; and well do I prove the same. Tamely written down, it may seem incredible that I should lend any ear to this proposition; but, in spite of his unnatural ugliness, there was something fascinating in a being whose voice could govern earth, air, and sea. I felt a keen desire to comply; for with that chest I could command the world. My only hesitation resulted from a fear that he would not be true to his bargain. Then, I thought, I shall soon die here on these lonely sands, and the limbs he covets will be mine no more: – it is worth the chance. And, besides, I knew that, by all the rules of art-magic, there were formula and oaths which none of its practisers dared break. I hesitated to reply; and he went on, now displaying his wealth, now speaking of the petty price he demanded, till it seemed madness to refuse. Thus is it: place our bark in the current of the stream, and down, over fall and cataract it is hurried; give up our conduct to the world torrent of passion, and we are away, we know not whither.

He swore many an oath, and I adjured him by many a sacred name; till I saw this wonder of power, this ruler of the elements, shiver like an autumn leaf before my words; and as if the spirit spake unwillingly and per force within him, at last, he, with broken voice, revealed the spell whereby he might be obliged, did he wish to play me false, to render up the unlawful spoil. Our warm life-blood must mingle to make and to mar the charm.

Enough of this unholy theme. I was persuaded – the thing was done. The morrow dawned upon me as I lay upon the shingles, and I knew not my own shadow as it fell from me. I felt myself change to a shape of horror, and cursed my easy faith and blind credulity. The chest was there – there the gold and precious stones for which I had sold the fame of flesh which nature had given me. The sight a little stilled my emotion: three days would soon be gone.

They did pass. The dwarf had supplied me with a plenteous store of food. At first I could hardly walk, so strange and out of joint were all my limbs; and my voice – it was that of the fiend. But I kept silent, and turned my face to the sun, that I might not see my shadow, and counted the hours, and ruminated on my future conduct. To bring Torella to my feet – to possess my Juliet in spite of him – all this my wealth could easily achieve. During dark night I slept, and dreamt of the accomplishment of my desires. Two suns had set – the third dawned. I was agitated, fearful. Oh expectation, what a frightful thing art thou, when kindled more by fear than hope! How dost thou twist thyself round the heart, torturing its pulsations! How dost thou dart unknown pangs all through our feeble mechanism, now giving us a fresh strength, which can *do* nothing, and so torments us by a sensation, such as the strong man must feel who cannot break his fetters, though they bend in his grasp. Slowly paced the bright, bright orb up the eastern sky; long it lingered in the zenith, and still more slowly wandered down the west: it touched the horizon's verge – it was lost! Its glories were on the summits of the cliff – they grew dun and grey. The evening star shone bright. He will soon be here.

He came not! – By the living heavens, he came not! – and night dragged out its weary length, and, in its decaying age, 'day began to grizzle its dark hair,' and the sun rose again on the most miserable wretch that ever upbraided its light. Three days thus I passed. The jewels and the gold – oh, how I abhorred them!

Well, well – I will not blacken these pages with demoniac ravings. All too terrible were the thoughts, the raging tumult of ideas that filled my soul. At the end of that time I slept; I had not before since the third sunset; and I dreamt that I was at Juliet's feet, and she smiled, and then she shrieked – for she saw my transformation – and again she smiled, for still her beautiful lover knelt before. But it was not I – it was he, the fiend, arrayed in my limbs, speaking with my voice, winning her with my looks of love. I strove to warn her, but my tongue refused its office; I strove to tear him from her, but I was rooted to the ground – I awoke with the agony. There were the solitary hoar precipices – there the splashing sea, the quiet strand, and the blue sky over all. What did it mean? Was my dream but a mirror of the truth? Was he wooing and winning my betrothed? I would on the instant back to Genoa – but I was banished. I laughed – the dwarf's yell burst from my lips – *I* banished! Oh, no! they had not exiled the foul limbs I wore; I might with these enter, without fear of incurring the threatened penalty of death, my own, my native city.

I began to walk towards Genoa. I was somewhat accustomed to my distorted limbs; none were ever so ill adapted for a straight-forward movement; it was with infinite difficulty that I proceeded. Then, too, I desired to avoid all the hamlets strewed here and there on the sea-beach, for I was unwilling to make a display of my hideousness. I was not quite sure that, if seen, the mere boys would not stone me to death as I passed, for a monster: some ungentle salutations I did receive from the few peasants or fishermen I chanced to meet. But it was dark night before I approached Genoa. The weather was so balmy and sweet that it struck me that the Marchese and his daughter would very probably have quitted the city for their county retreat. It was from Villa Torella that I had attempted to carry off Juliet; I had spent many an hour reconnoitring the spot, and knew every inch of ground in its vicinity. It was beautifully situated, embosomed in trees, on the margin of a stream. As I drew near, it became evident that my conjecture was right nay, moreover, that the hours were being then devoted to feasting and merriment. For the house was lighted up; strains of soft and gay music were wafted towards me by the breeze. My heart sank within me. Such was the generous kindness of Torella's heart that I felt sure that he would not have indulged in public manifestations of rejoicing just after my unfortunate banishment, but for a cause I dared not dwell upon.

The county people were all alive and flocking about it; it became necessary that I should study to conceal myself; and yet I longed to address some one, or to hear others discourse, or in any way to gain intelligence of what was really going on. At length, entering the walks that were in immediate vicinity to the mansion, I found one dark enough to veil my excessive frightfulness; and yet others as well as I were loitering in its shade. I soon gathered all I wanted to know – all that first made my very heart die with horror, and then boil with indignation. To-morrow Juliet was to be given to the penitent, reformed, beloved Guido – to-morrow my bride was to pledge her vows to a fiend from hell! And I did this! – my accursed pride – my demoniac violence and wicked self-idolatry had caused this act. For if I had acted as the wretch who had stolen my form had acted – if, with a mien at once yielding and dignified, I had presented myself to Torella, saying, I have done wrong, forgive me; I am unworthy of your angel-child, but permit me to claim her hereafter, when my altered conduct shall manifest that I abjure my vices, and endeavour to become in some sort worthy of her. I go to serve against the infidels; and when my zeal for religion and my true penitence for the past shall appear to you to cancel my crimes, permit me again to call myself your son. Thus had he spoken; and the penitent was welcomed even as the prodigal son of scripture: the fatted calf was killed for him; and he, still pursuing the same path, displayed such open-hearted regret for his follies, so humble a concession of all his rights, and so ardent a resolve to reacquire them by a life of contrition and virtue, that he quickly conquered the kind, old man; and full pardon, and the gift of his lovely child, followed in swift succession.

O! had an angel from Paradise whispered to me to act thus! But now, what would be the innocent Juliet's fate? Would God permit the foul union – or, some prodigy destroying it, link the dishonoured name of Carega with the worst of crimes? Tomorrow at dawn they were to be married: there was but one way to prevent this – to meet mine enemy, and to enforce the ratification of our agreement. I felt that this could only be done by a mortal struggle. I had no sword – if indeed my distorted arms could wield a soldier's weapon – but I had a dagger, and in that lay my every hope. There was no time for pondering or balancing nicely the question: I might die in the attempt; but besides the burning jealousy and despair of my own heart, honour, mere humanity, demanded that I should fall rather than not destroy the machinations of the fiend.

The guests departed – the lights began to disappear; it was evident that the inhabitants of the villa were seeking repose. I hid myself among the trees – the garden grew desert – the gates were closed – I wandered round and came under a window – ah! Well did I know the same! – a soft twilight glimmered in the room – the curtains were half withdrawn. It was the temple of innocence and beauty. Its magnificence was tempered, as it were, by the slight disarrangements occasioned by its being dwelt in, and all the objects scattered around displayed the taste of her who hallowed it by her presence. I saw her approach the window – she drew back the curtain yet further, and looked out into the night. Its breezy freshness played among her ringlets, and wafted them from the transparent marble of her brow. She clasped her hands, she raised her eyes to Heaven. I heard her voice. Guido! She softly murmured, Mine own Guido! and then, as if overcome by the fullness of her own heart, she sank on her knees: – her upraised eyes – her negligent but graceful attitude – the beaming thankfulness that lighted up her face – oh, these are tame words!

Heart of mine, thou imagest ever, though thou canst not portray, the celestial beauty of that child of light and love.

I heard a step – a quick firm step along the shady avenue. Soon I saw a cavalier, richly dressed, young and, methought, graceful to look on, advance. – I hid myself yet closer. – The youth approached; he paused beneath the window. She arose, and again looking out she saw him, and said – I cannot, no, at this distant time I cannot record her terms of soft silver tenderness; to me they were spoken, but they were replied to by him.

'I will not go,' he cried: 'here where you have been, where your memory glides like some Heaven-visiting ghost, I will pass the long hours till we meet, never, my Juliet, again, day or night, to part. But do thou, my love, retire; the cold morn and fitful breeze will make thy cheek pale, and fill with languor thy love-lighted eyes. Ah, sweetest! Could I press one kiss upon them, I could, methinks, repose.'

And then he approached still nearer, and methought he was about to clamber into her chamber. I had hesitated, not to terrify her; now I was no longer master of myself. I rushed forward – I threw myself on him – I tore him away – I cried, 'O loathsome and foul-shaped wretch!'

I need not repeat epithets, all tending, as it appeared, to rail at a person I at present feel some partiality for. A shriek rose from Juliet's lips. I neither heard nor saw – I *felt* only mine enemy, whose throat I grasped, and my dagger's hilt; he struggled, but could not escape: at length hoarsely he breathed these words: 'Do! – strike home! Destroy this body – you will still live: may your life be long and merry!'

The descending dagger was arrested at the word, and he, feeling my hold relax, extricated himself and drew his sword, while the uproar in the house, and flying of torches from one room to the other, showed that soon we should be separated – and I – oh! Far better die: so that he did not survive, I cared not. In the midst of my frenzy there was much calculation: – fall I might, and so that he did not survive I cared not for the death-blow I might deal again myself. While still, therefore, he thought I paused, and while I saw the villainous resolve to take advantage of my hesitation, in the sudden thrust he made at me, I threw myself on his sword, and at the same moment plunged my dagger, with a true desperate aim, in his side. We fell together, rolling over each other, and the tide of blood that flowed from the gaping wound of each mingled on the grass. More I know not – I fainted.

Again I returned to life: weak almost to death, I found myself stretched upon a bed – Juliet was kneeling beside it. Strange! My first broken request was for a mirror. I was so wan and ghastly, that my poor girl hesitated, as she told me afterwards; but, by the mass! I thought myself a right proper youth when I saw the dear reflection of my own well-known features. I confess it is a weakness, but I avow it, I do entertain a considerable affection for the countenance and limbs I behold, whenever I look at a glass; and have more mirrors in my hours, and consult them oftener than any beauty in Venice. Before you too much condemn me, permit me to say that no one better knows than I the value of his own body; no one, probably, except myself, ever having had it stolen from him.

Incoherently I at first talked of the dwarf and his crimes, and reproached Juliet for her too easy admission of his love. She thought me raving, as well she might, and yet it was some time before I could prevail on myself to admit that the Guido whose penitence had won her back for me was myself: and while I cursed bitterly the monstrous dwarf, and blest the well-directed blow that had deprived him of life, I suddenly checked myself when I heard her say – Amen! knowing that him whom she reviled was my very self. A little reflection taught me silence – a little practice enabled me to speak of that frightful night without any very excessive blunder. The wound I had given myself was no mockery of one – it was long before I recovered – and as the benevolent and generous Torella sat besides me, talking such wisdom as might win friends to repentance, and mine own dear Juliet hovered near me, administering to my wants, and cheering me by her smiles, the work of my bodily cure and mental reform went on together. I have never, indeed, wholly recovered my strength – my cheek is paler since – my person a little bent. Juliet sometimes ventures to allude bitterly to the malice that caused this change, but I kiss her on the moment, and tell her all is for the best. I am a fonder and more faithful husband – and true is this – but for that wound, never had I called her mine.

I do not revisit the sea-shore, nor seek for the fiend's treasure; yet, while I ponder on the past, I often think, and my confessor was not backward in favouring the idea, that it might be a good rather than an evil spirit, sent by my guardian angel, to show me the folly and misery of pride. So well at least did I learn this lesson, roughly taught as I was, that I am known now by all my friends and fellow-citizens by the name of Guido il Cortese.

The Tell-Tale Heart

Edgar Allan Poe

True! – nervous – very, very dreadfully nervous I had been and am; but why *will* you say that I am mad? The disease had sharpened my senses – not destroyed – not dulled them. Above all was the sense of hearing acute. I heard all things in the heaven and in the earth. I heard many things in hell. How, then, am I mad? Hearken! And observe how healthily – how calmly I can tell you the whole story.

It is impossible to say how first the idea entered my brain; but once conceived, it haunted me day and night. Object there was none. Passion there was none. I loved the old man. He had never wronged me. He had never given me insult. For his gold I had no desire. I think it was his eye! Yes! It was this! One of his eyes resembled that of a vulture – a pale blue eye with a film over it. Whenever it fell upon me, my blood ran cold; and so by degrees – very gradually – I made up my mind to take the life of the old man, and thus rid myself of the eye for ever.

Now this is the point. You fancy me mad. Madmen know nothing. But you should have seen *me*. You should have seen how wisely I proceeded – with what caution – with what foresight – with what dissimulation I went to work! I was never kinder to the old man than during the whole week before I killed him. And every night, about midnight, I turned the latch of his door and opened it – oh, so gently! And then, when I had made an opening sufficient for my head, I put in a dark lantern, all closed, closed, so that no light shone out, and then I thrust in my head. Oh, you would have laughed to see how cunningly I thrust it in! I moved it slowly – very slowly, so that

I might not disturb the old man's sleep. It took me an hour to place my whole head within the opening so far that I could see him as lay upon his bed. Ha! – would a madman have been so wise as this? And then, when my head was well in the room, I undid the lantern, cautiously – oh, so cautiously – cautiously (for the hinges creaked) I undid it just so much that a single thin ray fell upon the vulture eye. And this I did for seven long nights – every night just at midnight – but I found the eye was always closed; and so it was impossible to do the work; for it was not the old man who vexed me, but his Evil Eye. And every morning, when the day broke, I went boldly into the chamber, and spoke courageously to him, calling him by name in a hearty tone, and inquiring how he had passed the night. So you see he would have been a very profound old man, indeed, to suspect that every night, just at twelve, I looked in upon him while he slept.

Upon the eighth night I was more than usually cautious in opening the door. A watch's minute hand moves more quickly than did mine. Never before that night had I *felt* the extent of my own powers – of my sagacity. I could scarcely contain my feelings of triumph. To think that there I was, opening the door, little by little, and he not even to dream of my secret deeds or thoughts. I fairly chuckled at the idea; and perhaps he heard me – for he moved on the bed suddenly, as if startled. Now you may think that I drew back – but no. His room was as black as pitch with the thick darkness (for the shutters were close-fastened, through fear of robbers), and so I knew that he could not see the opening of the door, and I kept pushing it on steadily, steadily.

I had my head in, and was about to open the lantern, when my thumb slipped upon the tin fastening, and the old man sprang up in the bed, crying out, 'Who's there?'

I kept quite still and said nothing. For a whole hour I did not move a muscle, and in the meantime I did not hear him lie down. He was still sitting up in the bed, listening – just as I have done, night after night, hearkening to the death-watches in the wall.

Presently I heard a groan, and I knew it was the groan of mortal terror. It was not a groan of pain or of grief – oh, no! – it was the low stifled sound that arises from the bottom of the soul when overcharged with awe. I knew the sound well. Many a night, just at midnight, when all the world slept, it has welled up, from my own bosom, deepening with its dreadful echo, the terrors that distracted me. I say I knew it well. I knew what the old man felt, and pitied him, although I chuckled at heart. I knew that he had been awake ever since the first slight noise, when he had turned in the bed. His fears had been ever since growing upon him. He had been trying to fancy them causeless, but could not. He had been saying to himself, 'It is nothing but the wind in the chimney – it is only a mouse crossing the floor,' or, 'It is merely a cricket which has made a single chirp.' Yes, he had been trying to comfort himself with these suppositions; but he had found all in vain. *All in vain*; because Death, in approaching him, had stalked with his black shadow before him, and enveloped the victim. And it was the mournful influence of the unperceived shadow that caused him to feel – although he neither saw nor heard – to *feel* the presence of my head within the room.

When I had waited a long time, very patiently, without hearing him lie down, I resolved to open a little – a very, very little crevice in the lantern. So I opened it – you cannot imagine how stealthily, stealthily – until, at length, a single dim ray, like the thread of the spider, shot from out the crevice and fell upon the vulture eye.

It was open – wide, wide open – and I grew furious as I gazed upon it. I saw it with perfect distinctness – all a dull blue, with a hideous veil over it that chilled the very marrow in my bones; but I could see nothing else of the old man's face or person, for I had directed the ray, as if by instinct, precisely upon the damned spot.

And now have I not told you that what you mistake for madness is but over-acuteness of the senses? – now, I say, there came to my ears a low, dull, quick sound, such as a water makes when enveloped in cotton. I knew *that* sound, well, too. It was the beating of the old man's heart. It increased my fury, as the beating of a drum stimulates the soldier into courage.

But even yet I refrained and kept still. I scarcely breathed. I held the lantern motionless. I tried how steadily I could maintain the ray upon the eye. Meantime the hellish tattoo of the heart increased. It grew quicker and quicker, and louder and louder every instant. The old man's terror *must* have been extreme! It grew louder, I say, louder every moment! – do you mark me well? I have told you that I am nervous: so I am. And now, at the dead hour of the night, amid the dreadful silence of that old house, so strange a noise as this excited me to uncontrollable terror. Yet, for some minutes longer, I refrained and stood still. But the beating grew louder, louder! I thought the heart must burst. And now a new anxiety seized me – the sound would be heard by a neighbour! The old man's hour had come! With a loud yell I threw open the lantern and leaped into the room. He shrieked once – once only. In an instant I dragged him to the floor, and pulled the heavy bed over him. I then smiled gaily, to find the deed so far done. But, for many minutes, the heart beat on with a muffled sound. This, however, did not vex me; it would not be heard through the wall. At length it ceased. The old man was dead. I removed the bed and examined the corpse. Yes, he was stone, stone dead. I placed my hand upon the heart and held it there many minutes. There was no pulsation. He was stone dead. His eye would trouble me no more.

If still you think me mad, you will think so no longer when I describe the wise precautions I took for the concealment of the body. The night waned, and I worked hastily, but in silence. First of all I dismembered the corpse. I cut off the head and the arms and the legs.

I then took up three planks from the flooring of the chamber and deposited all between the scantlings. I then replaced the boards so cleverly, so cunningly, that no human eye – not even *his* – could have detected anything wrong. There was nothing to wash out – no stain of any kind – no blood-spot whatever. I had been too wary for that. A tub had caught it all – ha! ha!

When I had made an end of these labours, it was four o'clock – still dark as midnight. As the bell sounded the hour, there came a knocking at the street door. I went down to open it with a light heart – for what had I *now* to fear? There entered three men, who introduced themselves, with perfect suavity, as officers of the police. A shriek had been heard by a neighbour during the night; suspicion of foul play had been aroused; information had been lodged at the police office, and they (the officers) had been deputed to search the premises.

I smiled – for *what* had I to fear? I bade the gentlemen welcome. The shriek, I said, was my own in a dream. The old man, I mentioned, was absent in the country. I took my visitors all over the house. I bade them search – search *well*. I led them, at length, to his chamber. I showed them his treasures, secure, undisturbed. In the enthusiasm of my confidence, I brought chairs into the room, and desired them *here* to rest from their fatigues, while I myself, in the wild audacity of my perfect triumph, placed my own seat upon the very spot beneath which reposed the corpse of the victim.

The officers were satisfied. My manner had convinced them. I was singularly at ease. They sat, and while I answered cheerily, they chatted of familiar things. But, ere long, I felt myself getting pale and wished them gone. My head ached, and I fancied a ringing in my ears; but still they sat and still chatted. The ringing became more distinct – it continued and became more distinct. I talked more freely to get rid of the feeling; but it continued and gained definitiveness – until, at length, I found that the noise was not within my ears.

No doubt I now grew very pale; but I talked more fluently, and with a heightened voice. Yet the sound increased – and what could I do? It was a *low, dull, quick sound* – much such a sound as a watch makes when enveloped in cotton. I gasped for breath – and yet the officers heard it not. I talked more quickly – more vehemently; but the noise steadily increased. I arose and argued about trifles, in a high key and with violent gesticulations; but the noise steadily increased. Why *would* they not be gone? I paced the floor to and fro with heavy strides, as if excited to fury by the observations of the men – but the noise steadily increased. O God! What *could* I do? I foamed – I raved – I swore! I swung the chair upon the boards, but the noise arose over all and continually increased. It grew louder – louder – *louder*! And still the men chatted pleasantly, and smiled. Was it possible they heard not? Almighty God! – no, no! They heard! – they suspected! – they *knew*! – they were making a mockery of my horror! – this I thought, and this I think. But anything was better than this agony! Anything was more tolerable than this derision! I could bear those hypocritical smiles no longer! I felt that I must scream or die! – and now – again! Hark! louder! louder! louder! *louder*! –

'Villains!' I shrieked, 'dissemble no more! I admit the deed! – tear up the planks! – here, here! – it is the beating of his hideous heart!'

Some Terrible Letters from Scotland

James Hogg

Dear Sir, – As I knew you once, and think you will remember me, – I having wrought on your farm for some months with William Colins that summer that Burke was hanged, – I am going to write you on a great and trying misfortune that has befallen to myself, and hope you will publish it, before you leave London for the benefit of all those concerned.

You must know that I have served the last three years with Mr. Kemp, miller, of Troughlin and my post was to drive two carts, sometimes with corn to Dalkeith market, and sometimes with flourmeal to all the bakers in Musselburgh and the towns round about. I did not like this very well; for I often thought to myself, if I should take that terrible Cholera Morbus, what was to become of me, as I had no home to go to, and nobody would let me within their door. This constant fright did me ill, for it gave my constitution a shake: and I noticed, whenever I looked in my little shaving-glass, that my face was grown shilpit and white, and blue about the mouth; and I grew more frightened than ever.

Well, there was one day that I was at Musselburgh with flour; and when I was there the burials were going by me as thick as droves of Highland cattle; and I thought I sometimes felt a saur as if the air had thickened around my face. It is all over with me now, thought I, for I have breathed the Cholera! But when I told this to Davison, the baker's man, he only laughed at me, which was very ungracious and cruel in him; for before I got home I felt myself manifestly affected, and knew not what to do.

When I came into the kitchen, there was none in it but Mary Douglas: she was my sweetheart like, and we had settled to be married. 'Mary, I am not well at all tonight,' said I, 'and I am afraid I am taking that deadly Cholera Morbus.'

'I hope in God that is not the case!' said Mary, letting the tongs fall out of her hand; 'but we are all in the Almighty's hands, and he may do with us as seemeth good in his sight.'

She had not well repeated this sweet, pious submission, before I fell a-retching most terribly, and the pains within were much the same as if you had thrust seven or eight red-hot pokers through my stomach. 'Mary, I am very ill,' said I, 'and I well know Mr. Kemp will not let me abide here.'

'Nay, that he will not,' said she; 'for he has not dared to come in contact with you for weeks past; but, rather than you should be hurried off to an hospital, if you think you could walk to my mother's, I will go with you, to assist you.'

'Alas! I cannot walk a step at present,' said I: 'but the horses are both standing yoked in the carts at the stable-door, as I was unable to loose them.' In a few minutes she had me in a cart, and drove me to her mother's cot, where I was put to bed, and continued to be very ill. There was never any trouble in this world like it: to be roasted in a fire, or chipped all to pieces with a butcher's knife, is nothing to it. Mary soon had a doctor at me, who bled me terribly, as if I had been a bullock, and gave me great doses of something, which I suppose was laudanum; but neither of them did me any good: I grew worse and worse, and wished heartedly that I were dead.

But now the rest of the adjoining cotters rose in a body, and insisted on turning me out. Is it not strange, Sir, that this most horrible of all pestilences should deprive others, not only of natural feeling, but of reason? I could make no resistance although they had flung me over the dunghill, as they threatened to do; but the two women acted with great decision, and dared them to touch me or any one in their house. They needed not have been so frightened; for no one durst have touched me more than if I had been an adder or a snake. Mary, and her mother, old Margaret, did all they could for me: they bathed the pit of my stomach with warm camomile, and rubbed my limbs and hands with hard cloths, shedding many tears over me; but the chillness of death had settled on my limbs and arms, and all the blood in my body had retreated to its conquered citadel; and a little before daylight I died.

For fear of burying me alive, and for fear of any violence being done to my body by the affrighted neighbours, the two women concealed my death; but poor Mary took the sheets, which had been bought for her bridal bed, and made them into dead-clothes for me; and in the afternoon the doctor arrived, and gave charges that I should be coffined and buried without loss of time. At this order, Mary wept abundantly, but there was no alternative; for the doctor ordered a coffin to be made with all expedition at the wright's, as he went by, and carried the news through the parish, that poor Andrew, the miller's man, had died of a most malignant Cholera.

The next morning very early, Johnie, the elder, came up with the coffin, his nose plugged with tobacco, and his mouth having a strong smell of whisky; and, in spite of Mary's entreaties, nailed me in the coffin. Now, Sir, this was quite terrible; for all the while I had a sort of half-consciousness of what was going on, yet had not power to move a muscle of my whole frame. I was certain that my soul had not departed quite away, although my body was seized with this sudden torpor, and refused to act. It was a sort of dream, out of which I was struggling to awake, but could not; and I felt as if a fall on the floor, or a sudden jerk of any kind, would once more set my blood a-flowing, and restore animation. I heard my beloved Mary Douglas weeping and lamenting over me, and expressing a wish that, if it were not for the dreadfulness of the distemper, that she had shared my fate. I felt her putting the robes of death on me, and tying the napkin round my face; and, O, how my spirit longed to embrace and comfort her! I had great hopes that the joiner's hammer would awake me; but he only used it very slightly, and wrought with an inefficient screw-driver: yet I have an impression that if any human eye had then seen them, I should have been shivering; for the dread of being buried alive, and struggling to death in a deep grave below the mould, was awful in the extreme!

The wright was no sooner fairly gone, than Mary unscrewed the lid, and took it half off, letting it lie along the coffin on one side. O, how I wished that she would tumble me out on the floor, or dash a pail of water on me! But she did neither, and there I lay, still a sensitive corpse. I determined, however, to make one desperate effort, before they got me laid into the grave.

But between those who are bound together by the sacred ties of love, there is, I believe, a sort of electrical sympathy even in a state of insensibility. At the still hour of midnight, as Mary and her mother were sitting reading a chapter of the New Testament, my beloved all at once uttered a piercing shriek, – her mother having fallen down motionless, and apparently lifeless. That heart-rending shriek awakened me from the sleep of death! – I sat up in the coffin, and the lid rattled on the floor. Was there ever such a scene in a cottage at midnight? I think never in this island. Mary shrieked again, and fainted, falling down motionless across her mother's feet. These shrieks, which were hardly earthly, brought in John Brunton and John Sword, who came rushing forward toward the women, to render them some assistance; but when they looked towards the bed, and saw me sitting in my winding-sheet, struggling in the coffin, they simultaneously uttered a howl of distraction and betook them to their heels. Brunton fainted, and fell over the threshold, where he lay groaning till trailed away by his neighbour.

My ankles and knees being tied together with tapes, and my wrists bound to my sides, which you know is the custom here, I could not for a while get them extricated, to remove the napkin from my face, and must have presented a very awful appearance to the two men. Debilitated as I was, I struggled on, and in my efforts overturned the coffin, and, falling down upon the floor, my face struck the flags, which stunned me, and my nose gushed out blood abundantly. I was still helpless; and when the two women began to recover, there was I lying wallowing and struggling in my bloody sheet. I wonder that my poor Mary did not lose her reason that night; and I am sure she would, had she not received supernatural strength of mind from Heaven. On recovering from her swoon, she ran out, and called at every door and window in the hamlet; but not one would enter the cottage of the plague. Before she got me divested of my stained grave-clothes and put to bed, her mother was writhing in the Cholera, her mild countenance changed into the appearance of withered clay, and her hands and feet as if they had been boiled. It is amazing that the people of London should mock at the fears of their brethren for this terrible and anomalous plague; for though it begins with the hues and horrors of death, it is far more frightful than death itself; and it is impossible for any family or community to be too much on their guard against its baleful influence. Old Margaret died at nine next morning; and what could I think but that I had been her murderer, having brought infection to her homely and healthy dwelling? And the calamity will hang as a weight on my heart for ever. She was put into my coffin, and hurried away to interment; and I had no doubt that she would come alive again below the earth; – but the supposition is too horrible to cherish!

For my part, as far as I can remember, I did not suffer any more pain, but then I felt as if I had been pounded in a mill, – powerless, selfish, and insensible. I could not have remembered aught of the funeral, had it not been that my Mary wept incessantly, and begged of the people that they would suffer the body of her parent to remain in the house for one night; but they would not listen to her, saying that they dared not disobey the general order, and even for her own sake it was necessary the body should be removed.

Our cottage stood in the middle of a long row of labourers'

houses, all of the same description; and the day after the funeral of old Margaret, there were three people in the cottage next to ours seized with distemper, and one of them died. It went through every one of the cottages in that direction, but all those in the other end of the row escaped. On the Monday of the following week my poor Mary fell down in it, having, like myself and her mother, been seized with it in its worst form; and in a little time her visage and proportions were so completely changed, that I could not believe they were those of my beloved. I for a long time foolishly imagined that she was removed from me, and a demon had taken her place; but reason at length resumed her sway and convinced me of my error. There was no one to wait on or assist Mary but me, and I was so feeble that I could not do her justice: I did all that I was able, however; and the doctor gave me hopes that she would recover. She soon grew so ill, and her pangs, writhings, and contortions, became so terrible, that I wished her dead: – yes, I prayed that death would come and release her! But it was from a conviction that she would revive again, and that I should be able to wake her from the sleep of death. I did not conceive my own revival as any thing supernatural, but that which might occur to every one who was suddenly cut off by the plague of Cholera; and I prayed that my dear woman would die. She remained quite sensible; and, taking my hand, she squeezed it and said, 'Do you really wish me dead, Andrew?' I could make no reply; but she continued to hold my hand, and added, 'Then you will not need to wish for it long. O Lord, thy will be done in earth as it is in heaven!'

She repeated this last sentence in a whisper, and spoke no more, for the icy chillness had by this time reached the region of the heart; and she expired as in a drowsy slumber. Having no doubts of her revival I did not give the alarm of her death, but continued my exertions to restore animation. When the doctor arrived he was wroth with me, and laughed me to scorn, ordering the body to be directly laid out by matrons, preparatory for the funeral; and that night he sent two hired nurses for the purpose. They performed their task; but I would in no wise suffer the body to be coffined after what had happened to myself, until I saw the farthest. I watched her night and day, continuing my efforts to the annoyance of my neighbours until the third day, and then they would allow it no longer; but, despite all my entreaties, they took my beloved from me, nailed her in the coffin, and buried her; and now I am deprived of all I loved and valued in this world, and my existence is a burden I cannot bear, as I must always consider myself accessory to the deaths of those two valuable women.

The worst thing of all to suffer is the dreadful apprehension that they would come alive again below the earth, which I cannot get quit of; and though I tried to watch Mary's grave, I was so feeble and far-spent, that I could not but always fall asleep on it. There being funerals coming every day, when the people saw me lying on the grave with my spade beside me, they, half by force, took me away; but no one offered me an asylum in his house, for they called me the man that was dead and risen again, and shunned me as a being scarcely of this earth.

Still the thought that Mary would come alive haunts me, – a terror which has probably been engendered within me by the circumstances attending my own singular resuscitation. And even so late as the second night after her decease, as I was watching over her with prayers and tears, I heard a slight gurgling in her throat, as if she had been going to speak; there was also, I thought, a movement about the breast, and one of the veins of the neck started three or four times. How my heart leaped for joy as I breathed my warm breath into her cold lips! But movement there was no more. And now, Sir, if you publish this letter, let it be with an admonition for people to be on their guard when their friends are suddenly cut off by this most frightful of all diseases, for it is no joke to be buried alive.

I have likewise heard it stated, that one boy fell a-kicking the coffin on his way to the grave, who is still living and lifelike, and that a girl, as the doctors were cutting her up, threw herself off the table. I cannot vouch for the truth of these singular and cruel incidents, although I heard them related as facts; but with regard to my own case there can be no dispute.

It does a great deal of ill to the constitution to be too frightened for this scourge of God; but temerity is madness, and caution prudence: for this may be depended on, that it is as infectious as fire. But then, when fire is set to the mountain, it is only such parts of its surface as are covered with decayed garbage that is combustible, while over the green and healthy parts of the mountain the flame has no power; and any other reasoning than this is worse than insanity.

For my part, I have been very hardly used, there having been few harder cases than my own. In Lothian every one shunned me; and the constables stopped me on the road, and would not even suffer me to leave the county, – the terror of infection is so great. So dreadful are the impressions of fear on some minds, that it has caused a number of people in Scotland and England to hang themselves, or otherwise deprive themselves of life, as the only sure way of escaping its agonies.

Finding myself without a home and without employment, I made my escape over the tops of the Lammermuirs, keeping out of sight of any public road, and by that means escaped into Teviotdale, where I changed my name to Ker, and am now working at day-labour in the town of Roxburgh, and on the farms around; and though my name was Clapperton when I wrought with you, I must now sign myself your humble servant,

Andrew Ker

(The next is in some degree different, though likewise narrating very grievous circumstances. It is written by the mate of The Jane Hamilton of Port Glasgow.)

Sir, – I now sit down to give you the dismal account of the arrival of the Cholera in the west of Scotland. I sent it a month ago to a friend in London, to put into the newspapers, but it never appeared; so if you think it worth while, you may publish it. But if there be any paper or periodical that Campbell or Galt is connected with, I would rather it were sent to one of them, as they are both acquaintances and old schoolfellows, and will remember me very well.

Well then, Sir, you must know that in our passage from Riga to Liverpool, in January, we were attacked by very squally weather off the western coast of Scotland, and were obliged to put into one of those interminable narrow bays denominated lochs, in Argyleshire, where we cast anchor on very bad ground.

I cannot aver that our ship was perfectly clean, for we lost one fine old fellow by the way, and several others were very bad; so I was sent off to a mining or fishing village, to procure some medicine and fresh meat. Our captain had an immensely large black Newfoundland dog, whose name was Oakum, and who always attached himself to me, and followed me; but that day he chanced not to go ashore with me. Some time afterwards, some of the sailors going on shore to play themselves, Oakum went with them, and coming on the scent of my track he followed it. Now the natives had some way heard that the Cholera was come with the ship; but so little did they conceive what it was, that they were nothing afraid of coming in contact with me.

The village grocer, draper, hatter, and apothecary, had no medicines on hand, save Glauber's salts, and of these he had two corn-sacks full. I bought some; and while I was standing and bargaining about the price of a pig, I beheld a terrible commotion in the village: the men were stripped, and running after them, some of them having a child on their backs, and one below each arm, while the Gaelic was poured and shouted from every tongue. 'What is it? What in the world is it?' said I to the merchant, who had a little broken English. 'Oh, she pe tat tam bhaist te Collara Mòr,' said he; and away he ran with the rest.

It so happened that one Donald M'Coll was going down the coast on some errand, and meeting with Oakum with his broad gilded collar about his neck, he instantly knew who he was; and, alarmed beyond expression, he took to his heels, threw off his coat and bonnet and ran, giving the alarm all the way as he went; and men, women, and children, betook them to flight into the recesses of the mountains, where they lay peeping over the rocks and the heath, watching the progress of this destroying angel.

Honest Oakum was all the while chopping out of one cottage into another, enjoying the scraps exceedingly, which people had left behind them in their haste. Yea, so well satisfied was he with his adventure, that he did not return until after dark, so that the Highlanders did not know he had returned at all. The people had not returned to their houses when we came away.

But the most singular circumstances is yet to relate. On our return to the Clyde from Liverpool, where we rode quarantine, we learnt that the Cholera Morbus had actually broken out in that village, – at least a most inveterate diarrhoea, accompanied with excessive pains and vomiting, which carried off a number of the inhabitants; but, the glen being greatly overstocked, they were not much missed. Such a thing as Cholera Morbus or sending for a doctor never entered their heads, but a terrible consumption of the merchant's Glauber's salts ensued; and when no more could be done for their friends, they buried them, and then there was no more about it. Whether the disease was communicated to them by the dog, by myself, by the fright, or the heat they got in running, I cannot determine; but it is certain the place suffered severely. They themselves alleged as the cause, their having 'peen raiter, and te raiter too heafy on te herring and pothato.' It was from thence that the disease was communicated to Kirkintilloch by a single individual. Oakum continues in perfect health; but was obliged to undergo fumigation and a bath, by way of quarantine, which he took highly amiss.

I am, Sir, your obedient servant,

Alexander M'Alister

(The next is the most hideous letter of all. We wish the writer may be quite in his right mind. But save in a little improvement in the orthography and grammar, we shall give it in his own words.)

Sir, – Although I sent the following narrative to an Edinburgh newspaper, with the editor of which I was well acquainted; yet he refused to give it publicity, on the ground that it was only a dream of the imagination: but if a man cannot be believed in what he hears and sees, what is he to be believed in? Therefore, as I am told that you have great influence with the printers in London, I will thank you to get this printed; and if you can get me a trifle for it, so much the better.

I am a poor journeyman tradesman in the town of Fisherrow, and I always boarded with my mother and two sisters, who were all in the trade; but my mother was rather fond of gossiping and visiting, and liked to get a dram now and then. So when that awful plague of Cholera came on us for the punishment of our sins, my mother would be running to every one that was affected; and people were very glad of her assistance, and would be giving drams and little presents; and for all that my sisters and I could say to her, she would not be hindered.

'Mother,' said I to her, one night, 'gin ye winna leave aff rinning to infectit houses this gate, I'll be obliged to gang away an' leave ye an' shift for mysel' some gate else; an' my sisters shall gang away an' leave ye too. Do ye no consider, that ye are exposing the whole o' your family to the most terrible of deaths; an' if ye should bring infection among us, an' lose us a', how will ye answer to God for it?'

'Hout, Jamie, my man, ye make aye sic a wark about naething!' quoth she; 'I am sure ye ken an' believe that we are a' in our Maker's hand, and that he can defend us frae destruction that walketh at noonday, and from the pestilence that stealeth in by night?'

'I allow that, mother,' quoth I; 'I dinna misbelieve in an overruling Providence. But in the present instance, you are taking up an adder, and trusting in Providence that the serpent winna sting you and yours to death.'

'Tush! Away wi' your grand similitudes, Jamie,' said she; 'ye were aye ower-learned for me. I'll tell ye what I believe. It is, that if we be to take the disease an' dee in it, we'll take the disease an' dee in it; and if it is otherwise ordained, we'll neither take it nor dee in it: for my part, I ken fu' weel that I'll no be smittit, for the wee drap drink, whilk ye ken I always take in great moderation, will keep me frae taking the infection; an' if ye keep yoursels a' tight an' clean, as ye hae done, the angel o' Egypt will still pass by your door an' hurt you not.'

'I wot weel,' said my sister Jane, 'I expect every day to be my last, for my mither will take nae body's advice but her ain. An' weel do I ken that if I take it I'll dee in it. I hae the awfu'est dreams about it! I dreamed the last night that I dee'd o' the plague, an' I thought I set my head out o' the cauld grave at midnight, an' saw the ghosts of a' the Cholera fok gaun trailing about the kirk-yard wi' their white withered faces an' their glazed een; an' I thought I crap out o' my grave an' took away my mother and brother to see them, an' I had some kind o' impression that I left Annie there behind me.'

'O! for mercy's sake, haud your tongue, lassie,' cried Annie; 'I declare ye gar a' my flesh creep to hear you. It is nae that I'm only feared for death in ony other way but that. But the fearsome an' loathsome sufferings, an' the fearsome looks gars a' ane's heart grue to think o'. An' yet our mither rins the hale day frae ane to anither, and seems to take a pleasure in witnessing their cries, their writhings, and contortions. I wonder what kind o' heart she has, but it fears me it canna be a right ane.'

My poor dear sister Anne! She fell down in the Cholera the next day, and was a corpse before midnight; and, three days after, her sister followed her to the kirkyard, where their new graves rise side by side thegither among many more. To describe their sufferings is out of my power, for the thoughts of them turns me giddy, so that I lose the power of measuring time, sometimes feeling as if I had lost my sisters only as it were yesterday, and sometimes an age ago. From the moment that Annie was seized, my state of mind has been deplorable: I expected every hour to fall a victim to it myself: but as for mother, she bustled about as if it had been some great event in which it behoved her to make an imposing figure. She scolded the surgeon, the officers of the Board of Health, and even the poor dying girls, for their unhealthy looks and cries. 'Ye hae muckle to cry for,' cried she; 'afore ye come through what I hae done in life, ye'll hae mair to cry for nor a bit cramp i' the stomach.'

When they both died she was rather taken short, and expressed herself as if she weened that she had not been fairly dealt with by Providence, considering how much she had done for others; but she had that sort of nature in her that nothing could daunt or dismay, and continued her course – running to visit every Cholera patient within her reach, and going out and coming in at all times of the night.

After nine or ten days, there was one Sabbath night that I was awoke by voices which I thought I knew; and on looking over the bed, I saw my two sisters sitting one on each side of my mother, conversing with her, while she was looking fearfully first to the one and then to the other; but I did not understand their language, for they seemed to be talking keenly of a dance.

My sisters having both been buried in their Sunday clothes, and the rest burnt, the only impression I had was, that they had actually come alive and risen from the grave; and if I had not been naked at the time I would have flown to embrace them, for there were reports of that kind going. But when I began to speak, Jane held up her hand and shook her head at me; and I held my peace, for there was a chilness and terror came over me; yet it was not for my sisters, for they had no appearance of being ghosts: on the contrary, I thought I had never saw them look so beautiful. They continued talking of their dance with apparent fervour; and I heard one of them saying, it was a dance of death, and held in the churchyard. And as the plague of Cholera was a breath of hell, they who died of it got no rest in their graves, so that it behoved all, but parents in particular, to keep out of its influences till the vapour of death passed over.

'But now, dear mother, you must go with us and see,' said Annie.

'O, by all means!' said Jane, 'since you have introduced us into such splendid company, you must go with us, and see how we act our parts.' 'Come along, come along,' cried the both of them at the same time; and they led my mother off between them: she never spoke, but continued to fix the most hideous looks first on the one and then on the other. She was apparently under the power of resistance, but walked peaceably away between them. I cried with a tremulous voice, 'Dear, dear sisters, will you not take me with you too?' But Annie, who was next to me, said, 'No, dearest brother, lie still and sleep till your Redeemer wakes you – We will come for you again.'

I then felt the house fall a-wheeling round with me, swifter than a mill-wheel, the bed sank, and fell I knew not whither. The truth is, that I had fainted, for I remember no more until next day. As I did not go to work at my usual time, my master had sent his 'prentice-boy to inquire about me, thinking I had been attacked by Cholera. He found me insensible, lying bathed in cold sweat, and sent some of the official people to me, who soon brought me to myself. I said nothing of what I had seen; but went straight to the churchyard, persuaded that I would find my sisters' graves open, and they out of them; but, behold! They were the same as I left them, and I have never seen my mother or sisters more. I could almost have persuaded myself that I had been in a dream, had it not been for the loss of my mother; but as she has not been seen or heard of since that night, I must believe all that I saw to have been real. I know it is suspected both here and in Edinburgh, that she has been burked, as she was always running about by night; but I know what I saw, and must believe in it though I cannot comprehend it.

Yours most humbly,

James M'L–

Lost Face

Jack London

It was the end. Subienkow had travelled a long trail of bitterness and horror, homing like a dove for the capitals of Europe, and here, farther away than ever, in Russian America, the trail had ceased. He sat in the snow, arms tied behind him, waiting the torture. He stared curiously before him at a huge Cossack, prone in the snow, moaning his pain. The men had finished handling the giant and turned him over to the women. That they exceeded the fiendishness of the men the man's cries attested.

Subienkow looked on and shuddered. He was not afraid to die. He had carried his life too long in his hands, on that weary trail from Warsaw to Nulato, to shudder at mere dying. But he objected to torture. It offended his soul. And this offence, in turn, was not due to the mere pain he must endure, but to the sorry spectacle the pain would make him. He knew that he would pray, and beg, and entreat, even as Big Ivan and the others had gone before. This would not be nice. To pass out bravely and cleanly, with a smile and a jest – ah, that would have been the way. But to lose control, to have his soul upset by the pangs of the flesh, to screech and gibber like an ape, to become the veriest beast – ah, that was what was so terrible.

There had been no chance of escape. From the beginning, when he dreamed the fiery dream of Poland's independence, he had become a puppet in the hands of fate. From the beginning, at Warsaw, at St Petersburg, in the Siberian mines, in Kamchatka, on the crazy boats of the fur thieves, fate had been driving him to this end. Without doubt, in the foundations of the world was graved this end for him – for him, who was so fine and sensitive, whose nerves scarcely sheltered under his skin, who was a dreamer and a poet and an artist. Before he was dreamed of, it had been determined that the quivering bundle of sensitiveness that constituted him should be doomed to live in raw and howling savagery, and to die in this far land of night, in this dark place beyond the last boundaries of the world.

He sighed. So that thing before him was Big Ivan – Big Ivan the giant, the man without nerves, the man of iron, the Cossack turned freebooter of the seas, who was as phlegmatic as an ox, with a nervous system so low that what was pain to ordinary men was scarcely a tickle to him. Well, well, trust these Nulato Indians to find Big Ivan's nerves and trace them to the roots of his quivering soul. They were certainly doing it. it was inconceivable that a man could suffer so much and yet live. Big Ivan was paying for his low order of nerves. Already he had lasted twice as long as the others.

Subienkow felt that he could not stand the Cossack's suffering much longer. Why didn't Ivan die? He would go mad if that screaming did not cease. But when it did cease, his turn would come. And there was Yakaga awaiting him, too, grinning at him even now in anticipation – Yakaga, whom only last week he had kicked out of the fort, and upon whose face he had laid the lash of his dog whip. Yakaga would attend to him. Doubtlessly Yakaga was saving for him more refined tortures, more exquisite nerve-racking. Ah! That must have been a good one, from the way Ivan screamed. The squaws bending over him stepped back with laughter and clapping of hands. Subienkow saw the monstrous thing that had been perpetrated, and began to laugh hysterically. The Indians looked at him in wonderment that he should laugh. But Subienkow could not stop.

This would never do. He controlled himself, the spasmodic twitching slowly dying away. He strove to think of other things, and began reading back in his own life. He remembered his mother and his father, and the little spotted pony, and the French tutor who had taught him dancing and sneaked him an old worn copy of Voltaire. Once more he saw Paris, and dreary London, and gay Vienna, and Rome. And once more he saw that wild group of youths who had dreamed, even as he, the dream of an independent Poland with a king of Poland on the throne at Warsaw. Ah, there it was that the long trail had began. Well, he had lasted longest. One by one, beginning with the two executed at St Petersburg, he took up the count of the passing of those brave spirits. Here one had been beaten to death by a jailer, and there, on that bloodstained highway of the exiles, where they had marched for endless months, beaten and maltreated by their Cossack guards, another had dropped by the way. Always it had been savagery – brutal, bestial savagery. They had died – of fever, in the mines, under the knout. The last two had died after the escape, in the battle with the Cossacks, and he alone had won to Kamchatka with the stolen papers and the money of a traveller he had left lying in the snow.

It had been nothing but savagery. All the years, with his heart in studios and theatres and courts, he had been hemmed in by savagery. He had purchased his life with blood. Everybody had killed. He had killed a traveller for his passports. He had proved that he was a man of parts by duelling with two Russian officers on a single day. He had to prove himself in order to win a place among the fur thieves. He had had to win to that place. Behind him lay the thousand-years-long road across all Siberia and Russia. He could not escape that way. The only way was ahead, across the dark and icy sea of Bering to Alaska. The way had led from savagery to deeper savagery. On the scurvy-rotten ships of the fur thieves, out of food and out of water, buffeted by the interminable storms of that stormy sea, men had become animals. Thrice he had sailed east from Kamchatka. And thrice, after all manner of hardship and suffering, the survivors had come back to Kamchatka. There had been no outlet for escape, and he could not go back the way he had come, for the mines and the knout awaited him.

Again, the fourth and last time, he had sailed east. He had been with those who first found the fabled Seal Islands; but he had not returned with them to share the wealth of furs in the mad orgies of Kamchatka. He had sworn never to go back. He knew that to win to those dear capitals of Europe he must go on. So he had changed ships and remained in the dark new land. His comrades were Slavonian hunters and Russian adventurers, Mongols and Tartars and Siberian aborigines; and through the savages of the New World they had cut a path of blood. They had massacred whole villages that had refused to furnish the fur tribute; and they in turn had been massacred by ships' companies. He, with one Finn, had been the sole survivors of such a company. They had spent a winter of solitude and starvation on a lonely Aleutian isle, and their rescue in the spring by another fur ship had been one chance in a thousand.

But always the terrible savagery had hemmed him in. Passing from ship to ship, and ever refusing to return, he had come to the ship that explored south. All down the Alaskan coast they had encountered nothing but hosts of savages. Every anchorage among the beetling islands or under the frowning cliffs of the mainland had meant a battle or a storm. Either the gales blew, threatening destruction, or the war canoes came off, manned by howling natives with the war paint on their faces, who came to learn the bloody virtues of the sea rovers' gunpowder. South, south they had coasted, clear to the myth land of California. Here, it was said, were Spanish adventurers who had fought their way up from Mexico. He had had hopes of those Spanish adventurers. Escaping to them, the rest would have been easy – a year or two, what did it matter more or less? – and he would win to Mexico, then a ship, and Europe would be his. But they had met no Spaniards. Only had they encountered the same impregnable wall of savagery. The denizens of the confines of the world, painted for war, had driven them back from the shores. At last, when one boat was cut off and every man killed, the commander had abandoned the quest and sailed back to the North.

The years had passed. He had served under Tebenkoff when Michaelovski Redoubt was built. He had spent two years in the Kuskokwim country. Two summers, in the month of June, he had managed to be at the head of Kotzebue Sound. Here, at this time, the tribes assembled for barter; here were to be found spotted deerskins from Siberia, ivory from the Diomedes, walrus skins from the shores of the Artic, strange stone lamps, passing in trade from tribe to tribe, no one knew whence, and, once, a hunting knife of English make; and here, Subienkow knew, was the school in which to learn geography. For he met Eskimos from Norton Sound, from King Island and St Lawrence Island, from Cape Prince of Wales, and Point Barrow. Such places had other names, and their distances were measured in days.

It was a vast region these trading savages came from, and a vaster region from which, by repeated trade, their stone lamps and that steel knife had come. Subienkow bullied and cajoled and bribed. Every far journeyer or strange tribesman was brought before him. Perils unaccountable and unthinkable were mentioned, as well as wild beasts, hostile tribes, impenetrable forests, and mighty mountain ranges; but always from beyond came the rumour and the tale of white-skinned men, blue of eye and fair of hair, who fought like devils and who sought always for furs. They were to the east – far, far to the east. No one had seem them. It was the word that had been passed along.

It was a hard school. One could not learn geography very well through the medium of strange dialects, from dark minds that mingles fact and fable and that measured distances by 'sleeps' that varied according to the difficulty of the going. But at last came the whisper that gave Subienkow courage. In the east lay a great river where were these blue-eyed men. The river was called the Yukon. South of Michaelovski Redoubt emptied another great river which the Russians knew as the

Kwikpak. These two rivers were one, ran the whisper.

Subienkow returned to Michaelovski. For a year he urged an expedition up the Kwikpak. Then arose Malakoff, the Russian half-breed, to lead the wildest and most ferocious of the hell's broth of mongrel adventurers who had crossed from Kamchatka. Subienkow was his lieutenant. They threaded the mazes of the great delta of the Kwikpak, picked up the first low hills on the northern bank, and for half a thousand miles, in skin canoes loaded to the gunwales with trade goods and ammunition, fought their way against the five-knot current of a river that ran from two to ten miles wide in a channel many fathoms deep. Malakoff decided to build the fort at Nulato. Subienkow urged to go farther. But he quickly reconciled himself to Nulato. The long winter was coming on. It would be better to wait. Early the following summer, when the ice was gone, he would disappear up the Kwikpak and work his way to the Hudson's Bay Company's posts. Malakoff had never heard the whisper that the Kwikpak was the Yukon, and Subienkow did not tell him.

Came the building of the fort. It was enforced labour. The tiered walls of logs arose to the sighs and groans of the Nulato Indians. The lash was laid upon their backs, and it was the iron hand of the freebooters of the sea that laid on the lash. There were Indians that ran away, and when they were caught they were brought back and spread-eagled before the fort, where they and their tribe learned the efficiency of the knout. Two died under it; others were injured for life; and the rest took the lesson to heart and ran away no more. The snow was flying ere the fort was finished, and then it was the time for furs. A heavy tribute was laid upon the tribe. Blows and lashings continued, and that the tribute should be paid, the women and children were held as hostages and treated with the barbarity that only fur thieves knew.

Well, it had been a sowing of blood, and now was come the harvest. The fort was gone. In the light of its burning, half the fur thieves had been cut down. The other half had passed under the torture. Only Subienkow remained, or Subienkow and Big Ivan. Subienkow caught Yakaga grinning at him. There was no gainsaying Yakaga. The mark of the lash was still on his face. After all, Subienkow could not blame him, but he disliked the thought of what Yakaga would do to him. He thought of appealing to Makamuk, the head chief; but his judgement told him that such appeal was useless. Then, too, he thought of bursting his bonds and dying fighting. Such an end would be quick. But he could not break his bonds. Caribou thongs were stronger than he. Still devising, another thought came to him. He signed for Makamuk, and that an interpreter who knew the coast dialects should be brought.

'Oh, Makamuk,' he said, 'I am not minded to die. I am a great man, and it were foolishness for me to die. In truth, I shall not die. I am not like these other carrion.'

He looked at the moaning thing that had once been Big Ivan, and stirred it contemptuously with his toe.

'I am too wise to die. Behold, I have a great medicine. I alone know this medicine. Since I am going to die, I shall exchange this medicine with you.'

'What is this medicine?' Makumuk demanded.

'It is a strange medicine.'

Subienkow debated with himself for a moment, as if loath to part with the secret.

'I will tell you. A little bit of this medicine rubbed on the skin makes the skin hard like rock, hard as iron, so that no cutting weapon can cut it. The strongest blow of a cutting weapon is a vain thing against it. A bone knife becomes like a piece of mud; and it will turn the edge of the iron knives we have brought among you. What will you give me for the secret of the medicine?'

'I will give you your life,' Makumuk made answer through the interpreter.

Subienkow laughed scornfully.

'And you shall be a slave in my house until you die.'

The Pole laughed more scornfully.

'Untie my hands and feet and let us talk,' he said.

The chief made the sign; and when he was loosened Subienkow rolled a cigarette and lighted it.

'This is foolish talk,' said Makumuk. 'There is no such medicine. It cannot be. A cutting edge is stronger than any medicine.'

The chief was incredulous, and yet he wavered. He had seen too many deviltries of fur thieves that worked. He could not wholly doubt.

'I will give you your life; but you shall not be a slave,' he announced.

'More than that.'

Subienkow played his game coolly as if he were bartering for a fox skin.

'It is a very great medicine. It has saved my life many times. I want a sled and dogs, and six of your hunters to travel with me down the river and give me safety to one day's sleep from Michaelovski Redoubt.'

'You must live here, and teach us all of your deviltries,' was the reply.

Subienkow shrugged his shoulders and remained silent. He blew cigarette smoke out on the icy air, and curiously regarded what remained of the big Cossack.

'That scar!' Makumuk said suddenly, pointing to the Pole's neck, where a livid mark advertised the slash of a knife in a Kamchatkan brawl. 'The medicine is not good. The cutting edge was stronger than the medicine.'

'It was a strong man that drove that stroke.' (Subienkow considered.) 'Stronger than you, stronger than your strongest hunter, stronger than he.'

Again, with the toe of his moccasin, he touched the Cossack – a grisly spectacle, no longer conscious – yet in whose dismembered body the pain-racked life clung and was loath to go.

'And the medicine was weak. For at that place there were no berries of a certain kind, of which I see you have plenty in this country. The medicine here will be strong.'

'I will let you go downriver,' said Makumuk; 'and the sled and the dogs and the six hunters to give you safety shall be yours.'

'You are slow,' was the cool rejoinder. 'You have committed an offence against my medicine in that you did not at once accept my terms. Behold, I now demand more. I want one hundred beaver skins.' (Makumuk sneered.) 'I want one hundred pounds of dried fish.' (Makumuk nodded, for fish were plentiful and cheap.) 'I want two sleds – one for me and one for my furs and fish. And my rifle must be returned to me. If you do not like the price, in a little while it will grow.'

Yakaga whispered to the chief.

'But how can I know your medicine is true medicine?' Makumuk asked.

'It is very easy. First, I shall go into the woods – '

Again Yakaga whispered to Makumuk, who made a suspicious dissent.

'You can send twenty hunters with me,' Subienkow went on. 'You see, I must get the berries and the roots with which to make the medicine. Then, when you have brought the two sleds and loaded on them the fish and the beaver skins and the rifle, and when you have told off the six hunters who will go with me – then, when all is ready, I will rub the medicine on my neck, so, and lay my neck there on that log. Then can your strongest hunter take the axe and strike three times on my neck. You yourself can strike the three times.'

Makumuk stood with gaping mouth, drinking in this latest and most wonderful magic of the fur thieves.

'But first,' the Pole added hastily, 'between each blow I must put on fresh medicine. The axe is heavy and sharp, and I want no mistakes.'

'All that you have asked shall be yours,' Makumuk cried in a rush of acceptance. 'Proceed to make your medicine.'

Subienkow concealed his elation. He was playing a desperate game and there must be no slips. He spoke arrogantly.

'You have been slow. My medicine is offended. To make the

offence clean you must give me your daughter.'

He pointed to the girl, an unwholesome creature, with a cast in one eye and a bristling wolf tooth. Makumuk was angry, but the Pole remained imperturbable, rolling and lighting another cigarette.

'Make haste,' he threatened. 'If you are not quick, I shall demand yet more.'

In the silence that followed, the dreary Northland scene faded from behind him, and he saw once more his native land, and France, and once, as he glanced at the wolf-toothed girl, he remembered another girl, a singer and a dancer, whom he had known when first as a youth he came to Paris.

'What do you want with the girl?' Makumuk asked.

'To go down the river with me.' Subienkow glanced her over critically. 'She will make a good wife, and it is an honour worthy of my medicine to be married to your blood.'

Again he remembered the singer and dancer and hummed aloud a song she had taught him. He lived the old life over, but in a detached, impersonal sort of way, looking at the memory pictures of his own life as if they were pictures in a book of anybody's life. The chief's voice, abruptly breaking the silence, startled him.

'It shall be done,' said Makumuk. 'The girl shall go down the river with you. But be it understood that I myself strike the three blows with the axe on your neck.'

'But each time I shall put on the medicine,' Subienkow answered, with a show of ill-concealed anxiety.

'You shall put the medicine on between each blow. Here are the hunters who shall see you do not escape. Go into the forest and gather your medicine.'

Makumuk had been convinced of the worth of the medicine by the Pole's rapacity. Surely nothing less than the greatest of medicines could enable a man in the shadow of death to stand up and drive an old woman's bargain.

'Besides,' whispered Yakaga, when the Pole, with his guard, had disappeared among the spruce trees, 'when you have learned the medicine you can easily destroy him.'

'But how can I destroy him?' Makumuk argued. 'His medicine will not let me destroy him.'

'There will be some part where he has not rubbed the medicine,' was Yakaga's reply. 'We will destroy him through that part. It may be his ears. Very well; we will thrust a spear in one ear and out the other. Or it may be his eyes. Surely the medicine will be much too strong to rub on his eyes.'

The chief nodded. 'You are very wise, Yakaga. If he possess no other devil things, we will then destroy him.'

Subienkow did not waste time in gathering the ingredients for his medicine. He selected whatsoever came to hand such as spruce needles, the inner bark of the willow, a strip of birch bark, and a quantity of mossberries, which he made the hunters dig up for him from beneath the snow. A few frozen roots completed his supply, and he led the way back to camp.

Makumuk and Yakaga crouched beside him, noting the quantities and kinds of the ingredients he dropped into the pot of boiling water.

'You must be careful that the mossberries go in first,' he exclaimed.

'And – oh yes, one other thing – the finger of a man. Here, Yakaga, let me cut off your finger.'

But Yakaga put his hands behind him and scowled.

'Just a small finger,' Subienkow pleaded.

'Yakaga give him your finger,' Makumuk commanded.

'There must be plenty of fingers lying around,' Yakaga grunted, indicating the human wreckage in the snow of the score of persons who had been tortured to death.

'It must be the finger of a live man,' the Pole objected.

'Then shall you have the finger of a live man.' Yakaga strode over to the Cossack and sliced off a finger.

'He is not yet dead,' he announced, flinging the bloody trophy in the snow at the Pole's feet. 'Also, it is a good finger, because it is large.'

Subienkow dropped it into the fire under the pot and began

to sing. It was a French love song that with great solemnity he sang into the brew.

'Without these words I utter into it the medicine is worthless,' he explained. 'The words are the chiefest strength of it. Behold, it is ready.'

'Name the words slowly, that I may know them,' Makamuk commanded.

'Not until after the test. When the axe flies back three times from my neck, then will I give you the secret of the words.'

'But if the medicine is not good medicine?' Makumuk queried anxiously.

Subienkow turned upon him wrathfully.

'My medicine is always good. However, if it is not good, then do by me as you have done to the others. Cut me up a bit at a time, even as you have cut him up.' He pointed to the Cossack. 'The medicine is now cool. Thus I rub it on my neck, saying this further medicine.'

With great gravity he slowly intoned a line of the 'Marseillaise', at the same time rubbing the villainous brew thoroughly into his neck.

An outcry interrupted his play acting. The giant Cossack, with a last resurgence of his tremendous vitality, had arisen to his knees. Laughter and cries of surprise and applause arose from the Nultos, as Big Ivan began flinging himself about in the snow with mighty spasms.

Subienkow was made sick by the sight, but he mastered his qualms and made believe to be angry.

'This will not do,' he said. 'Finish him, and then we will make the test. Here, you, Yakaga, see that his noise ceases.'

While this was being done, Subienkow turned to Makumuk.

'And remember, you are to strike hard. This is not baby work. Here take the axe and strike the log, so that I can see you strike like a man.'

Makumuk obeyed, striking twice, precisely and with vigour, cutting out a large chip.

'It is well.' Subienkow looked about him at the circle of

savage faces that somehow seemed to symbolize the wall of savagery that had hemmed him about ever since the Czar's police had first arrested him in Warsaw. 'Take your axe, Makumuk, and stand so. I shall lie down. When I raise my hand, strike, and strike with all your might. And be careful that no one stands behind you. The medicine is good, and the axe may bounce off my neck and right out of your hands.'

He looked at the two sleds, with the dogs in harness, loaded with furs and fish. His rifle lay on top of the beaver skins. The six hunters who were to act as his guard stood by the sleds.

'Where is the girl?' the Pole demanded. 'Bring her up to the sleds before the test goes on.'

When this had been carried out, Subienkow lay down in the snow, resting his head on the log like a tired child about to sleep. He had lived so many dreary years that he was indeed tired.

'I laugh at you and your strength, O Makumuk.' he said. 'Strike, and strike hard.'

He lifted his hand. Makumuk swung the axe, a broadaxe for the squaring of logs. The bright steel flashed through the frosty air, poised for a perceptible instant above Makumuk's head, then descended upon Subienkow's bare neck. Clear through the flesh and bone it cut its way, biting deeply into the log beneath. The amazed savages saw the head bounce a yard away from the blood-spouting trunk.

There was great bewilderment and silence, while slowly it began to dawn in their minds that there had been no medicine. The fur thief had outwitted them. Alone, of all their prisoners, he had escaped the torture. That had been the stake for which he had played. A great roar of laughter went up. Makumuk bowed his head in shame. The fur thief had fooled him. He had lost face before his people. Still they continued to roar out their laughter. Makumuk turned, and with bowed head stalked away. He knew that thenceforth he would no longer be known as Makumuk. He would be Lost Face; the record of his shame would be with him until he died; and whenever the tribes gathered in the spring for the salmon, or in the summer for the trading, the story would pass back and forth across the camp-fires of how the fur thief died peaceably, at a single stroke, by the hand of Lost Face.

'Who was Lost Face?' he could hear, in anticipation, some insolent young buck demand. 'Oh, Lost Face,' would be the answer, 'he who was once Makumuk in the days before he cut off the fur trader's head.'

True Relation of the Apparition of One Mrs Veal

Daniel Defoe

This thing is so rare in all its circumstances, and on so good authority, that my reading and conversation have not given me anything like it. It is fit to gratify the most ingenious and serious inquirer. Mrs Bargrave is the person to whom Mrs Veal appeared after her death; she is my intimate friend, and I can avouch for her reputation for these fifteen or sixteen years, on my own knowledge; and I can affirm that good character she had from her youth to the time of my acquaintance. Though, since this relation, she is calumniated by some people that are friends to the brother of Mrs Veal who appeared to think this relation of this appearance to be a reflection, and endeavour what they can to blast Mrs Bargrave's reputation and to laugh the story out of countenance. But by the circumstances thereof, and the cheerful disposition of Mrs Bargrave, notwithstanding the ill usage of a very wicked husband, there is not yet the least sign of dejection in her face; nor did I ever hear her let fall a desponding or murmuring expression; nay, not when actually under her husband's barbarity, which I have been a witness to, and several other persons of undoubted reputation.

Now you must know Mrs Veal was a maiden gentlewoman of about thirty years of age, and for some years past had been troubled with fits, which were perceived coming on her by her going off from her discourse very abruptly to some impertinence. She was maintained by an only brother, and kept his house in Dover. She was a very pious woman, and her brother a very sober man, to all appearance; but now he does all he can to null and quash the story. Mrs Veal was intimately acquainted with Mrs Bargrave from her childhood. Mrs Veal's circumstances were then mean; her father did not take care of his children as he ought, so that they were exposed to hardships. And Mrs Bargrave in those days had as unkind a father, though she wanted neither for food nor clothing; while Mrs Veal wanted for both, insomuch that she would often say, 'Mrs Bargrave, you are not only the best, but the only friend I have in the world; and no circumstance of life shall ever dissolve my friendship.' They would often condole each other's adverse fortunes, and read together *Drelincourt upon Death*, and other books; and so, like two Christian friends, they comforted each other under their sorrow.

Some time after, Mr Veal's friends got him a place in the custom-house at Dover, which occasioned Mrs Veal, by little and little, to fall off from her intimacy with Mrs Bargrave, though there was never any such thing as a quarrel; but an indifferency came on by degrees, till at last Mrs Bargrave had not seen her in two years and a half, though about a twelvemonth of the time Mrs Bargrave hath been absent from Dover, and this last half-year has been in Canterbury about two months of the time, dwelling in a house of her own.

In this house, on the eighth of September, one thousand seven hundred and five, she was sitting alone in the forenoon, thinking over her unfortunate life, and arguing herself into a due resignation to Providence, though her condition seemed hard: 'And,' she said, 'I have been provided for hitherto, and doubt not but I shall be still, and am well satisfied that my afflictions shall end when it is most fit for me.' And then took up her sewing work, which she had no sooner done but she hears a knocking at the door; she went to see who was there, and this proved to be Mrs Veal, her old friend, who was in a riding habit. At that moment of time the clock struck twelve at noon.

'Madam,' says Mrs Bargrave, 'I am surprised to see you, you who have been so long a stranger'; but told her she was glad to see her, and offered to salute her, which Mrs Veal complied with, till their lips almost touched, and then Mrs Veal drew her hand across her own eyes, and said, 'I am not very well,' and so waived it. She told Mrs Bargrave she was going on a journey, and had a great mind to see her first. 'But,' says Mrs Bargrave, 'how can you take a journey alone? I am amazed at it, because I know you have a fond brother.' 'Oh,' says Mrs Veal, 'I gave my brother the slip, and came away, because I had so great a desire to see you before I took my journey.' So Mrs Bargrave went in with her into another room within the first, and Mrs Veal sat her down in an elbow-chair, in which Mrs Bargrave was sitting when she heard Mrs Veal knock. 'Then,' says Mrs Veal, 'my dear friend, I am come to renew our old friendship again and beg your pardon for my breach of it; and if you can forgive me, you are the best of women.' 'Oh,' says Mrs Bargrave, 'do not mention such a thing; I have not had an uneasy thought about it.' 'What did you think of me?' says Mrs Veal. Says Mrs Bargrave, 'I thought you were like the rest of the world, and that prosperity had made you forget yourself and me.' Then Mrs Veal reminded Mrs Bargrave of the many friendly offices she did her in former days, and much of the conversation they had with each other in the times of their adversity; what books they read, and what comfort in particular they received from Drelincourt's *Book of Death*, which was the best, she said, on the subject ever wrote. She also mentioned Dr Sherlock, and two Dutch books, which were translated, wrote upon death, and several others. But Drelincourt, she said, had the clearest notions of death and of the future state of any who had handled that subject. Then she asked Mrs Bargrave whether she had Drelincourt. She said, 'Yes.' Says Mrs Veal, 'Fetch it.' And so Mrs Bargrave goes upstairs and brings it down. Says Mrs Veal, 'Dear Mrs Bargrave, if the eyes of our faith were as open as the eyes of our body, we should see numbers of angels about us for our guard. The notions we have of Heaven now are nothing like what it is, as Drelincourt says; therefore be comforted under your afflictions, and believe that the Almighty has a particular regard to you, and that your afflictions are marks of God's favour; and when they have done the business they are sent for, they shall be removed from you. And believe me, my dear friend, believe what I say to you, one minute of future happiness will infinitely reward you for all your sufferings. For I can never believe' (and claps her hand upon her knee with great earnestness, which, indeed, ran through most of her discourse) 'that ever God will suffer you to spend all your days in this afflicted state. But be assured that your afflictions shall leave you, or you them, in a short time.' She spake in that pathetical and heavenly manner that Mrs Bargrave wept several times, she was so deeply affected with it.

Then Mrs Veal mentioned Doctor Kendrick's *Ascetic*, at the end of which he gives an account of the lives of the primitive Christians. Their pattern she recommended to our imitation, and said, 'Their conversation was not like this of our age. For now,' says she, 'there is nothing but vain, frothy discourse, which is far different from theirs. Theirs was to edification, and to build one another up in faith, so that they were not as we are, nor are we as they were. But,' she said, 'we ought to do as they did; there was a hearty friendship among them; but where is it now to be found?' Says Mrs Bargrave, 'It is hard indeed to find a true friend in these days.' Says Mrs Veal, 'Mr Norris has a fine copy of verses, called *Friendship in Perfection*, which I wonderfully admire. Have you seen the book?' says Mrs Veal. 'No,' says Mrs Bargrave, 'but I have the verses of my own writing out.' 'Have you?' says Mrs Veal; 'then fetch them'; which she did from above stairs, and offered them to Mrs Veal to read, who refused, and waived the thing, saying 'holding down her head would make it ache'; and then desiring Mrs Bargrave to read them to her, which she did. As they were admiring *Friendship*, Mrs Veal said, 'Dear Mrs Bargrave, I shall love you forever.' In these verses there is twice used the word Elysian. 'Ah!' says Mrs Veal, 'these poets have such names for Heaven.' She would often draw her hand across her own eyes, and say,

'Mrs Bargrave, do not you think I am mightily impaired by my fits?' 'No,' says Mrs Bargrave; 'I think you look as well as ever I knew you.'

After this discourse, which the apparition put in much finer words than Mrs Bargrave said she could pretend to, and as much more as she can remember – for it cannot be thought that an hour and three quarters' conversation could all be retained, though the main of it she thinks she does – she said to Mrs Bargrave she would have her write a letter to her brother, and tell him she would have him give rings to such and such; and that there was a purse of gold in her cabinet, and that she would have two broad pieces given to her cousin Watson.

Talking at this rate, Mrs Bargrave thought that a fit was coming upon her, and so placed herself on a chair just before her knees, to keep her from falling to the ground, if her fits should occasion it; for the elbow-chair, she thought, would keep her from falling on either side. And to divert Mrs Veal, as she thought, took hold of her gown-sleeve several times, and commended it. Mrs Veal told her it was a scoured silk, and newly made up. But, for all this, Mrs Veal persisted in her request, and told Mrs Bargrave she must not deny her. And she would have her tell her brother all their conversation when she had the opportunity. 'Dear Mrs Veal,' says Mrs Bargrave, 'it is much better, methinks, to do it yourself.' 'No,' says Mrs Veal, 'though it seems impertinent to you now, you will see more reasons for it hereafter.' Mrs Bargrave, then, to satisfy her importunity, was going to fetch a pen and ink, but Mrs Veal said, 'Let it alone now, but do it when I am gone; but you must be sure to do it'; which was one of the last things she enjoined her at parting, and so she promised her.

Then Mrs Veal asked for Mrs Bargraves's daughter. She said she was not at home. 'But if you have a mind to see her,' says Mrs Bargrave, 'I'll send for her.' 'Do,' says Mrs Veal; on which she left her, and went to a neighbour's to see her; and by the time Mrs Bargrave was returning, Mrs Veal was without the door in the street, in the face of the beast-market, on a Saturday (which is market-day), and stood ready to part as soon as Mrs Bargrave came to her. She said she must be going, though perhaps she might not go her journey till Monday; and told Mrs Bargrave she hoped she should see her again at her cousin Watson's before she went whither she was going. Then she said she would take her leave of her, and walked from Mrs Bargrave, in her view, till a turning interrupted the sight of her, which was three-quarters after one in the afternoon.

Mrs Veal died the seventh of September, at twelve o'clock at noon, of her fits, and had not above four hours' senses before her death, in which time she received the sacrament. The next day after Mrs Veal's appearance, being Sunday, Mrs Bargrave was mightily indisposed with a cold and sore throat, that she could not go out that day; but on Monday morning she sends a person to Captain Watson's to know if Mrs Veal was there. They wondered at Mrs Bargrave's inquiry, and sent her word she was not there, nor was expected. At this answer, Mrs Bargrave told the maid she had certainly mistook the name or made some blunder. And though she was ill, she put on her hood and went herself to Captain Watson's, though she knew none of the family, to see if Mrs Veal was there or not. They said they wondered at her asking, for that she had not been in town; they were sure, if she had, she would have been there. Says Mrs Bargrave, 'I am sure she was with me on Saturday almost two hours.' They said it was impossible, for they must have seen her if she had. In comes Captain Watson, while they were in dispute, and said that Mrs Veal was certainly dead, and the escutcheons were making. This strangely surprised Mrs Bargrave, when she sent to the person immediately who had the care of them, and found it true. Then she related the whole story to Captain Watson's family; and what gown she had on, and how striped; and that Mrs Veal told her that it was scoured. Then Mrs Watson cried out. 'You have seen her indeed, for none knew but Mrs Veal and myself that the gown was scoured.' And Mrs Watson owned that she described the gown exactly; 'for,' she said, 'I helped her to make it up.' This Mrs Watson blazed all about the town, and avouched the demonstration of truth of Mrs Bargrave's seeing Mrs Veal's apparition. And Captain Watson carried two gentlemen immediately to Mrs Bargrave's house to hear the relation from her own mouth. And when it spread so fast that gentlemen and persons of quality, the judicious and sceptical part of the world, flocked in upon her, it at last became such a task that she was forced to go out of the way; for they were in general extremely satisfied of the truth of the thing, and plainly saw that Mrs Bargrave was no hypochondriac, for she always appears with such a cheerful air and pleasing mien that she has gained the favour and esteem of all the gentry, and it is thought a great favour if they can but get the relation from her own mouth. I should have told you before that Mrs Veal told Mrs Bargrave that her sister and brother-in-law were just come down from London to see her. Says Mrs Bargrave, 'How came you to order matters so strangely?' It could not be helped,' said Mrs Veal. And her brother and sister did come to see her, and entered the town of Dover just as Mrs Veal was expiring. Mrs Bargrave asked her whether she would drink some tea. Says Mrs Veal, 'I do not care if I do; but I'll warrant you this mad fellow' – meaning Mrs Bargrave's husband – 'has broke all your trinkets.' 'But,' says Mrs Bargrave, 'I'll get something to drink in for all that'; but Mrs Veal waived it, and said, 'It is no matter; let it alone,' and so it passed.

All the time I sat with Mrs Bargrave, which was some hours, she recollected fresh sayings of Mrs Veal. And one material thing more she told Mrs Bargrave, that old Mr Bretton allowed Mrs Veal ten pounds a year, which was a secret, and unknown to Mrs Bargrave till Mrs Veal told her.

Mrs Bargrave never varies her story, which puzzles those who doubt of the truth, or are unwilling to believe it. A servant in the neighbour's yard adjoining to Mrs Bargrave's house heard her talking to somebody an hour of the time Mrs Veal was with her. Mrs Bargrave went out to her next neighbour's the very moment she parted with Mrs Veal, and told her what ravishing conversation she had had with an old friend, and told the whole of it. Drelincourt's *Book of Death* is, since this happened, bought up strangely. And it is to be observed that, notwithstanding all the trouble and fatigue Mrs Bargrave has undergone upon this account, she never took the value of a farthing, nor suffered her daughter to take anything of anybody, and therefore can have no interest in telling the story.

But Mr Veal does what he can to stifle the matter, and said he would see Mrs Bargrave; but yet it is certain matter of fact that he has been at Captain Watson's since the death of his sister, and yet never went near Mrs Bargrave; and some of his friends report her to be a liar, and that she knew of Mr Bretton's ten pounds a year. But the person who pretends to say so has the reputation to be a notorious liar among persons whom I know to be of undoubted credit. Now, Mr Veal is more of a gentleman than to say she lies, but says a bad husband has crazed her; but she needs only present herself, and it will effectually confute that pretence. Mr Veal says he asked his sister on her death-bed whether she had a mind to dispose of anything. And she said no. Now the things which Mrs Veal's apparition would have disposed of were so trifling, and nothing of justice aimed at in her disposal, that the design of it appears to me to be only in order to make Mrs Bargrave satisfy the world of the reality thereof as to what she had seen and heard, and to secure her reputation among the reasonable and understanding part of mankind. And then again, Mr Vela owns that there was a purse of gold; but it was not found in her cabinet, but in a comb-box. This looks improbable; for that Mrs Watson owned that Mrs Veal was so very careful of the key of her cabinet that she would trust nobody with it; and if so, no doubt she would not trust her gold out of it. And Mrs Veal's often drawing her hands over her eyes, and asking Mrs Bargrave whether her fits had not impaired her, looks to me as if she did it on purpose to remind Mrs Bargrave of her fits, to prepare her not to think it strange that she should put her upon writing to her brother, to dispose of rings and gold, which looks so much like a dying person's bequest; and it took accordingly with Mrs Bargrave as the effect of her fits coming upon her, and was one of the many instances of her wonderful love to her and care of her, that she should not be affrighted, which, indeed, appears in her whole management, particularly in her coming to her in the daytime, waiving the salutation, and when she was alone; and then the manner of her parting, to prevent a second attempt to salute her.

Now, why Mr Veal should think this relation a reflection – as it is plain he does, by his endeavouring to stifle it – I cannot imagine; because the generality believe her to be a good spirit, her discourse was so heavenly. Her two great errands were, to comfort Mrs Bargrave in her affliction, and to ask her forgiveness for her breach of friendship, and with a pious discourse to encourage her. So that, after all, to suppose that Mrs Bargrave could hatch such an invention as this, from Friday noon to Saturday noon – supposing that she knew of Mrs Veal's death the very first moment – without jumbling circumstances, and without any interest too, she must be more witty, fortunate, and wicked too, than any indifferent person, I dare say, will allow. I asked Mrs Bargrave several times if she was sure she felt the gown. She answered, modestly, 'If my senses be to be relied on, I am sure of it.' I asked her if she heard a sound when she clapped her hand upon her knee. She said she did not remember she did, but said she appeared to be as much a substance as I did who talked with her. 'And I may,' said she, 'be as soon persuaded that your apparition is talking to me now as that I did not really see her; for I was under no manner of fear, and received her as a friend, and parted with her as such. I would not,' says she, 'give one farthing to make any one believe it; I have no interest in it; nothing but trouble is entailed upon me for a long time, for aught I know, and, had it not come to light by accident, it would never have been made public.' But now she says she will make her own private use of it, and keep herself out of the way as much as she can; and so she has done since. She says she had a gentleman who came thirty miles to her to hear the relation; and that she had told it to a roomful of people at the time. Several particular gentlemen have had the story from Mrs Bargrave's own mouth.

This thing has very much affected me, and I am as well satisfied as I am of the best-grounded matter of fact. And why we should dispute matter of fact, because we cannot solve things of which we can have no cerain or demonstrative notions, seems strange to me; Mrs Bargrave's authority and sincerity alone would have been undoubted in any other case.

The Blast of the Book

GK Chesterton

Professor Openshaw always lost his temper, with a loud bang, if anybody called him a Spiritualist; or a believer in Spiritualism. This, however, did not exhaust his explosive elements; for he also lost his temper if anybody called him a disbeliever in Spiritualism. It was his pride to have given his whole life to investigating Psychic Phenomena; it was also his pride never to have given a hint of whether he thought they were really psychic or merely phenomenal. He enjoyed nothing so much as to sit in a circle of devout Spiritualists and give devastating descriptions of how he had exposed medium after medium and detected fraud after fraud: for indeed he was a man of much detective talent and insight, when once he had fixed his eye on an object, and he always fixed his eye on a medium, as a highly suspicious object. There was a story of his having spotted the same spiritualistic mountebank under three different disguises: dressed as a woman, a white-bearded old man, and a Brahmin of a rich chocolate brown. These recitals made the true believers rather restless, as indeed they were intended to do; but they could hardly complain, for no Spiritualist denies the existence of fraudulent mediums; only the Professor's flowing narrative might well seem to indicate that all mediums were fraudulent.

But woe to the simple-minded and innocent Materialist (and Materialists as a race are rather innocent and simple-minded) who, presuming on this narrative tendency, should advance the thesis that ghosts were against the laws of nature, or that such things were only old superstitions; or that it was all tosh, or, alternately, bunk. Him would the Professor, suddenly reversing all his scientific batteries, sweep from the field with a cannonade on unquestionable cases and unexplained phenomena, of which the wretched rationalist had never heard in his life, giving all the dates and details, stating all the attempted and abandoned natural explanations; stating everything, indeed, except whether he, John Oliver Openshaw, did or did not believe in Spirits; and that neither Spiritualist nor Materialist could ever boast of finding out.

Professor Openshaw, a lean figure with pale leonine hair and hypnotic blue eyes, stood exchanging a few words with Father Brown, who was a friend of his, on the steps outside the hotel where both had been breakfasting that morning and sleeping the night before. The Professor had come back rather late from one of his grand experiments, in general exasperation, and was still tingling with the fight that he always waged alone and against both sides.

'Oh, I don't mind you,' he said laughing. 'You don't believe in it even if its true. But all these people are perpetually asking me what I'm trying to prove. They don't seem to understand that I'm a man of science. A man of science isn't trying to prove anything. He's trying to find out what will prove itself.'

'But he hasn't found out yet,' said Father Brown.

'Well, I have some little notions of my own, that are not quite so negative as most people think,' answered the Professor, after an instant of frowning silence; 'anyhow, I've begun to fancy that if there is something to be found, they're looking for it along the wrong line. It's all too theatrical; it's showing off, all their shiny ectoplasm and trumpets and voices and the rest; all on the model of old melodramas and mouldy historical novels about the Family Ghost. If they'd go to history instead of historical novels, I'm beginning to think they'd really find something. But not apparitions.'

'After all,' said Father Brown, 'apparitions are only Appearances. I suppose you'd say the Family Ghost is only keeping up appearances.'

The Professor's gaze, which had commonly a fine abstracted character, suddenly fixed and focussed itself as it did on a dubious medium. It had rather the air of a man screwing a strong magnifying-glass into his eye. Not that he thought the priest was in the least like a dubious medium; but he was startled into attention by his friend's thought following so closely on his own.

'Appearances!' he muttered, 'crikey, but it's odd you should say that just now. The more I learn, the more I fancy they lose by merely looking for appearances. Now if they'd look a little into Disappearances – '

'Yes,' said Father Brown, 'after all, the real fairy legends weren't so very much about the appearance of famous fairies; calling up Titania or exhibiting Oberon by moonlight. But there were no end of legends about people *disappearing*, because they were stolen by fairies. Are you on the track of Kilmeny or Thomas the Rhymer?'

'I'm on the track of ordinary modern people you've read of in the newspapers,' answered Openshaw. 'You may well stare; but that's my game just now; and I've been on it for a long time. Frankly, I think a lot of psychic appearances could be explained away. It's the disappearances I can't explain, unless they're psychic. These people in the newspapers who vanish and are never found – if you knew the details as I do … and now only this morning I got confirmation; an extraordinary letter from an old missionary, quite a respectable old boy. He's coming to see me at my office this morning. Perhaps you'd lunch with me or something; and I'd tell the results – in confidence.'

'Thanks; I will – unless,' said Father Brown modestly, 'the fairies have stolen me by then.'

With that they parted and Openshaw walked round the corner to a small office he rented in the neighbourhood; chiefly for the publication of a small periodical, of psychical and psychological notes of the driest and most agnostic sort. He had only one clerk, who sat at a desk in the outer office, totting up figures and facts for the purposes of the printed report; and the Professor paused to ask if Mr Pringle had called. The clerk answered mechanically in the negative and went on mechanically adding up figures; and the Professor turned towards the inner room that was his study. 'Oh, by the way, Berridge,' he added, without turning round, 'if Mr Pringle comes, send him straight in to me. You needn't interrupt your work; I rather want those notes finished to-night if possible. You might leave them on my desk to-morrow, if I am late.'

And he went into his private office, still brooding on the problem which the name of Pringle had raised; or rather, perhaps had ratified and confirmed in his mind. Even the most perfectly balanced of agnostics is partially human; and it is possible that the missionary's letter seemed to have greater weight as promising to support his private and still tentative hypothesis. He sat down in his large and comfortable chair, opposite the engraving of Montaigne; and read once more the short letter from the Rev. Luke Pringle, making the appointment for that morning. No man knew better than Professor Openshaw the marks of the letter of the crank; the crowded details; the spidery handwriting; the unnecessary length and repletion. There were none of these things in this case; but a brief and businesslike typewritten statement that the writer had encountered some curious cases of Disappearance, which seemed to fall within the province of the Professor as a student of psychic problems. The Professor was favourably impressed; nor had he any unfavourable impression, in spite of a slight movement of surprise, when he looked up and saw that the Rev. Luke Pringle was already in the room.

'Your clerk told me I was to come straight in,' said Mr Pringle apologetically, but with a broad and rather agreeable grin. The grin was partly masked by masses of reddish-grey beard and whiskers; a perfect jungle of a beard, such as is sometimes grown by white men living in jungles; but the eyes above the snub nose had nothing about them in the least wild or outlandish. Openshaw had instantly turned on them that concentrated spotlight or burning-glass of sceptical scrutiny which he turned on many men to see if they were mountebanks or maniacs; and, in this case, he had a rather unusual sense of reassurance. The wild beard might have belonged to a crank, but the eyes completely contradicted the beard; they were full of that quite frank and friendly laughter which is never found in the faces of those who are serious frauds or serious lunatics. He would have expected a man with those eyes to be a Philistine, a jolly sceptic, a man who shouted our shallow but hearty contempt for ghosts and spirits; but anyhow, no professional humbug could afford to look as frivolous as that. The man was buttoned up to the throat in a shabby old cape, and only his broad limp hat suggested the cleric; but missionaries from wild places do not always bother to dress like clerics.

'You probably think all this is another hoax, Professor,' said Mr Pringle, with a sort of abstract enjoyment, 'and I hope you will forgive my laughing at your very natural air of disapproval. All the same, I've got to tell my story to somebody who knows, because it's true. And, all joking apart, it's tragic as well as true. Well, to cut it short, I was a missionary in Nya-Nya, a station in West Africa, in the thick of the forests, where almost the only other white man was the officer in command of the district, Captain Wales; and he and I grew rather thick. Not that he liked missions; he was, if I may say so, thick in many ways; one of those square-headed, square-shouldered men of action who hardly need to think, let alone believe. That's what makes it all the queerer. One day he came back to his tent in the forest, after a short leave, and said he had gone through a jolly rum experience, and didn't know what to do about it. He was holding a rusty old book in a leather binding, and he put it down on a table beside his revolver and an old Arab sword he kept, probably as a curiosity. He said this book had belonged to a man on the boat he had just come off; and the man swore that nobody must open the book, or look inside it; or else they would be carried off by the devil, or disappear, or something.

Wales said that this was all nonsense, of course; and they had a quarrel; and the upshot seems to have been that this man, taunted with cowardice or superstition, actually did look into the book; and instantly dropped it; walked to the side of the boat – '

'One moment,' said the Professor, who had made one or two notes. 'Before you tell me anything else. Did this man tell Wales where he got the book, or who it originally belonged to?'

'Yes,' replied Pringle, now entirely grave. 'It seems he said he was bringing it back to Dr Hankey, the Oriental traveller now in England, to whom it originally belonged, and who had warned him of its strange properties. Well, Hankey is an able man and a rather crabbed and sneering sort of man; which makes it queerer still. But the point of Wales's story is much simpler. It is that the man who had looked into the book walked straight over the side of the ship, and was never seen again.'

'Do you believe it yourself?' asked Openshaw after a pause.

'Well, I do,' replied Pringle. 'I believe it for two reasons. First, that Wales was an entirely unimaginative man; and he added one touch that only an imaginative man could have added. He said that the man walked straight over the side on a still and calm day; but there was no splash.'

The Professor looked at his notes for some seconds in silence; and then said: 'And your other reason for believing it?'

'My other reason,' answered the Rev. Luke Pringle, 'is what I saw myself.'

There was anther silence; until he continued in the same matter-of-fact way. Whatever he had, he had nothing of the eagerness with which the crank, or even the believer, tried to convince others.

'I told you that Wales put down the book on the table beside the sword. There was only one entrance to the tent; and it happened that I was standing in it, looking out into the forest, with my back to my companion. He was standing by the table grumbling and growling about the whole business; saying it was tomfoolery in the twentieth century to be frightened of opening a book; asking why the devil he shouldn't open it himself. Then some instinct stirred in me and I said that he had better not do that, it had better be returned to Dr. Hankey. 'What harm could it do?' he said restlessly. 'What harm did it do?' I answered obstinately. 'What happened to your friend on the boat?' He didn't answer, indeed I didn't know what he could answer; but I pressed my logical advantage in mere vanity. 'If it comes to that,' I said, 'what is your version of what really happened on the boat?' Still he didn't answer; and I looked round and saw that he wasn't there.

'The tent was empty. The book was lying on the table; open, but on its face, as if he had turned it downwards. But the sword was lying on the ground near the other side of the tent; and the canvas of the tent showed a great slash, as if somebody had hacked his way out with the sword. The gash in the tent gaped at me; but showed only the dark glimmer of the forest outside. And when I went across and looked through the tent I could not be certain whether the tangle of the tall plants and the undergrowth had been bent or broken; at least not farther than a few feet. I have never seen or heard of Captain Wales from that day.

'I wrapped the book up in brown paper, taking good care not to look at it; and I brought it back to England, intending at first to return it to Dr Hankey. Then I saw some notes in your paper suggesting a hypothesis about such things; and I decided to stop on the way and put the matter before you; as you have a name for being balanced and having an open mind.'

Professor Openshaw laid down his pen and looked steadily at the man on the other side of the table; concentrating in that single stare all his long experience of many entirely different types of humbug, and even some eccentric and extraordinary types of honest men. In the ordinary way, he would have begun with the healthy hypothesis that the story was a pack of lies. And yet he could not fit the man into his story; if it were only that he could not see that sort of liar telling that sort of lie. The man was not trying to look honest on the surface, as most quacks and imposters do; somehow, it seemed all the other way; as if the man was honest, in spite of something else that was merely on the surface. He thought of a good man with one innocent delusion; but again the symptoms were not the same; there was even a sort of virile indifference; as if the man did not care much about his delusion, if it was a delusion.

'Mr Pringle,' he said sharply, like a barrister making a witness jump, 'where is this book of yours now?'

The grin reappeared on the bearded face which had grown grave during the recital.

'I left it outside,' said Mr Pringle. 'I mean in the outer office. It was a risk, perhaps; but the less risk of the two.'

'What do you mean?' demanded the Professor. 'Why didn't you bring it straight in here?'

'Because,' answered the missionary, 'I knew that as soon as you saw it, you'd open it – before you had heard the story. I thought it possible you might think twice about opening it – after you'd heard the story.'

Then after a silence he added: 'There was nobody out here but your clerk; and he looked a stolid steady-going specimen, immersed in business calculations.'

Openshaw laughed unaffectedly. 'Oh, Babbage,' he cried, 'your magic tomes are safe enough with him, I assure you. His name's Berridge – but I often call him Babbage; because he's so exactly like a Calculating Machine. No human being, if you can call him a human being, would be less likely to open other people's brown paper parcels. Well, we may as well go and bring it in now; though I assure you I will consider seriously the course to be taken with it. Indeed, I tell you frankly,' and he stared at the man again, 'that I'm not quite sure whether we ought to open it here and now, or send it to this Dr Hankey.'

The two had passed together out of the inner into the outer office; and even as they did so, Mr Pringle gave a cry and ran forward towards the clerk's desk. For the clerk's desk was there; but not the clerk. On the clerk's desk lay a faded old leather book, torn out of its brown-paper wrappings, and lying closed, but as if it had just been opened. The clerk's desk stood against the wide window that looked out into the street; and the window was shattered with a huge ragged hole in the glass; as if a human body had been shot through it into the world without. There was no other trace of Mr Berridge.

Both the two men left in the office stood as still as statues; and then it was the Professor who slowly came to life. He looked even more judicial than he had ever looked in his life; as he slowly turned and held out his hand to the missionary.

'Mr Pringle,' he said, 'I beg your pardon. I beg your pardon only for thoughts that I have had; and half-thoughts at that. But nobody could call himself a scientific man and not face a fact like this.'

'I suppose,' said Pringle doubtfully, 'that we ought to make some enquiries. Can you ring up his house and find out if he has gone home?'

'I don't know that he's on the telephone,' answered Openshaw, rather absently; 'he lives somewhere up Hampstead way I think. But I suppose somebody will enquire here, if his friends or family miss him.'

'Could we furnish a description,' asked the other, 'if the police want it?'

'The police!' said the Professor, starting from his reverie. 'A description … Well, he looked awfully like everybody else, I'm afraid, except for goggles. One of those clean-shaven chaps. But the police … look here, what are we going to do about this mad business?'

'I know what I ought to do,' said the Rev. Mr Pringle firmly, 'I am going to take this book straight to the only original Dr Hankey, and ask him what the devil it's all about. He lives not very far from here, and I'll come straight back and tell you what he says.'

'Oh, very well,' said the Professor at last, as he sat down rather wearily; perhaps relieved for the moment to be rid of the responsibility. But long after the brisk and ringing footsteps of the little missionary had died away down the street, the Professor sat in the same posture, staring into vacancy like a man in a trance.

He was still there in the same seat and almost the same attitude, when the same brisk footsteps were heard on the pavement without and the missionary entered, this time, as a glance assured him, with empty hands.

'Dr Hankey,' said Pringle gravely, 'wants to keep the book for an hour and consider the point. Then he asks us both to call, and he will give us his decision. He specially desired, Professor, that you should accompany me on the second visit.'

Openshaw continued to stare in silence; then he said, suddenly:

'Who the devil is Dr Hankey?'

'You sound rather as if you meant he was the devil,' said Pringle smiling, 'and I fancy some people have thought so. He had quite a reputation in your own line; but he gained it mostly in India, studying local magic and so on, so perhaps he's not so well known here. He is a yellow skinny little devil with a lame leg, and a doubtful temper; but he seems to have set up in an ordinary respectable practice in these parts, and I don't know anything definitely wrong about him – unless it's wrong to be the only person who can possibly know anything about all this crazy affair.'

Professor Openshaw rose heavily and went to the telephone; he rang up Father Brown, changing his luncheon engagement to a dinner, that he might hold himself free for the expedition to the house of the Anglo-Indian doctor; after that he sat down again, lit a cigar and sank once more into his own unfathomable thoughts.

Father Brown went round to the restaurant appointed for dinner, and kicked his heels for some time in a vestibule full of mirrors and palms in pots; he had been informed of Openshaw's afternoon engagement, and as the evening closed in dark and stormy round the glass and green plants, guessed that it had produced something unexpected and unduly prolonged. He even wondered for a moment whether the Professor would turn up at all; but when the Professor eventually did, it was clear that his own more general guesses had been justified. For it was a very wild-eyed and even wild-haired Professor who eventually drove back with Mr Pringle from the expedition to the North of London, where suburbs are still fringed with heathy wastes and scraps of common, looking more sombre under the rather thunderstorm sunset. Nevertheless, they had apparently found the house, standing a little apart though within hail of other houses; they had verified the brass-plate duly engraved: 'J.I. Hankey, M.D., M.R.C.S.' Only they did not find J.I. Hankey, M.D., M.R.C.S. They found only what a nightmare whisper had already subconsciously prepared them to find: a commonplace parlour with the accursed volume lying on the table, as if it had just been read; and beyond, a backdoor burst open and a faint trail of footsteps that ran a little way up so steep a garden-path that it seemed no lame man could have run up so lightly. But it was a lame man who had; for in those few steps there was the misshapen unequal mark of some sort of surgical boot; then two marks of that boot alone (as if the creature had hopped) and then nothing. There was nothing further to be learnt from Dr J.I. Hankey, except that he had made his decision. He had read the oracle and received the doom.

When the two came into the entrance under the palms, Pringle put the book down suddenly on a small table, as if it burned his fingers. The priest glanced at it curiously; there was only some rude lettering on the front with a couplet:

They that looked into this book
Them the Flying Terror took;

and underneath, as he afterwards discovered, similar warnings in Greek, Latin and French. The other two had turned away with a natural impulsion towards drinks, after their exhaustion and bewilderment; and Openshaw had called to the waiter, who brought them cocktails on a tray.

'You will dine with us, I hope,' he said. 'I'm going off to wrestle with this book and this business myself somewhere. I suppose I couldn't use your office for an hour or two?'

'I suppose – I'm afraid it's locked,' said Openshaw in some surprise.

'You forget there's a hole in the window.' The Rev. Luke Pringle gave the very broadest of all his broad grins and vanished into the darkness without.

'A rather odd fellow, that, after all,' said the Professor, frowning.

He was rather surprised to find Father Brown talking to the waiter who had brought the cocktails, apparently about the waiter's most private affairs; for there was some mention of a baby who was now out of danger. He commented on the fact with some surprise, wondering how the priest came to know the man; but the former only said, 'Oh, I dine here every two or three months, and I've talked to him now and then.'

The Professor, who himself dined there about five times a week, was conscious that he had never thought of talking to the man; but his thoughts were interrupted by a strident ringing and a summons to the telephone. The voice on the telephone said it was Pringle; it was rather a muffled vice, but it might well be muffled in all those bushes of beard and whisker. Its message was enough to establish identity.

'Professor,' said the voice, 'I can't stand it any longer. I'm going to look for myself. I'm speaking from your office and the book is in front of me. If anything happens to me, this is to say good-bye. No – it's no good trying to stop me. You wouldn't be in time anyhow. I'm opening the book now. I ...'

Openshaw thought he heard something like a sort of thrilling or shivering yet almost soundless crash; then he shouted the name of Pringle again and again; but he heard no more. He hung up the receiver, and, restored to a superb academic calm, rather like the calm of despair, went back and quietly took his seat at the dinner-table. Then, as coolly as if he were describing the failure of some small trick at a séance, he told the priest every detail of this monstrous mystery.

'Five men have now vanished in this impossible way,' he said. 'Every one is extraordinary; and yet the one case I simply can't get over is my clerk, Berridge. It's just because he was the quietest creature that he's the queerest case.'

'Yes,' replied Father Brown, 'it was a queer thing for Berridge to do, anyway. He was awfully conscientious. He was always so jolly careful to keep all the office business separate from any fun of his own. Why, hardly anybody knew he was quite a humorist at home and – '

'Berridge!' cried the Professor. 'What on earth are you talking about? Did you know him?'

'Oh, no,' said Father Brown carelessly, 'only as you say I know the waiter. I've often had to wait in your office, till you turned up; and of course I passed the time of day with poor Berridge. He was rather a card. I remember he once said he would like to collect valueless things, as collectors did the silly things they thought valuable. You know the old story about the woman who collected valueless things.'

'I'm not sure I know what you're talking about,' said Openshaw. 'But even if my clerk was eccentric (and I never knew a man I should have thought less so), it wouldn't explain what happened to him; and it certainly wouldn't explain the others.'

'What others?' asked the Priest.

The Professor stared at him and spoke distinctly, as if to a child:

'My dear Father Brown, Five Men have disappeared.'

'My dear Professor Openshaw, no men have disappeared.'

Father Brown gazed back at his host with equal steadiness and spoke with equal distinctness. Nevertheless, the Professor required the words repeated, and they were repeated as distinctly.

'I say that no men have disappeared.'

After a moment's silence, he added, 'I suppose the hardest thing is to convince anybody that O + O + O = O. Men believe the oddest things if they are in a series; that is why Macbeth believed the three words of the three witches; though the first was something he knew himself; and the last something he could only bring about himself. But in your case the middle term is the weakest of all.'

'What do you mean?'

'You saw nobody vanish. You did not see the man vanish from the boat. You did not see the man vanish from the tent. All that rests on the word of Mr Pringle, which I will not discuss just now. But you'll admit this; you would never have taken his word yourself, *unless* you had seen it confirmed by your clerk's disappearance; just as Macbeth would never have believed he would be king, if he had not been confirmed in believing he would be Cawdor.'

'That may be true,' said the Professor, nodding slowly. 'But when it was confirmed, I knew it was the truth. You say I saw nothing myself. But I did; I saw my own clerk disappear. Berridge did disappear.'

'Berridge did not disappear,' said Father Brown. 'On the contrary.'

'What the devil do you mean by "on the contrary"?'

'I mean,' said Father Brown, 'that he never disappeared. He appeared.'

Openshaw stared across at his friend, but the eyes had already altered in his head, as they did when they concentrated on a new presentation of a problem. The priest went on:

'He appeared in your study, disguised in a bushy red beard and buttoned up in a clumsy cape, and announced himself as the Rev. Luke Pringle. And you never noticed your own clerk enough to know him again, when he was in so rough-and-ready disguise.'

'But surely,' began the Professor.

'Could you describe him to the police?' asked Father Brown. 'Not you. You probably knew he was clean-shaven and wore tinted glasses; and merely taking off those glasses was a better disguise than putting on anything else. You had never seen his eyes any more than his soul; jolly laughing eyes. He had planted his absurd book and all the properties; then he calmly smashed the window, put on the beard and cape and walked into your study; knowing that you had never looked at him in your life.'

'But why should he play me such an insane trick?' demanded Openshaw.

'Why, *because* you had never looked at him in your life,' said Father Brown; and his hand slightly curled and clinched, as if he might have struck the table, if he had been given to gesture. 'You called him the Calculating Machine, because that was all you ever used him for. You never found out even what a stranger strolling into your office could find out, in five minutes' chat: that he was a character; that he was full of antics; that he had all sorts of views on you and your theories and your reputation for 'spotting' people. Can't you understand his itching to prove that you couldn't spot your own clerk? He has nonsense notions of all sorts. About collecting useless things, for instance. Don't you know the story of the woman who bought the two most useless things: an old doctor's brass-plate and a wooden leg? With those your ingenious clerk created the character of the remarkable Dr Hankey; as easily as the visionary Captain Wales. Planting them in his own house –'

'Do you mean that place we visited beyond Hampstead was Berridge's own house?' asked Openshaw.

'Did you know his house – or even his address?' retorted the priest. 'Look here, don't think I'm speaking disrespectfully of you or your work. You are a great servant of truth and you know I could never be disrespectful to that. You've seen through a lot of liars. Do, just occasionally, look at honest men – like the waiter.'

'Where is Berridge now?' asked the Professor, after a long silence.

'I haven't the least doubt,' said Father Brown, 'that he is back in your office. In fact, he came back into your office at the exact moment when the Rev. Luke Pringle read the awful volume and faded into the void.'

There was another long silence and then Professor Openshaw laughed; with the laugh of a great man who is great enough to look small. Then he said abruptly:

'I suppose I do deserve it; for not noticing the nearest helpers I have. But you must admit the accumulation of incidents was rather formidable. Did you *never* feel just a momentary awe of the awful volume?'

'Oh, that,' said Father Brown. 'I opened it as soon as I saw it lying there. It's all blank pages. You see, I am not superstitious.'